CURFEW

CURFEW

JAYNE COWIE

Berkley

New York

BERKLEY
An imprint of Penguin Random House LLC
penguinrandomhouse.com

Library of Congress Cataloging-in-Publication Data

Names: Cowie, Jayne, author.
Title: Curfew / Jayne Cowie.
Description: First edition. | New York: Berkley, 2022.
Identifiers: LCCN 2021032636 (print) | LCCN 2021032637 (ebook) |
ISBN 9780593336786 (trade paperback) | ISBN 9780593336793 (ebook)
Subjects: LCGFT: Thrillers (Fiction)
Classification: LCC PR6103.O97134 C87 2022 (print) |
LCC PR6103.O97134 (ebook) | DDC 823/.92—dc23
LC record available at https://lccn.loc.gov/2021032636
LC ebook record available at https://lccn.loc.gov/2021032637

First Edition: March 2022

Printed in the United States of America
1st Printing

Book design by Ashley Tucker

For my family

Pamela

Present Day
6:20 a.m.

When I was a young woman at the police training academy, I learned two important things. First was that you never forget your first dead body. And second was that behind every dead woman was a man who would swear that she was the love of his life, even as he stood there in a blood-soaked T-shirt with the knife still gripped firmly in his hand. But that was a long time ago, thirty years to be exact, and things have changed since then. We're safe in our homes, because it's easy to escape a bad relationship now. And we're safe in public, too.

That's what makes today unusual.

She's been found on an otherwise normal October morning, when the sky is a soft gray, the ground is littered with crisp autumn leaves, and men are still under Curfew. The call came in just after six a.m. It was short and to the point. I was the most senior officer on duty at the time, and so I'm the first at the scene. Whoever dumped her body tried to hide it behind the glossy green leaves of a stretch of laurel and didn't do a very good job. If they had, it might have been days before she was found instead of a few hours.

I don't want to be here. I'm only a few weeks away from retirement. I expected to finish with a bit of shoplifting and perhaps an act or two of vandalism, an abandoned puppy, a domestic dispute. But this is the job.

I cross the park with two of my officers, our dark uniforms and heavy boots a stark contrast to the lush spread of grass and the pansies and violas bursting from the flower beds. It's beautiful here, especially when it's just starting to get light. It's peaceful. Quiet. Clean.

The three of us automatically pick up speed when we see a couple of women huddled together on a bench next to the lake. One is wearing a white jacket stretched around a full middle-aged body. The other is much younger, dressed in leggings and bright pink trainers, her hair pulled up into a messy bun on the top of her head. Early birds, getting their daily exercise before the men are allowed out at seven a.m. "I guess they found her," says Rachel. She's only been a police officer for a few years. She's keen, but she's young, and she's only ever done this job with Curfew in place. She doesn't know what it was like before. She doesn't know. She's trying to be calm, professional, but inside, I can tell that she's excited, and it worries me. For Rachel, this is something new. Something big. Adrenaline is pumping. I can feel it, too, but I'm not excited. I'm afraid.

"I'll speak to them first," I say. "They'll be in shock."

"I know how they feel," Rachel replies. "I just . . . how can this have happened?"

"We don't know," I say. "So let's keep an open mind until we do. For all we know, she's had some sort of accident. It might not be anything more complicated than that." Even as I'm saying the words, I know they don't fit. Women who have accidents don't end up half-buried in the bushes in the park.

The younger woman has her arm around the shoulders of the older one. They turn as I approach. The younger unsticks herself and gets unsteadily to her feet. "She's over there," she says, pointing shakily toward the clump of bushes. "I . . . I put my jacket over her. I didn't know what else to do."

"You did the right thing," I lie. I don't want to cause either of them any further distress. I ask Alison, the other officer, to note down their details and offer what comfort she can. I take out my slate and start recording. Slates replaced smartphones years ago. Everyone has them now. They do everything, which is both a blessing and a curse because you've got everything in one spot, but you're screwed if you lose the damn thing or you can't afford one in the first place.

I steady myself and walk down toward that dense mass of leaves. The first I see of the body is a pair of bare feet. The toenails are peachy pink. Such a pretty color. It reminds me of flowers and lipsticks and the summer dresses of little girls, lovely, happy things that have no place here. She's been partially wrapped in a white sheet, and her shoulders and face are covered by a blue sports jacket.

I know, as I crouch down next to her, that this is a tipping point, just as the murders of the MP Susan Lang and four other women were the tipping point of things sixteen years ago. They were all bludgeoned to death in a public place over the course of five awful months.

Women were told to stay indoors until the killer was caught, the implication being that it would be our fault if it happened to us. But we'd had enough of being blamed for things that men did. We said no. We started to organize online. We marched in the streets. When that didn't work, we went on strike and stopped doing all the unpaid domestic labor that kept society going. We wanted change and we got it. It's not a stretch to say that those murders gave us Curfew, and I can't help but wonder what this one will do.

I quickly push that thought away. This situation is totally different. Men have to stay in their houses overnight now, their movements between seven and seven tracked by the tag on their ankle that alerts us immediately if they break Curfew. If a man had anything to do with this, I'd already know.

Even though it's been a long time since I dealt with a situation like this, the training is still there, and when it kicks in, I'm grateful. I angle my slate so that I can record everything I see. I take a pair of latex gloves from my pocket, put them on, and gently lift the edge of the jacket that covers her face and shoulders.

Bile rises in the back of my throat. I swallow it down. It leaves a sour, acidic taste behind. I straighten up, lifting my face to the rapidly lightening sky, and let myself breathe. Then I move back a little so that Rachel can take a look.

"That didn't happen to her by accident," Rachel says. She sounds upset.

I don't have time to comfort her. "We need to get the park closed off," I tell her. "Get officers on every entrance. Don't let anyone in." We won't be able to keep this quiet for long. But I have to buy us as much time as possible. We need to move the body. We need to comb every inch of this park. And we need to find out who this woman is and tell her family. Oh, god, her family.

"On it," Rachel says. She reaches in her pocket for her slate and taps in a message with trembling fingers. The station is only a few minutes away, so it won't take long to get more officers on-site. "What about identification?"

"The pathologist will have to do that."

I won't be able to use my slate to scan her face and get a name that way. Whoever did this wanted to make sure that we couldn't easily identify her. But we will. And then we'll identify them.

CHAPTER ONE

Sarah

Four Weeks Earlier

I t was a long drive to the prison. Sarah had the music up loud. She tapped her thumb against the steering wheel, moving her shoulders in time with the beat. She wanted to think of nothing but the drive, of her hand on the wheel, the flex in her thighs as she switched lanes and shifted gear. She would not think about him.

But she did.

It was almost three months since she'd last seen her ex-husband. She wondered if he'd changed. She certainly had. She risked a glance at herself in the rearview mirror, one hand rising to touch the dark strands of her hair, and found herself regretting the new cut. She'd been planning this visit for weeks. She'd wanted to show him that she was managing fine without him. That he no longer had any hold over her. The haircut was meant to be part of that, as were the new clothes.

Now she found that she wanted the changes she'd made to be a secret, hers and hers alone. She should just turn around and go home. There was nothing to stop her. She didn't have to go and see him.

But she kept driving.

She had to face him one last time. She needed confirmation

that she'd done the right thing, something to push away the doubts that crept in sometimes, when she had yet another row with their daughter, Cass, or when she lay awake in the early hours of the morning as her mind refused to stop replaying memories she would rather forget.

She flicked the indicator and took the slip road, easing off the accelerator and rolling up to the lights at the top of the slope. She waited for the red to turn green, then set off again, peripherally aware that four other cars were following her, a sorry train of women going to visit their men.

She followed the white markings that led the way to the prison. The conifers that grew at the side of the road were tall and thick, hiding the building from the road. Sarah was grateful for the huge orange signs that told her where to go. She parked the car in the first empty spot. It took considerable effort to unbuckle her seat belt and open the door, and when she did, she found that her parking was so bad that she'd barely left herself enough room to get out. She thought about reversing and having another go, but that would only delay things and give her too much of an opportunity to chicken out.

Slinging her bag over her shoulder, she began the walk toward the entrance. Barriers funneled visitors into a single-file queue and in through an automatic door. Sarah couldn't see anything behind the frosted glass. She didn't look directly at the other women. To make eye contact was to be seen, and to be seen was to admit that you had reason to be here, and she didn't want to do that.

Ahead of her, a woman in a green blouse was waved through, and Sarah stepped forward to take her place. A guard about her own age wearing a navy blue uniform with a radio clipped at the shoulder held Sarah back until the door slid open. Once inside, it quickly became obvious what she was expected to do. She still managed to stumble as she made her way over to an empty counter where a bored-looking woman waited, a large slate in one hand. "Who are you here to see?"

"Greg Johnson."

The woman checked the name on the slate. "And your name?"

"Sarah Wallace."

"Relationship to Greg Johnson?"

"Ex-wife."

The divorce had been quick, painless, and cheap, requested online four weeks after Greg had broken Curfew and confirmed within twenty-four hours. That had been a good day.

The woman gestured to a conveyor belt that led to a scanning machine. "Bag on there, please."

Sarah did as she was told. Then she was directed through a metal archway. Stepping through it felt like crossing a threshold, outside to inside, innocent to guilty. She waited for the machine to spit out her bag. When it did, another guard held out a scuffed yellow tray. "In there," she said, gesturing to the bag.

"You want me to empty it?"

"Yes, please."

Sarah hastily opened her bag and upended it over the tray, keen to show that she'd got nothing to hide. The noisy clatter of pens and lipsticks and keys made her wince. The guard poked at them, then shone her torch into the empty bag. There was nothing more than another little wave of a hand to tell Sarah this step was done. She scooped up her things and then she was funneled down a corridor, long, gray blue, and windowless with a squeaky floor. She followed the peeling black arrows until she found herself in a stuffy room filled with small square tables and plastic chairs.

What was the routine here? Should she pick a table or wait to be shown to one? She took a couple of steps forward and her heart started to thump loudly in her ears, and the air seemed suddenly heavy and the walls too close, because he was there.

Greg sat down at an empty table, rested his hands on the table-top, and looked at her.

Her lips parted and her tongue, which had been a normal size only moments before, felt too big for her mouth. She could feel saliva gathering around her gums and wanted to swallow but couldn't. She couldn't remember how.

This was the man she'd shared her home, her bed, her life with. The man who had lain on top of her, heavy and sweating as, inside her body, their daughter had been created. She saw every moment of their life together flash before her eyes, from the first time she'd seen him to the moment he had been driven away in the back of a police car, and the room spun.

Someone touched her on the shoulder. Sarah blinked, pulled back to the present. It was the woman in the green blouse. "Are you all right?"

"I . . ." Sarah swallowed. "I don't know."

"First time visiting?"

Sarah nodded.

"Shit, isn't it?" The woman had a sharp nose and wore earrings shaped like starfish. "Just tell yourself ten minutes. Say whatever it is that you need to say, then leave. You can survive anything for ten minutes."

She'd survived Greg for eighteen years. "I will," Sarah said. "Thank you."

The woman gave her a pat on the shoulder and then made her way over to a table where a young man with the same sharp nose sat staring into space.

Ten minutes. That was all. Sarah turned her head, forcing herself to look in Greg's direction. He was familiar, and yet she barely recognized him. He'd lost weight. His hair was completely gray and much thinner than she remembered, emphasizing his shiny scalp. His sweatshirt was the same dirty yellow as the walls. She had to make herself walk over to where he sat.

"Sarah," he said. She'd forgotten the way he said her name, like it left a sour taste in his mouth. Suddenly all the things she'd intended to say disappeared from her mind. She groped for them but found nothing more than a blank space. The days of rehearsal, of talking to herself in the shower and the car, had been for nothing. For several long, drawn-out seconds, they simply looked at each other. Sarah registered fury first of all, tightly packed into his stocky body. It didn't surprise her.

She was, after all, the one who had put him in here.

She sat down, putting their faces level, and immediately wished that she'd remained standing. "I've asked for you to be relocated after you're released," she told him. She didn't bother with a greeting. She didn't ask him how he was. She didn't want to know.

He didn't let her get away with it. "Hello, Sarah," he said. "How are you? How is my daughter?"

"She's fine. Did you hear what I said?"

"I heard."

"Don't you have anything to say about it?"

He sat back in his chair and sighed. "What do you want me to say? Thank you for letting me know?"

"I just thought—"

He interrupted her. "Where are they sending me?"

"I don't know. Wherever there's a space for you, I suppose." But it wouldn't be at Riverside, the block of flats in town that housed men who had recently been released, and that was all that mattered.

"So away from Cassie."

Sarah gritted her teeth. His possessiveness over their daughter, even now, made her want to kick him. You didn't get to behave the way he had and then play the caring parent. "She's almost eighteen."

"I know how old my daughter is."

"Parental responsibility ends at eighteen. You don't need to live near us."

"You came all the way here just to tell me that you're cutting me off from my daughter?" he asked.

Sarah refused to take the bait. "Yes."

"Why?"

"I thought you should know."

Greg lifted one of his hands from the table and inspected his nails. They were short and clean. "I'm sure someone here could have passed the message on." The bitterness that edged his voice was unmistakable.

"I wanted you to hear it from me," Sarah told him.

"It was always about what you wanted, wasn't it?"

Don't do it, Sarah. Don't do it. "What do you mean?"

He folded his arms. "Cass and I needed you, but you weren't interested. You were never there. You were always too busy."

"That's not true!"

"Isn't it?"

"I had to work," she told him. She could feel her face getting hot, but the words kept on rolling right out of her mouth. "We had bills to pay. The mortgage. Curfew . . ."

"Go on, blame Curfew. I suppose it's easier than facing the truth. You weren't cut out to be a wife, and you certainly weren't cut out to be a mother. Why do you think I did what I did? It would never have happened if you'd been there, if we'd had anything even resembling a good marriage."

Sarah stopped. She made herself take one last look at him, at the creases at the corners of his eyes and the patch of hair on his neck where he'd missed a spot shaving. She made herself remember how her life had been. She thought about the tears shed in secret, the crushing exhaustion due to working so many hours, the constant pressure in her head when she thought about the mortgage and the never-ending credit card bills. She'd always put on a positive face in front of Greg because he had given up so much due to

Curfew, and she knew it couldn't be easy for him, having to carry the load of most of the childcare. What a fool she'd been. She remembered what had happened on that final day and wondered how he could be so arrogant as to think that any of this was her fault.

She leaned in. "Actually," she whispered, "I don't blame Curfew. I blame you, and my only regret is that I didn't push you out the door sooner." She got to her feet. Her heart was pounding. The woman in the green blouse gave her a little smile and a guard shifted restlessly at the edge of the room, but no one else took any notice.

"Good-bye, Greg," she said, and she walked out, grateful that she never had to see him again.

CHAPTER TWO

Cass

n a school thirty miles away, Cass Johnson was busy trying to work out if she had enough money in her account to buy a magazine from the secondhand bookshop on the way home. Old *Cosmopolitan*s were her favorite, although she'd settle for a pre-Curfew *Grazia* if they had nothing else.

Twenty minutes of the lesson remained. Officially the subject was women's history, but everyone called it Curfew class. None of them took it seriously apart from Amy Hill, who sat near the front with her expensive slate and her perfect hair and got on Cass's nerves.

Their teacher, Miss Taylor, was flapping a bony hand at a photo on the screen and droning on about the Prevention of Femicide Act of 2023, also known as the Curfew Laws. They had been brought in six months after an MP called Susan Lang was murdered in the street by an ex-boyfriend. According to the government at the time, the appropriate response to this was to lock men in their homes overnight.

It was surprising how something so major could be so boring.

Cass pulled up a cat video on her slate and nudged her best friend, Billy. He looked, but only for a second. Cass poked him again and angled the slate so that he could see it more easily. This time he turned his full attention to the video. Cass held the slate steady, half watching Billy, half watching Miss Taylor, making sure they didn't get caught.

"Ha ha," Billy muttered at the end.

Then he picked up his stylus and scribbled something on his own slate. Cass assumed it was a message for her. It wasn't. He was making notes. She rolled her eyes and tried to jab at him with her own stylus, but he moved at the last second and she hit the edge of the table instead. The noise caught Miss Taylor's attention. She stopped talking and stared at them.

"Is there a problem?" she asked.

"No," Billy mumbled, blushing furiously.

As only ten minutes of the lesson remained, Cass decided to have a little fun. "Yes, actually, there is," she said.

"Which is?" Miss Taylor asked her, raising an eyebrow.

Cass sat back in her chair and folded her arms. "Curfew. I just don't see what society gained by tagging men and making them stay at home at night."

A murmur went round the class. Miss Taylor silenced it with a look. "You're not the first person to voice that opinion, Cass. Lots of people, male and female, thought the same when Curfew was first suggested. But there's no disputing the fact that since Curfew was introduced, the number of violent offenses committed has fallen dramatically."

"That doesn't mean that Curfew is the reason."

"Curfew is the reason."

This was said so firmly and with such conviction that Cass laughed out loud. She couldn't help it. "You can't prove that."

"Typically men commit more violent crimes," Miss Taylor continued calmly. "Before Curfew, they were responsible for close to eighty percent of all murders. Seventy-five percent of all other violent crimes. Even in children, the data shows that boys carried out more assaults than girls."

"But you can make statistics show anything you want. Everyone knows that."

"On average, three women a week died at the hands of men."

"Women killed men, too!"

"Yes, they did, roughly one a month, but the pattern of offending was different. Women kill in self-defense, or because they have psychiatric problems. Men kill because they can."

"That doesn't make Curfew a good idea. What's the point in locking men inside? Most women were killed by someone they knew, not by men in the street out after seven p.m."

"Susan Lang was killed in the street by a man she knew."

Cass sighed. It always came back to Saint Susan, and her crazy boyfriend, who had thought he could get away with killing her by killing four other women as well so that the police would think they were random stranger murders and not look too closely at him. "And that was horrible," Cass said. "No one is denying that. I just don't believe that the Curfew Laws were an appropriate response. We locked up all men because of one lunatic."

Including her father, who should never have gone to prison, who would never have gone to prison if it weren't for the tag on his ankle.

"What do other people think?" Miss Taylor asked. "Was Curfew the way to deal with male violence?"

"Yes," said Amy Hill, her arms folded tightly across her chest. Her mouth was set in a hard line. "It works, doesn't it?"

Some of the girls were downright vicious in their defense of Curfew. Cass thought they were idiots. Some of the boys said that they supported Curfew, but things couldn't possibly have been as bad as Miss Taylor claimed, that women had never carried the weight of society on their backs, unpaid. They insisted that it was common for women to lie about being sexually assaulted and they said that the gender pay gap existed because women didn't work as hard as men, especially not after they had children. They said that not all men were like Susan Lang's boyfriend, that male violence was rare. Miss Taylor told them they didn't understand, because they had never seen it.

"The one thing we can be sure of is that the Prevention of Femicide Act revolutionized women's lives," Miss Taylor continued. "How many of you have ever been catcalled by a man in the street in the evening? Taken the long way home because it's a safer route? Got a taxi you couldn't afford because it was the safer option, knowing that even that choice was still risky?"

The girls looked at one another, but no one raised their hand.

"It was the springboard for all sorts of other changes," Miss Taylor continued. "Cohab counseling, for example, so we can identify those couples most at risk of developing abusive patterns within their relationship and prevent them from living together. Escape funds, so that no woman is trapped due to a lack of money if she decides to end a relationship."

"Cohab certificates just make women look weak," Cass pointed out. "Like we can't figure out for ourselves who the decent men are."

Miss Taylor set down the remote for the projector and walked over to Cass and Billy's table. She was wearing red velvet shoes with a tiger face embroidered on the toe, and Cass was spitefully jealous of them. "I can see that you've got some strong opinions on this. That's good. It's important to know where you stand on these things. But it's also important to know why things are as they are."

"We know why," Cass said.

"No," Miss Taylor replied. "I don't think you do. Let's have a real-world demonstration. Billy, I want you to arm-wrestle Cass."

"What?" Billy shuffled in his seat.

"Go on," Miss Taylor said, seemingly oblivious to Billy's discomfort. "Arm-wrestle Cass."

"Why?" Cass asked. "It won't prove anything."

"Then there's no reason not to do it, is there?"

There were lots of reasons, but in that moment, Cass couldn't think of any of them. It didn't help that Billy was sitting there like an idiot.

"Go on," Amy Hill called out. "Do it!"

"Fine." Cass thumped her elbow down on the tabletop. She was wearing a pale blue blouse, which had looked pretty in the mirror at home. Now she was painfully aware that her armpit was damp and on display to everyone, and that made her even more annoyed.

Billy slowly set his elbow on the table, too. He spread his fingers, his palm facing out. His little finger twitched as Cass angled her hand forward and carefully fit it to his. She had a plan. Do this slow, then catch him off guard and slam his hand straight into the table. Point made, thank you very much.

As her palm grazed against his, she put her plan into action, stiffening her biceps and shoving as hard as she could. His hand barely moved an inch before his fingers tightened around hers and with what seemed like no effort at all, he pressed her hand back against the desk. She resisted, but it didn't make any difference. It was like pushing against a brick wall.

As soon as the back of her hand hit the table, he let go. "He cheated!" Cass declared, looking around, trying to catch the eyes of the other girls. "You all saw it!"

"No, I didn't!" Billy exclaimed, and no one jumped in to argue with him.

"I think I've made my point," Miss Taylor said as she wound her way back to the front of the classroom. "Men are physically stronger than women, and that's the key thing that makes them a threat. It's not their fault. But that doesn't change it."

Cass didn't get a chance to argue further because the bell went. But it seemed that Miss Taylor had something to say to her. "Cass," she called softly, just before Cass could reach the door and freedom. Cass would be lying if she said that she didn't think, just for a moment, of pretending she hadn't heard. She turned. She wouldn't walk out, but that didn't mean she was going to be polite. "What?"

Miss Taylor was perched on the corner of her desk. "That was a difficult lesson for you."

"I think that says more about your teaching than about me, Miss." Cass held her breath, waiting to see how Miss Taylor would respond to that, hoping for a raised voice or a flushed cheek. She was disappointed.

"I'm sorry you think so," Miss Taylor said calmly. She was wearing dark blue chinos that went irritatingly well with the shoes, and there were no damp patches under her arms.

"Curfew is stupid," Cass told her. "It's unfair and we should be working to get rid of it."

"I understand why you feel that way."

"Do you?" Cass asked.

"Yes, of course. But I hope that demonstration with Billy helped you to see why Curfew is so important. It isn't fair that men are physically stronger than we are, but these are the cards that life has dealt us, and Curfew is a way of trying to balance the scales."

I hate this class, Cass thought to herself as she turned and walked out without bothering to reply. The corridors were already empty, but it was busy outside, as parents waited to collect younger children from the primary school next door. She watched as a man in a red Ford Focus flew past, pushing right against the speed limit, death grip on the wheel. Crazy hour, her mum called it, the time of day when men rushed to get home. It was worst between six and seven, but even now, close to five, the charge had begun.

Crazy bloody country, more like. No other country electronically tagged half the population from the age of ten just because they'd been born with a Y chromosome. Some people had emigrated when Curfew came in, gone to live in places where men weren't re-stricted. Cass had asked her dad once why they couldn't move abroad. He'd said her mother didn't want to.

Billy was waiting for her at the bus stop. "I don't know why you do that," he said. "Why do you always try to argue with Miss Taylor? What's the point?"

"Someone has to," she told him. "Do you really want to spend the rest of your life living under Curfew, Billy?"

He didn't answer.

CHAPTER THREE

Sarah

S arah loved Curfew. She hoped that it would carry on indefinitely. There had been times when she'd found it tricky, there was no denying that, but now that Greg was out of her life, it was wonderful. She was free. For a long time, she hadn't even known she was trapped. It hadn't felt like it at first. There had been a courtship, and there had been a wedding and a white dress, and eighteen months later, right on time, a tiny pink ball of a baby. Sarah had welcomed all of it.

Then Curfew had come along. Greg had quit his job and become a stay-at-home father, and she'd gone from a part-time job to working more hours than she ever had before. In many ways it made sense; he couldn't increase his hours, but Sarah could, and that meant there was always someone at home to take care of Cass, which they both agreed was important. Sarah had just always assumed it would be her because that was the way these things worked, and although that was patriarchy and it was wrong, at the same time, secretly, quietly, she had wanted it that way. But that job had passed to Greg. She couldn't remember when she'd first started to hate him for it.

She'd buried that feeling, ashamed of it, and she'd let Greg get away with things that he shouldn't have. Greg had done his part by lying about everything, but Sarah couldn't escape the fact that she'd been willing to believe him. She'd refused to see what was happening.

At least not everything in her life was a disaster. After Greg had gone to prison, she'd quit her job and retrained as a tagger. It was going well. She had passed her probationary month with flying colors. She worked sensible hours now, she was paid well for her time, and she liked the other women she worked with. She felt like what she was doing had a purpose, that it made a difference.

Cass didn't agree. But then Cass didn't seem to agree with anything Sarah said or did.

The day after she'd been to see Greg, Sarah got to work early. The center manager, Hadiya, was already there. Sarah asked Hadiya about her new car, and Hadiya asked her about Cass, and Sarah said, oh, you know, teenagers, and rolled her eyes. Hadiya grinned back and said she knew exactly what Sarah meant and that she was glad that her own daughters were past that stage. Sarah wondered what Hadiya would say if she told her the truth: that her tiny pink ball of a baby had turned into a thoroughly unpleasant teen.

After that, Sarah went into her room to make sure that everything was set up. She opened the window to let in the song of the blackbirds that liked to sit in the tree outside before turning on her slate and logging into the tagging center appointment system. She looked at names, addresses, and dates of birth and built a picture of each man in her mind. There was a knock against the open door, and she looked up to see Hadiya, closely followed by Mabel, the other new tagger, who had started a couple of weeks after Sarah. They had formed a friendship based on their inexperience.

"I need to check your tags and keys," Hadiya said. Sarah gestured to the top drawer of her desk. Hadiya crouched down next to it and began the process of counting the unused tags and testing the keys. It didn't take long. "All sorted," she said, tapping her slate as she sailed out of the room.

Mabel sat down on the big padded chair in the middle of the room, put one leg up on the leg rest, and leaned back. She was wearing gold hoop earrings and a baggy black sweatshirt. "How's Cass?"

"Difficult," Sarah admitted. "She keeps asking about Greg's release date."

"Does she know that he's going somewhere else?"

"Not yet. And I'm not looking forward to her finding out. She's her daddy's girl. Always has been."

"Even now? After he broke Curfew?"

"Especially now," Sarah said. "As far as Cass is concerned, Curfew is the evil that took her dad away from her and left her stuck with her witch of a mother."

Mabel laughed. "You should ask Hadiya if you can bring her here for a day, let her see what it's all about. It might change her mind." She swung her leg to the floor and sat up, then looked at the clock on the wall. "Time to get to work." Her room was just next door, and after she left, Sarah could hear her singing to herself through the wall.

Like Mabel, Sarah had dressed plainly. They all did. The men who came into her room were presented with an easily forgettable experience. Her work uniform, as she thought of it, consisted of dark trousers and a loose-fitting shirt. She never said more than she had to, even with the lonely ones who wanted to chat. She preferred the ones who were angry, their resentment simmering just below the surface, leaking out through clenched teeth and flushed cheeks. Tagging them was easy. There was never any doubt that she was doing the right thing.

It was harder with the ones who came in with children in tow. They frequently told her Curfew was a good thing because they got to spend quality time together, as their offspring sat there grubby faced, glued to a slate. Sarah always smiled at the children as she checked their fathers' tags. When boys came in on their tenth birthday for their first tag, she offered them big fruity lollipops in colorful wrappers. They were just children, too young to understand what the tags really meant, and her heart ached a little for them. There wouldn't be any post-Curfew swimming lessons or scout camps for these boys. It would be a life of restriction.

But it was worth it. Sweet, good-natured ten-year-old boys became men, and men couldn't be trusted.

She could remember sitting on the brown corduroy sofa in their poky living room, perched right on the edge of the seat with her face in her hands as the MPs at Westminster voted to bring Curfew into law. Talk of it had been rumbling for months, but she hadn't believed it would happen. Surely a country with such a long history of talking about male violence but failing to do anything about it wouldn't take such a drastic step. But it did.

Sarah checked her watch and buzzed in her first appointment. He was in his late twenties, with a mop of dark hair deliberately arranged so that it fell down over his forehead, and two days' worth of stubble. She recognized his type immediately and inwardly rolled her eyes. "Hi," he said, smiling at her.

"Take a seat." Sarah turned to check her screen. "Can you confirm your name, please?"

"Tom Roberts," he said.

He settled into the chair and rolled up the cuff of his jeans, revealing a white sports sock and a tanned, hairy calf. His tag sat just above the sock. Sarah inspected it, examining the strap and the fastening.

"Everything all right?" he asked, in a way that told Sarah he was confident that it would be and was talking more to make conversation than because he wanted an answer.

"Fine."

"Good," he replied. He leaned closer, so that she caught a faint whiff of his cologne, which was not unpleasant, and examined the tag himself before pulling his jeans leg down. "How long until I need a new one?"

"Let me just check." Sarah wheeled her seat away and turned her attention back to the screen. "Not until next year."

"I guess I'll see you in another three months, then."

"I guess you will."

She updated his record and wiped down the seat, then picked up her water bottle only to find it empty. It would only take a minute to fill it at the water fountain just outside her room. In the corridor, she saw Mabel talking to Tom Roberts. Mabel caught Sarah's eye over his shoulder. She didn't look happy. He strolled off toward the exit. Curious, Sarah followed Mabel into her room.

"God, he's such a prick," Mabel said, before Sarah could even ask.

"How do you know him?"

"He's my best friend's boyfriend." Mabel sat on her chair, lifting her feet off the floor and letting it swivel. "She thinks the sun shines out of his backside. The problem is that she's got baby fever and she can't see past the pretty face."

"Have you tried talking to her about it?"

"No," Mabel admitted. "What would I even say? That I think she's so desperate for a baby that she's lost all common sense? She'd be really hurt. He's her choice and I've got to respect that. It's just . . ."

"He's a prick?" Sarah offered.

"Exactly. The thing is, I couldn't even tell you why I don't like him. Helen adores him, so there's obviously something good about him." She sighed. "It's probably just me."

"No," Sarah said. "I just did his tag. Didn't like him."

"You don't like any of them."

Sarah laughed. She made her way back to her own room, sipping her water as she went. A couple of men were late, but she accommodated them, and by the time she'd put her tag keys on to charge, restocked her drawer with new tags, and taken a quick look at her appointment list for the next day, it was ten to seven.

She stopped at the supermarket on the way home, lingering a little longer than necessary when all she wanted was a bag of salad and a cooked chicken, but she enjoyed these short spells of quiet freedom between work and home. They had become a habit long before Greg went to prison, and that habit had remained for one reason, and one reason only.

Cass.

Sarah paid for her shopping without bothering to check how much it cost. She dumped the bag on the passenger seat and thought about going back in for a bottle of wine but decided against it. Better to get back and see her daughter, even if the thought didn't exactly fill her with joy.

Seeing the Motherhouse helped. She and Cass had moved into the building two months back. It had once been a primary school, and the old Victorian building had been converted into a series of flats, complete with communal kitchen, dining room, and laundry. It was strictly female only, a place for women who wanted to live their lives without men.

"But what about Dad?" Cass had asked when Sarah had shown her around the quiet two-bedroom apartment that she'd been offered. "Where's he going to live when he gets out of prison?"

The walls were white, the carpets were a soft pink, and the bath was deep and new. Sarah wanted to live there as soon as she saw it. The icing on the cake was the shared spaces, where the women in the Motherhouse cooked and ate together. She had decided there and then that Greg's living arrangements were not her problem. "You'll have your own shower," she had said in reply, pointing to the en suite in the second bedroom. "Look."

Sarah had paid the deposit and they'd moved in three days later. The Motherhouse had turned out to be everything she'd hoped. Her relationship with Cass, however, was best described as a work in progress. She opened the door of their apartment to find Cass's boots on the mat, perfectly placed for her to trip over. She pushed them out of the way with the side of her foot and went into the kitchen, where she found a loaf of bread out on the counter next to an open packet of butter, a knife mark deep in the soft yellow. There was a dollop of jam on the worktop. When she went past Cass's bedroom, Cass was sitting on the bed, slate in hand, chewing on a sandwich.

"Chicken and salad for tea," Sarah called, as she continued on to her own room. She heard Cass get off the bed and come padding along the hallway.

"I thought we were having Chinese," Cass said, standing in the doorway. She was wearing skintight jeans with a rip in the knee and Sarah's new red jumper. She tugged at the hem, daring Sarah to notice.

Sarah didn't mind Cass borrowing the jumper. It suited her. But she wished that she'd asked first. "I didn't feel like it."

"What about what I felt like?"

Sarah eased off her shoes and wiggled her toes. "Feel free to cook something," she said, inwardly regretting the words as soon as they left her mouth. She waited for the explosion. She could feel the tension of it building in the room, thickening the air, heating her blood. She heard the hitch in Cass's breathing. She had the option to back down, to back off, to make this easier on both of them. She decided not to. She'd already let Cass get away with the mess in the kitchen and with stealing her jumper.

"I've got homework," Cass said in a hard, tight voice. "I haven't got time to make dinner as well."

"I work full-time," Sarah pointed out. "You still expect me to make dinner."

"Dad always made dinner."

"Well, Dad isn't here."

"Thanks to you," Cass said.

Sarah could see her daughter's temper building further, and she sighed. "Do we really have to do this again, Cass?"

Cass opened her mouth, closed it again, then turned and went back to her own bedroom, slamming the door behind her. No sound came through. She would be messaging Billy on her slate, no doubt telling him how awful Sarah was.

It pained Sarah to know that Cass thought so little of her, but then she was her father's daughter. He was there in the shape of her eyes and the way her hair peaked slightly in the middle of her forehead, and in the face she pulled when she was angry, which was most of the time.

Sarah went back into the kitchen, looked again at the mess on the worktop, then picked up her keys and went to the communal dining room. It wasn't her night to eat there, but the other women wouldn't mind. She needed good conversation and a friendly face, and she wasn't going to find it here. Maybe the others would know what to do with Cass. Sarah had no bloody idea anymore. She wanted to be close to her daughter, for Cass to trust her and tell her secret things, to laugh together, and she had hoped that living here, in this haven of women, would help her figure out how, but so far it wasn't working.

If anything, it had made things worse.

CHAPTER FOUR

Helen

In her classroom on the other side of town, Helen Taylor opened her bag and tucked her slate away before giving her classroom one last check. She found a broken stylus on the floor and a book that had been put back on the shelf upside down and swiftly dealt with both of them. She liked to leave things in an organized, tidy state.

Her slate buzzed as she was putting on her jacket. It was Mabel. They had dinner together every week and had done for years. Sometimes they went to a bar or a club afterward, dancing in a crowd of other women until their feet screamed at them to stop, though they'd been doing that less and less recently.

Still on for tonight?

Absolutely! Helen replied.

The town center was an easy walk from the school. Helen cut through the park, enjoying the early autumn sunshine and the way it made everything look alive. The flower beds had started to die down and some of the trees were shedding, but there was still a cheery amount of green. A middle-aged woman ran past in a shock of pink Lycra, headphones on, and she smiled at Helen as she passed. Helen smiled back.

Another group of women had gathered to do yoga and she saw a group of teenage girls setting out a picnic blanket. The world came to life after Curfew. Women ruled these public spaces. They were free to do what they wanted, say what they wanted, dress how they wanted. They were free to walk home drunk at midnight without being bothered.

Her slate buzzed again as she walked through the gates on the other side of the park. It was Tom. Where are you?

Dinner with Mabel, she replied.

Can't wait to see you this weekend. So close to Cohab Day
already! Have fun with M. Call me later???

The slate was still in her hand when someone caught her attention from the other side of the road. It was Mabel, one arm in the air, waving madly. As if Helen could miss her. As if anyone could miss her, given that she was almost six feet tall, plus hair.

Crossing the road, Helen ran up to Mabel and hugged her. They linked arms and Helen found herself being steered in the direction of the shops. She didn't resist. They looked in the window of the shoe shop, where Helen admired a pair of blue suede boots, and in the jeweler's and in the bookshop. They found a table outside their favorite restaurant, Puccino's, and the waitress brought them a jug of water with slices of lemon in it and a basket of breadsticks. Helen picked one up and snapped it in half. Huge heaters rained warmth down on her back.

"God, I love Curfew." Mabel sighed happily, looking around. "Did you ever think, when it came in, that it would be like this?"

"I was fifteen," Helen said. "I just wanted to walk home after swimming club without being shouted at by the boys who lived at the end of my road."

"Speaking of boys, I saw Tom today," Mabel said. "Came into the center to have his tag checked."

"He mentioned it was due," Helen said. The waitress reappeared, and they ordered cheap red wine and a salami pizza with extra cheese. "Did you check it?"

"No, someone else did. Why?"

"Just making conversation," Helen replied. She wanted to say *how did he look, did he mention me, what did you talk about?* But she held back. Mabel and Tom were the one area in her life that was sticky. Mabel didn't like Tom. She was nice enough to his face, but Tom hadn't been fooled, and once he'd pointed it out to Helen, it was so obvious that she didn't know how she'd missed it. Helen had taken to ignoring it, not knowing what else to do. Some people just didn't jell. "Work seems to be going well. You're obviously well suited to tagging."

Her slate buzzed again, and she took a moment to check it. Tom.

I miss you.

"I think so," Mabel said. "I'm starting to get the hang of it now, and it's good money. Plus, I help to make it possible for girls to walk home after swimming club without being shouted at, and you know I like that."

"Me too," Helen said, smiling as she tapped out a quick reply to the message from Tom.

Miss you too.

They finished the pizza and the wine, and then a second bottle of wine on top of that. It was more than Helen would usually have on a school night, but they were having such a lovely time, and it had been a stressful day. Cass Johnson was turning into a real pain. It hadn't been an easy few months for Cass, with her father in prison, but Helen had cut her enough slack. It was time that Cass got over herself and grew up.

Mabel held the empty bottle over her glass, watching as the last few drops fell out. Her cheeks were flushed with alcohol, and when she grinned at Helen, her teeth were purple.

"I'm glad that it's going well," Helen said. "Speaking of things going well, I wanted to talk to you about something."

"What?"

The wine felt lovely and warm inside Helen's belly. "Me and Tom."

"What about you and Tom?" Mabel asked.

"We're . . . we're thinking about moving in together."

Mabel sat back in her chair. "Already?"

"You make it sound like we've been together six weeks instead of six months," Helen said. She felt a bit dizzy. Perhaps too much wine. "We've already started the counseling. We're seeing Dr. Fearne at the therapy center in town. She's really good."

"This is major, Helen. I can't believe that you didn't tell me you were seeing a therapist."

"I didn't know if it would work out," Helen said, a little annoyed. As Tom kept reminding her, she was allowed a private life. She didn't have to share everything with Mabel. "I didn't see the point in telling you until I was sure we were going to get the certificate."

"Of course you should have told me!"

"I'm sorry." It was a knee-jerk reaction, the word slipping out because it was what you said in the face of anger. It was the safe word, the defuse-the-tension word, the word that promised you would take the blame as long as the other person stopped being mad at you. "You're right. I should have said something."

"It's just so quick," Mabel said. "I'm a bit surprised, that's all."

"I know," Helen replied. "And it is quick. It's really quick." She exhaled. Her slate buzzed again. This time she ignored it. "But we both feel this is right. We've talked about it loads and I know he feels the same way I do."

"How do you know?"

There it was again, the little angry jab, like the bite of a wasp sting. "Because I know him," Helen said.

"How can you possibly know him after six months?"

Helen could feel the beginnings of a headache. "Please, Mabel. I know you don't like him, but he's lovely. I don't know why you can't see it."

"I never said I didn't like him," Mabel told her.

The waitress came over with the bill. Helen paid it. The two of them picked up their bags and left, taking their usual route back through the park. They walked past the lake. The fountain was still running, sending ripples out across the surface.

"You don't like him, though, do you?" Helen asked. She didn't know why she was asking that question, or what answer she wanted.

"Don't do this," Mabel said.

"Do what?"

"Just don't." She unlinked her arm from Helen's, and with a small step, put what felt like a huge distance between them. "I'll call you later, okay?"

The joy of the evening leaked away into the darkening sky, and Helen stumbled home to her empty flat, hurt and sad. She turned on the lights and the kettle and left a cup of tea to stew on the work-top as she checked her phone and realized that she had several more messages from Tom. She slumped down on the sofa and messaged him back. In between messages, she looked at new posts on the pregnancy forum she'd started to haunt. Another three women had announced their pregnancies. All of them were having girls. Helen felt a pang of longing and envy. She imagined the day when she'd be able to put up her own message. Soon, she told herself. Soon. She'd already stopped taking the pill and started taking folic acid. She hadn't told Tom yet, because she didn't want to pressure him, but she was sure that he'd be thrilled if she got pregnant.

CHAPTER FIVE

Cass

Cass sat in the passenger seat of the car, leaning her head against the window. It was still dark outside. She yawned. She wouldn't normally have been up this early, and there hadn't been time for coffee. Sarah was making her do a day of work experience at the tagging center. Cass had been quite looking forward to the day off school until they'd had a row about her choice of clothes. Cass had won and was wearing the skirt she'd picked out rather than the loose trousers Sarah had wanted her to put on.

The world looked different at this time of day, before Curfew had ended. Cass saw a running group all dressed in matching purple T-shirts and a few women pushing buggies or holding hands with toddlers. One little boy, in a dark blue jacket and yellow wellies, was kicking at the leaves. *Enjoy it while it lasts, kid*, she thought to herself. There were no teenage boys. No adult men. They were all inside.

Sarah was talking, but her voice was just noise in the background. "... so it's really important that you follow my instructions to the letter. Tagging is a serious business, Cass. There are procedures to be followed. The last thing we want is for a man to leave the clinic with a tag that isn't functioning properly. Understand?"

"I'm not stupid."

"I didn't say you were."

They pulled into the car park for the tagging center. Before they went inside, Sarah gave Cass a once-over. "Lose the lipstick," she said.

Cass's mouth formed a hard pout. Her back teeth pressed together. "It's appropriate workwear," she said.

"Maybe according to those trash bag magazines you're so obsessed with, but not in the real world." Sarah pulled a few tissues from her pocket and held them out.

"Fine," Cass said. She snatched the tissues from her mother's hand, then she carefully reduced the lipstick, but she didn't remove it completely.

It wasn't her first visit to a tagging center. Greg had brought her with him to tag checks when she was little, although it had stopped once she started school. As she followed Sarah inside, she remembered the waiting room with wipe-clean plastic chairs and the TV tuned to a kids' channel. Always kids' TV. Never anything else. There was a reception desk shielded by Perspex and a vending machine. She remembered that, too. Greg would always let her have something, usually salt and vinegar crisps, and she had loved watching the machine work.

On one side of the waiting room was a row of closed doors, each identified by a different letter. A dark-skinned woman with curly hair stuck her head out of door H and smiled. "Morning!" she said cheerily.

"Hi, Mabel," Sarah said. "This is my daughter, Cass."

"Hello, Cass." Mabel came rushing forward, one hand outstretched. Cass shook it. "Lovely to meet you."

Cass straightened her shoulders. She gave Mabel a big smile. "Nice to meet you," she said. "I like your earrings." Although not the baggy black trousers, or the sweatshirt, which looked far too much like what her mother was wearing.

"Thanks!" Mabel replied.

She didn't comment on Cass's outfit in return, not even her carefully chosen necklace, but there was no time to dwell on it because Sarah had opened the door to another room and was waiting for her to go inside.

The room was small, one wall taken up by a large window half-obscured by a venetian blind with yellowed strings pulled higher at one side than the other. The window itself had a lovely view of a half-dead tree and the car park. There was a chair in the middle of the room that looked like the one at the dentist's, with thick padding and a headrest, and horrible strip lighting.

There were posters on the wall, a couple about compulsory tagging of ten-year-old boys, telling parents to Look Out for Your Letter! and Avoid a Fine! Another was about tagging checks. That one had been there for a while, judging by the haircut of the man on it. All the men on the posters were beaming away as if their tag was the best gadget they'd ever had. What a crock of shit.

Sarah's desk was just as grim. She didn't have a single nice thing. No spider plant, no pot of colored pens, no photos or little ornaments. As Cass looked at her mother, sitting there in her beige clothes in her beige room at her beige job, a wave of disgust washed over her. This wasn't a good job. It was awful. Cass promised herself there and then that she was never going to be a tagger like her mother. Never. She would do a job that helped people.

"We start at eight," Sarah said. "Most of the men will be here for a routine check to make sure the tag is in good condition and working properly. The aim is to get them in and out as quickly as possible. We're not their social worker or their friend, though some of them seem to think otherwise."

She had a small black case on the desk, which she deftly opened. She picked something out of it. "This is a tag key," she said, holding it up. It looked a bit like a memory stick for a laptop, except that it had a metal hook sticking out of one end. "It locks and unlocks the tags. If I need to replace a tag, new ones are in here." She leaned down and opened a drawer, which Cass saw was full of boxes, each containing the familiar black bands. "There are different sizes because it's important that the tag fits well and doesn't cause any irritation. Have you any questions so far?"

Yes, Cass thought to herself. *How can you do this? Don't you think tagging is wrong? Why shouldn't the men talk to you if they want to? Why do you hate men so much?* "No," she said.

"Okay," Sarah replied. She gestured to a seat in the corner. "You sit there. You'll just be watching. I'll explain why you're here. If any of them don't like it, then you'll have to wait outside until they're done, but I'm sure it'll be fine."

Cass looked at the floor and then the wall. Anything to avoid making eye contact with Sarah. Her gaze settled on the one bright thing in the room, a red button on the wall just above the desk. "What's that for?"

Sarah turned to see what Cass was pointing at. "That's an alarm."

"An alarm?"

"Yes. In case I need help."

"Oh."

There was no chance to ask anything else. Sarah clicked on the first name in a spreadsheet. A man entered a few moments later. He confirmed his name and sat in the big seat in the middle, pulling up one leg of his suit trousers to reveal a stripy sock and his tag. Sarah poked at it and clicked some more on her screen before telling the man he could leave, which he promptly did. She sprayed the seat with a smelly blue liquid and wiped it down, and then clicked on the list again. For the next two hours Cass watched a parade of men traipse in and out. They didn't complain about her presence. Most of them barely acknowledged her.

She got very bored.

There was a short break and then there was more of the same, and Cass began to feel stiff and uncomfortable in her skirt and boots. She longed for a pair of trousers so that she could sit with her knees a little farther apart and ease the growing stiffness in her back.

Another hour went by. The only time Cass saw a flicker of anything resembling emotion was when Sarah fitted a tag to a ten-year-old boy, his first one. He cried. Sarah gave him a lollipop as his father apologized profusely for his son's tears. "God, I hate doing kids," she said after the pair of them had left.

"So don't do them," Cass said. Sarah's reaction to the little boy had surprised her. She'd always thought of her mother as someone who didn't have much time for children. She'd certainly not had much time for Cass when she was little. She'd always been at work.

"It's my job," Sarah said. "And unfortunately, I don't get to pick and choose which parts of it I want to do. A bit like the rest of life."

Before Cass could respond, the sound of raised voices came filtering through the wall from the room next door.

"What the hell is that about?" Sarah muttered, already halfway out of her seat. She wrenched the door open and marched out of the room. Cass stayed where she was for approximately five seconds before deciding that she didn't want to miss whatever was going on, and rushed after Sarah.

Something was happening in Mabel's room, something big and exciting. The men in the waiting room were craning their necks to get a better view, some of them half out of their seats. Cass darted in through the open door. There was a large, meaty man with a very red face in the chair. "It's too tight!" he shouted, gesturing to his tag. "All I'm asking you to do is loosen the bloody thing!"

Mabel was standing next to the chair. "The fit is fine," she shouted back at him.

And then there was Sarah. She was standing just to the left of the doorway, and there was something in her hand. "This is your final warning," she said to the man. She didn't shout. Her voice was cold and sharp and it was somehow far worse.

The man took no notice. He grabbed at his tag, trying to pull it off.

"Stop that!" Sarah snapped at him as she took a step forward. Something flew from the end of the thing in her hand and hit the man squarely in the chest. His face twisted into a look of acute surprise, his mouth forming a vicious, angry word, and then he collapsed back on the chair. He lay there, twitching violently, making a strange animal sound unlike anything Cass had heard come from another person before. She looked at him and saw someone who was utterly helpless.

She looked at her mother and saw a monster.

CHAPTER SIX

Pamela

Present Day
8:30 a.m.

It takes two hours to move the body from the park to the morgue. We work as fast as we can because we're on a clock, and we all know it. Closing off the park has already generated a lot of online chatter. As soon as people find out that there's a body, difficult questions will be asked, which at the moment I can't answer. I still don't know who she is. But I do know that somewhere is a family that is about to receive the worst possible news about a daughter, or a sister, or a wife, and my heart hurts for them. They're strangers to me now. They won't be by the end of this.

The station is frantic. The officers who worked the night shift are still here, and the day shift is here, too. I've got officers at the homes of the two women who found the body, talking it through with them, making sure they don't tell anyone what they know or post anything online. No one has been reported missing yet, though I'm hoping that call will come in soon. Until I know who she is, trying to find the person who did this to her is like looking for a needle in a haystack.

That doesn't mean I'm not trying. But there's not much to go on. I'm waiting for a call from the pathologist telling me I can see the body and examine her clothes. There are officers at the park, sweeping for evidence there. Rachel and I are sitting together in a meeting room at the station. We're watching the CCTV footage of the park on the big screen. So far we've zipped through seven hours of nothing. The quality is pretty poor. The most interesting thing we've seen so far is a fox that ran across the path, head down, on the hunt for something.

The tagging program is so expensive that the council doesn't have much left over for camera maintenance, and with men indoors overnight and not tipping out of pubs and clubs half-cut and less able to behave themselves, we don't need CCTV as much.

The clock in the corner of the screen reads 2:48 a.m. when we finally see something that makes me sit up and take notice. The park is empty at that point, though the main pathways are still lit, making everything gray and white, so any movement at all is interesting. But this is far more than just a nocturnal animal looking for food.

This is something. This is definitely something. My mouth goes dry.

"Oh my god," Rachel says under her breath.

A figure in dark, loose clothing strides along the path. They've got something in their arms. Even wrapped up, I can tell that it's our victim. The figure appears for only a few brief seconds, then disappears out of view. It doesn't reappear. I rewind the recording, slow it down, and we watch it again and again. Whoever it is has their hood up and we don't get a clear look at their face.

"She's pretty strong, whoever she is," Rachel says.

"She?" The only "she" I can see on the screen is the one wrapped in a sheet. "That's a man."

"No, it's not." Rachel's confusion is obvious. "It's a woman."

I wonder if we're looking at the same image. To me, everything about it screams male. "Look at the height, the proportions of the body. The way they move."

But Rachel can't see it. "It can't be a man," she says. "His tag would have gone off and we'd have known. He would never have made it to the park."

She sounds so certain, and I know that if I spoke to any of the other young female officers, I'd get a similar answer. It's not their fault. They've been through an education system that teaches them that Curfew is infallible, and then they've had their police training, which reinforces that idea. To them, this is the way the world works. But it's not to me. Every system has broken edges. Rules are proved by the exceptions. Yes, Curfew keeps men indoors at night. But to blindly insist that there's no room for error, for failure? Only a fool would do that.

Although I suppose it could be a woman, if she was above average height. The clothes are baggy enough to hide breasts and hips. The walk could be distorted by the load being carried. "You're probably right," I say, thinking of the body currently lying on a slab at the morgue, the long day ahead, the energy I'm going to need to get through it that I don't want to waste on a fight with a junior officer.

"Probably?" Rachel asks. She shakes her head. "Honestly, Pamela."

"I simply don't think that we should rule anything out."

"We can rule out the possibility that it's a man!"

I want to point out that no system is unbreakable, that it's important not to dismiss anything at this stage, but I bite my tongue. I know what the other women think of me. I'm the oldest here, only a few weeks away from retirement. I'm considered old-fashioned, out of touch, a dinosaur still clinging to outdated fears. They believe in the tech, the tags, the slates. I like the tech, and I think it's made our lives better, easier, but I also believe in listening to my gut.

The image from the CCTV is still frozen on the big screen and I stare at it. Rachel's slate buzzes, shortly followed by mine. I've got two messages. One from the pathologist, telling me that I can visit our victim as soon as I'm able. The other is from the commissioner of police for our area.

"They're sending in a specialist team," Rachel says. "Does that mean we'll be taken off the investigation?"

"Probably," I say. But until I'm told otherwise, I'm going to keep doing my job.

CHAPTER SEVEN

Sarah

Sarah didn't tase a man very often. The first time had been awful. She'd barely slept the following night, pulled awake by vivid flashes of memory that left her shaken and breathless. The buzz of the device, the sound the man had made when he'd collapsed, the puddle of yellow that had spread across the floor. Before that, it had been an intellectual exercise. Reality had been a shock. The second time she'd been better prepared. This third one barely even registered.

But she'd forgotten one thing.

Cass.

It was Mabel who alerted her to Cass's presence in the doorway. "Oh, shit," she said, and Sarah turned to find her daughter standing there, face so pale that she looked like she might faint. She looked at Sarah, then at the man, then at Sarah again. Her bottom lip wobbled.

"Take her to the break room, will you?" Sarah asked Mabel. "I've got to deal with him."

Cass was quickly swept away. Hadiya came in, took one look at him, and sighed. The next thing she did was call the police. Sarah wasn't too concerned about that. It was routine. The important thing now was to keep everyone calm. The men in the waiting room would be upset. Some of them would want to leave without having their tags checked and would have to be rebooked.

What a pain in the arse men are, Sarah thought as she looked across at the one who was still sitting limply in the chair. As the person who had tased him, she was responsible for sitting with him until the police arrived, for making sure that he was conscious and breathing, if not exactly comfortable.

There was paperwork to do and forms to fill out, so she took a seat at Mabel's desk and made a start on it. According to the system, the man's name was Paul Townsend. He was sixty-three years old. Divorced with two adult children, he worked part-time at the sorting office on London Road. The last tagger who had dealt with him had made a note of his hostile attitude. That worked in Sarah's favor if he decided to kick up a fuss. She'd just started writing a short description of what had happened when the door opened. It was Hadiya again. "Police are here," she said.

The first of them breezed into the room, heavy-duty boots creaking. Sarah felt herself relax at the sight of her dark uniform. Everything would be all right now. The officer acknowledged Sarah with a nod, then turned to the man slumped in the chair. "Right, sir," she said. "Let's get you out of here, shall we?"

Another officer followed her in, this one younger and male. The two of them grabbed the man under the arms and tried to make him stand. He resisted.

"Put some effort into it," the male officer said to him. "There's an easy and a hard way to do this, you know. The easy way is that you walk out of here, with us, now, and get quietly into the back of the van. It'll be a couple of minutes of embarrassment, sure, making that trip through the waiting room, but you're a big guy. You can handle that. The alternative is that we cuff you, I bring in more officers, and we carry you out."

The man made a strangled noise, veins popping out in his neck. He took a strained breath and tried again. "Walk," he said.

"Good choice," the female officer told him. She didn't waste any more time and he was swiftly ushered out of sight. Sarah heard the silence that fell in the waiting room, felt the buildup of pressure as they all waited to see who would be the first to say something. It was a little boy. She heard his high, childish voice, the confusion and fear in it, the low, muttered response from his father.

She finished her report, then left Mabel's room and made her way past the waiting men, all of whom had seen her run in there, all of whom would know that it was her who had tased the man they had watched be escorted out. She liked that they knew. She hoped it would make them think twice about their own behavior. She hoped that they were even a little bit scared.

When she got to the break room, Cass was sitting at a table in the corner, playing with a can of Coke. Mabel was in front of one of the vending machines. She fed it some coins and then pushed a couple of buttons. Something clattered to the bottom. She bent down to retrieve it. Sarah walked over and gave her a reassuring squeeze on the arm.

"The tag was fine," Mabel said.

"I know," Sarah said. "Some men just like to argue." Then she turned to her daughter. "It's probably best if you go home, Cass."

Cass jerked upright. "What? Why?"

"Please don't argue," Sarah said. She didn't explain, didn't try to justify it. It didn't occur to her that she should. Cass was in the way. All of the taggers were behind on their appointments now, there were reports to write, and they would all need to talk about what had happened, to decompress. They couldn't do that in front of a teenager, especially not one in a miniskirt.

"I'm supposed to do a full day of work experience, otherwise it doesn't count," Cass complained.

"For god's sake, just go!" It was only half past eleven and Sarah had already had a full day's worth of stress. As she looked at her daughter in lipstick and a miniskirt, she only felt more annoyed. Why couldn't Cass accept that sometimes, Sarah knew better than she did?

"Fine," Cass said. She shoved her chair back so hard that it squeaked on the floor. "I left my bag in your room. I'll have to get it." She marched out without saying another word, the effect somewhat spoiled by her attempt to tug her skirt down without making it obvious.

"It was a lot for her to take in," Mabel said.

"It was a lot for all of us," Sarah said. She rubbed a hand over her face. "I'm glad it's Friday."

"What a way to end the week."

Sarah laughed. "I think I'll be having an extra-large glass of wine tonight."

She went back to her office, thinking about the first time she'd faced male anger. It hadn't been here at the tagging center but in her own home, and the man hadn't been a stranger, it had been her husband. But Greg wouldn't get the opportunity to do that to her again. She'd made sure of that. She could vividly remember him standing on the path outside their house, yelling at her to let him back in, how she'd stood in the hallway with her heart racing, almost too shocked to breathe. She'd only moved to stop Cass from opening the door. As far as Sarah was concerned, he'd deserved it, but that hadn't made his anger any less frightening.

As she crossed reception, Hadiya caught up with her and asked her if she wanted to go home. Sarah said no. She just wanted to get back to work. She didn't want to spend the rest of the day in her apartment at the Motherhouse, because Cass would be there, and Sarah was in no mood to talk to her daughter. She'd seen the way Cass had looked at her. She was sick of the fact that every time she tried to do something that she thought Cass would find useful or interesting, that would help bring the two of them together, it went wrong.

At least the men here had to listen to her.

CHAPTER EIGHT

Cass

C ass walked out of the building with her heart pounding. It sounded so loud in her ears that she was sure everyone could hear it, even though she knew that was impossible. The world around her seemed vivid and close, the fallen leaves a brighter orange and the sky a stiffer gray than they had been before. The air smelled tangy and repeated shallow breaths left her feeling oxygen starved.

In her hand, buried deep inside her pocket, was a tag key.

She could feel the hard shape of it pressing against her clammy fingers. It had been lying on the floor in her mother's room when she'd gone to get her things. She'd seen it as soon as she walked through the door. She'd taken her bag out of Sarah's drawer, checked for her purse and slate, and she'd tried to ignore the key, really she had. She hadn't intended to take it. She hadn't even known that she was going to do it until she did.

She'd scooped it up quickly and shoved it into her jacket pocket, and then she'd walked straight out of there. No one had tried to stop her, not even the woman on reception. She felt little guilt. It served them right for being so careless.

Cass wondered if the key would work.

She fleetingly considered how much men would pay to have their tags removed. She imagined setting up a service to do it. She'd pick and choose her clientele and treat them with the utmost respect. It wouldn't be like the tagging center. She knew, deep down, that it wasn't possible. She worked all the scenarios anyway, planning what she'd wear, what she'd say, what the men would be like, and soon she'd pushed away the horrible, grubby images of that morning.

There was one thought that she couldn't push away, however, and that was of Sarah tasing that man. The image that Cass had of her mother hadn't been particularly positive anyway. She already knew that Sarah was a cold-faced bitch. Look what she'd done to her dad. But now . . . Cass felt ashamed to be her daughter.

At least Greg would be released soon. Cass had the date marked on the calendar on her slate. She hadn't been allowed to visit him in prison, because she was under eighteen so couldn't go without Sarah, and Sarah had refused to take her. But she was sure that as soon as he was out, he'd make contact and then things would change. There'd be no more living in the stupid Motherhouse with Sarah, tied to their stupid rules. She couldn't even invite Billy over to do homework or watch a film because he wasn't allowed inside the building. She imagined Sarah's face when she told her that she was moving out of their apartment and moving in with her dad, and it made her feel better.

It made her feel so much better that she went all the way into town, and why not? It wasn't like she had anything else to do. Cass loved going into town. She could easily lose hours looking in boutique windows, imagining buying whatever she wanted. But the emotional fatigue from the morning kicked in after only half an hour, and with it, a craving for sugar. She went straight to the coffee shop in the town square that sold fresh croissants and hot chocolate with hazelnut syrup.

She was surprised to find it almost empty. It was much nicer than coming on a Saturday morning and having to sit at a dirty table with someone else's lipstick-smeared mug on it.

"Take a seat," called the man behind the counter. "I'll be with you in a sec."

Personal service, too? Cass sat on a seat toward the back, which had a good view of the counter, the rows of shiny cinnamon buns and chocolate macaroons and fruitcake. White mugs were stacked in precise rows. The counter was spotless, and the warm smell of butter and vanilla wafted from the worktop oven.

What to have, what to have.

Maybe a hot chocolate. Or a mocha with whipped cream.

But as the man came over from the other side of the counter, those thoughts slid completely out of Cass's head. It wasn't the first time she'd set eyes on him. He was sometimes here on a Saturday morning; not every time, but often enough. Then she'd only seen glimpses of him, mostly hidden by the chest-high counter or the silver bulk of the huge machine that hissed and spat as it steamed the milk. She knew the wave of dark hair that fell over his forehead, the dark eyes that matched it, the shoulders that stretched out the short-sleeved polo shirt with the green coffee shop logo on the right breast. The way his body shaped that shirt stirred something in Cass that she felt but couldn't examine too closely, not yet, because she was too young and the experience too overwhelming.

Her awareness of him had her tracking his movements as he stacked another row of cups alongside those already in place. The shape and size of his hands sent a sensual shiver running over her skin, both exhilarating and frightening all at once. She was glad now of the lipstick and the short skirt.

With the final cup put into position, he turned his attention to her and offered her a friendly smile. She smiled back. Did he recognize her? Had he noticed her on one of the many Saturdays she'd been in? She already knew his name. Bertie. She'd taken a sneaky photo and reverse searched the image on her slate weeks ago.

"Hi," he said. "What can I get you?"

"Hi," Cass replied, trying to sound casual. "I'd like a chai tea." She couldn't quite bring herself to ask for the extra-large luxury caramel hot chocolate that she really wanted. She straightened her back, trying to look a little taller, a little older.

"Anything to eat? The beignets are still warm."

She didn't want to look greedy, but then she didn't want to say no and have him think she was stuck-up. "Are they? Yes. Please."

"Sure," he said and reached for a mug. He was wearing jeans that were a little faded around the pockets, and a red belt. These details jumped out at her as if she were seeing him in high definition.

She took her slate from her bag and pretended to check her messages, wanting to look busy, wanting him to know that although she was in here alone, she wasn't a loner. He walked back behind the counter and got to work. He brought her tea over on a tray together with the beignet, warm as promised, and a neatly folded napkin and polished knife. She sent the payment from her slate and he lingered by the table until his own slate pinged to confirm that it had been received. He went back to polishing glasses on the other side of the counter. Cass ate her beignet in neat, tiny bites, a morsel at a time, instead of wolfing it down as she normally would. The air suddenly seemed heavy, her breathing too loud.

She kept playing with her slate. She checked her messages repeatedly, but she didn't get any new ones, so she sent a couple to herself, just to make it look like she had something to do. She sipped the tea slowly because it was horrible, but she'd ordered it, so she had to pretend to like it.

A couple of men in shirts and ties came in. They loitered at the counter before leaving with their take-out coffees. One of them gave Cass a sneaky glance on the way out. She raised an eyebrow at him, an expression she'd practiced in the mirror quite a few times, and he quickly looked away. She liked that. Men didn't need to be tagged. You just needed to know how to handle them. If her mother had any idea, she wouldn't have needed to tase that man. Cass took a big gulp of tea, forgetting in her triumph how horrible it was, and she must have made a noise because Bertie looked at her from behind the counter and grinned. Something about the way he smiled made Cass's insides feel funny.

"Is your drink all right?"

"It's fine."

"Oh. It's just that you don't strike me as the chai tea type."

"I don't?"

"No," he said. "Chai tea drinkers are always a bit . . . well. I shouldn't say it."

"A bit what?"

He shrugged. "Not like you."

That funny feeling in Cass's tummy got stronger. "Yeah," she said, because she couldn't think of anything else. She inwardly prayed that he didn't think she was an idiot.

"Why don't you let me choose something for you?" he asked.

"Oh, well . . ."

"On the house," he continued. "It's our policy. If you don't like it, we replace it for free."

"I suppose that would be okay," she said. "If it's policy."

He put his elbows on the counter and his chin on his hand and looked her over. "I know just the thing."

He turned and busied himself with syrups and milk and steam. Cass sat and watched him. She tried to think of witty things to say, but she couldn't come up with any, so she settled for trying to arrange herself in her seat so that she looked sexy and self-assured but hard to get. *Cosmopolitan* said that was important.

She could smell the caramel and a hint of something else when he brought her drink over, a thing of beauty in a tall glass topped with a perfect swirl of whipped cream. He set it down in front of her and held out a long-handled spoon. "Enjoy."

Cass took the spoon. "Thank you. I'm sure I will."

He moved back to the counter to serve new customers, leaving Cass to work on her drink and overanalyze the past few minutes. Had she imagined that he'd held on to the spoon for a second before she took it from him?

The clock on her slate told her that she'd been in the coffee shop for almost an hour. It didn't feel like that much time had passed. But the place was starting to get busy now, moving into lunch hour, and Cass started to worry. What if someone saw her and reported it to the school? Or worse still, to her mother?

She snuck a final glance at the man behind the counter. She was so sure that there had been something more than just the usual coffee shop service going on. Now, as she watched him, she wasn't sure at all. He glanced in her direction briefly and she dipped her chin and pouted, but he didn't look her way again. A woman in the queue looked over at her, and Cass could have sworn she laughed. The high she'd felt plunged into embarrassment that was so over-whelming she didn't even want to finish her drink.

She shoved her slate into her bag and slung the strap over her shoulder. Screw him. Screw all of them. She was fed up with people treating her as if she were nothing. Look at her mother, insisting she go to the tagging center and then kicking her out without even letting her do a full day. Her mood turned to thunder.

She went outside. The town center was busy, full of people of both sexes, not like the streets she'd seen on the way to the center that morning. She should feel happy here, but she didn't, not at all, and the events of the morning came crashing back in, and this time they didn't feel so good.

She'd taken a tag key from the center. No, not just taken. Stolen.

She put her hand in her pocket to check for it, feeling both sick and relieved when it made itself felt against the sensitive tips of her fingers. She had no idea what she was going to do with it. She couldn't keep it, but she couldn't bring herself to toss it into one of the nearby bins, paranoid that someone might see what she was doing.

She caught the bus home, sitting at the back, watching everyone else. No one took any notice of her, and eventually she was able to relax and think. She hadn't really stolen the key, she'd merely picked it up, and better her than one of the men.

The door of the Motherhouse opened before she could even get her key in the lock. Mrs. O'Brien looked out. "Home already?" she asked tartly.

Of all the women in the Motherhouse, Cass hated Mrs. O'Brien the most. She was the head of the residents' committee and got to decide who could live in the Motherhouse. Cass privately thought that the power had gone to her head. She didn't like the gym gear that Mrs. O'Brien seemed to live in, either. Dressing up your fleece top with pearls didn't make it look any better.

"Looks like it," Cass said, angling her way past the old bat and into the building.

"Shouldn't you be at school?"

"No." Cass didn't elaborate. It was none of her business. And she didn't say what she really wanted to say, because she knew that any attempt to tell Mrs. O'Brien to get stuffed would make its way back to her mother, and that would lead to an hour-long lecture on the importance of Being Nice to Other Women, especially the ones living in the Motherhouse. Cass thought they were pathetic, living in this place, refusing to have anything to do with men. They really needed to get over themselves. Not all men were awful.

She trekked along the hallway, her boots making marks in the pink carpet, then stomped up the stairs to their flat. She let herself in before any of the other behavior police who lived in the building could stick their heads out of their doors and find something to criticize. She hated living here. She wanted to be back in their old house with her dad. He was fun. He didn't care what she did or how she dressed. He didn't treat her like a child. She always felt like the women here were spying on her. She couldn't do anything.

Once inside her room, Cass kicked the door shut and flopped down on the bed. She took the tag key from her pocket and examined it more closely, then she hid it at the back of her underwear drawer and took a long bath. She was still shocked that Sarah had tased that man, but in hindsight, she should have been ready for it. She knew what her mother was like. She'd seen her push her dad out the door, after all.

The tag key was a problem, but only if she got caught with it, and the solution to that was simple. She wouldn't get caught. She thought about flushing it down the toilet, but what if it got stuck and blocked it? No. There had to be a better way, though she couldn't think of one. She spent an hour playing with her makeup, trying to get her eyeliner right. It was Friday, which meant that her mother would make her go downstairs to the communal dining room for dinner, so she wiped it off afterward because it wasn't worth the grief. She wished that she lived in a place where she could just be herself, somewhere without so many rules.

At least her dad would be out of prison soon. Then things would change. She was still thinking about that when Sarah arrived home from work. By that time Cass was stretched out on the sofa reading a magazine with the TV humming gently in the background. She tensed, expecting Sarah to ask her about the tag key, but Sarah went straight to her room. She didn't mention it when she came out, either, dressed in jeans and a cardigan. "Come on," she said. "We need to go downstairs and help with the food prep."

In what had been the old school kitchen, Cass was given a pile of potatoes to peel. She attacked the first few with vigor and dumped the skins into a plastic bucket. Sarah was supposed to help, but she was too busy talking to Mrs. O'Brien about the man she'd tased and so Cass had to do all of them, getting slower and more careless as her fingers grew wet and cold with the starchy juice. She'd have refused, but it was fish pie, her favorite, and she was hungry. By the time pudding was served and she was halfway through her portion of strawberry mousse, one thing was overwhelmingly clear. Sarah had no idea that Cass had taken the tag key. She hadn't even mentioned that it was missing. All she'd talked about was the man she'd tased. The other women had lapped it up. They acted like Sarah had been so brave, and they never once asked Cass how she'd felt.

And so Cass decided to keep it.

CHAPTER NINE

Helen

Helen woke early on Saturday morning, long before her alarm went off, and lay in bed staring at the ceiling and thinking about Tom. She pulled the duvet up to her chin and stretched her arm out across the empty half of the bed. Soon Tom would be on that side. She would wake in the morning and reach out and touch him, and it would be lovely.

She got up and dressed in a navy blouse and jeans. The blouse had mother-of-pearl buttons and a subtle stripe in the fabric, classy but not over the top. She'd taken great care with her outfits for each of the counseling sessions, keen to make a good impression. She didn't want to leave anything to chance. Dr. Fearne had to give them the certificate. She had to.

When Helen had stopped taking the pill six weeks before, the morning her reluctance to swallow it had escalated into a physical inability to put it in her mouth, she knew that she should tell Tom. But the right moment remained elusive. She told herself it wasn't a problem. It would take her body time to adjust, anyway. It wasn't like she was going to get pregnant straightaway. If anything, it was sensible, because by the time they got their Cohab certificate and were living together, her body would be free of the artificial hormones and ready to go.

There was still another hour before she was due to meet Tom. She decided to leave now to make sure she could find somewhere to park. Normally she would have saved the petrol money and walked. It wasn't far. But if she took her car, they'd have more time in bed that afternoon. They wouldn't have to rush. Maybe they'd even get to do it twice.

It took only a few minutes to drive into the town center, and she found a parking spot easily. Most of the shops were still closed. She looked in a couple of windows anyway, sighing over a green leather handbag and patent brogues, neither of which she needed. But maybe she should buy some new underwear. Tom was an attractive man, and Helen wasn't naive. She knew that he had other options. He didn't have to be with her. If she let herself go he would be straight back on the iDate app, looking for someone else.

She smoothed down the front of her blouse, trying to reassure herself. They loved each other. She had nothing to worry about. Yes, there had been some overlap between her and his previous girl-friend, but that was due to unfortunate timing, nothing more.

When she reached the counseling center, she sat on the wall outside and pulled out her slate. She stared at the same page of the book she was reading until the device switched itself off, and even then it was a while before she noticed, her mind far too busy with other things. What would Dr. Fearne ask them today? How was she going to answer? How would she feel if they got their certificate? How would she feel if they didn't?

Tom in her bed that night, and every night. A positive preg-nancy test. A baby girl.

Her slate pinged. It was a message from Tom, letting her know that he was on his way, but he'd probably be another twenty min-utes or so. The wall was hard and cold, and her bum wasn't happy about being seated on it, so Helen decided to kill the time with an-other walk around town. Things were starting to pick up. The cafés were open. The scent of cooking bacon wafted out of one of them. Helen contemplated going in for a sandwich, but the thought was pushed aside by her slate ringing. It was her mother.

Helen's parents had taken up permanent residence in their holiday home in the South of France as soon as Helen went to university. There had never been any suggestion that Helen go with them. She'd spent a couple of summers there while she'd been a student, not having anywhere else to stay, but she'd always felt like an intruder. Now she went for a week once a year, and sometimes even that felt like too much. Her parents were enthusiastic when she arrived, but by the third day, her father would have disappeared to play golf and her mother would be irritated by the change to her routine. They didn't come to visit her because her father refused to pay the fee to have a temporary tag fitted at the airport.

She decided not to answer the call. She turned on her heel and went back to the counseling center, taking up her spot on the wall. She didn't bother with her book this time. She sat, ankles crossed, hands clasped to keep in the nerves, and waited for Tom. He arrived at 8:30 on the dot, wearing a faded black sweatshirt and jeans. He smiled when he saw her.

Helen hopped down from the wall and ran over to him. "Tom!" she said and threw her arms around him, feeling the familiar spread of his shoulders beneath her hands, burying her face in his neck for just a moment so that she could breathe in his delicious smell, far better than the bacon.

"Are you ready?" he asked.

"Absolutely."

They still had a little time to kill before their appointment. Helen suggested that they go straight in anyway. The waiting room was comfortable enough and it was better than spending half an hour and twenty quid in one of the coffee shops in town.

The chairs were thinly padded, but the potted palm in the corner was flourishing. The woman on reception had the radio switched on and Helen hummed along with it. Tom kept her right hand firmly clasped between both of his, a gesture that she felt said many positive things about their relationship.

They chatted as they waited. Helen did most of the talking. It wasn't that she had anything to say, but her nerves were bubbly and huge and had to come out somewhere. She leaned into him. "Love you," she whispered, and he smiled at her and kissed the top of her head and made her feel like her heart was too big for her body.

A door opened on the other side of the corridor and a couple walked out. The woman came out first, arms folded, her walk stiff and fast. She was shortly followed by a man in a droopy jacket with a matching face. He shuffled out after her, moving at a much slower pace.

"Poor bloke," Tom said. "Doesn't look like he's having a good day."

"No," Helen replied, although she'd been thinking *poor woman, sleeping with that.* She put her thumb in her mouth and flexed the tip of her nail against her front teeth, a stress habit she'd thought broken years before.

"I wonder if they got turned down," Tom said.

"Maybe," Helen said. Not everyone got their certificate, it was true. At least she could say that the two of them had looked ill-suited. She couldn't decide if that made her feel better or worse. If a couple got turned down, they could apply again, but they would have to wait a year and show that there had been significant improvements in their relationship, whatever the hell that meant. The second round of counseling wasn't free, either. Helen patted her hair and wished she'd worn it differently.

The door opened again and Dr. Fearne stuck her head out. She had short hair dyed a fierce shade of red and matching glasses, and she wore big silver rings and long skirts. Helen often thought that she would have been a wonderful primary school teacher. "Morning!" she said brightly.

"Hello!" Helen said, trying to match her light tone. She got to her feet, glanced back at Tom to check that he was with her, then hurried into the now familiar office. She sat in the seat next to the window. There was a crystal vase with an arrangement of silk flowers in it on the windowsill, and a bookcase full of books with titles like *The Psychotherapy Toolbox* and *Counseling Techniques, Vol. 12* behind the desk.

Did she look nervous? She hoped not. She didn't want to do anything that might make Dr. Fearne think the two of them weren't compatible, because they were, they just were. Helen was certain of that. She would never do better than him.

Tom was the one.

He took the chair next to hers and sat back in his easy, comfortable way.

"How are you both today?" Dr. Fearne asked. She had her slate on a stand with a wireless keyboard in front of it, and she was tapping away as she spoke.

"We're good," Tom said.

"How about you, Helen?" Dr. Fearne asked, moving her glasses to the top of her head and turning to face them. "How was work this week?"

"Fine, thanks," Helen said. Her palms were damp, and she pressed them against her jeans. She didn't want Dr. Fearne to think that they were trying too hard. But she also didn't want her to think that they weren't trying at all, because surely that was just as bad.

"I imagine teaching teenagers must be a challenge. All those hormones. They always think they know everything when they don't know anything at all, don't they?"

"That just about sums it up," Helen replied. "I enjoy it, though. It's a good job."

"A very good job," Dr. Fearne agreed. "Well paid."

She looked at Tom when she said that. Helen noticed, and didn't like it. "Better than it used to be," she said.

"Yes," Dr. Fearne replied. She turned her gaze back to Helen. "Much better. I wouldn't want to go back to how things were before. Would you? All that unpaid housework and childcare and appalling wages for female-dominated professions, particularly if they had anything to do with children or care of the elderly. At least now what we do is taken seriously."

She moved her glasses from her head back to her nose and stabbed at her keyboard again. "So," she said. "Session nine! Today we'll be talking about domestic responsibilities and your thoughts on those. I find it always helps if a couple has thrashed out an agreement before they move in together."

"Well, we both work," Tom said. "So we'll both chip in."

Helen felt all the muscles in her back tighten up. Dr. Fearne didn't like vague answers. "Tom's already said that he's going to do most of the cooking, haven't you, darling?"

"Of course," he said, sliding his hand over hers. "I don't want my girl to go hungry."

"How many days a week do you work, Tom?" Dr. Fearne asked him.

"Three and a half, at the moment."

"Three and a half," Dr. Fearne said. "I see." She jotted something down on a notepad using a fountain pen. Helen couldn't make out what it was. "And Helen, you're full-time?"

"Yes," Helen said.

"I want to work more," Tom said, cutting in before Helen could say anything else. "Obviously with Curfew I can't work later shifts. But I'm hoping to make a career change once Helen and I move in together. It'll be much easier for me then."

"And why is that?"

"My flat is in a bit of a tricky location," he said, shifting in his seat. "Helen's is much closer to the town center, so I'll be able to work longer hours."

"I understand," Dr. Fearne said. "You're restricted by the travel times. It's a common problem."

"Exactly," Tom said. "And I've signed up to do a course at the college. Electrical engineering. Once I've finished that, I'll have all sorts of options."

Helen wasn't sure what Dr. Fearne thought of Tom's career plans. Her face gave nothing away. But it didn't matter how many times she told herself that a counseling session was not a test. She always felt like they'd not quite hit the mark. Today was no exception.

They endured Dr. Fearne's questions about washing-up rotas and bathroom schedules and laundry detergent preferences for an hour before they were able to escape. Dr. Fearne gave them a domestic work timetable, which they downloaded onto their slates and promised to fill in for their next session. Tom grabbed Helen's hand as they headed to the door and down the steps, out into the fresh air and the real world.

"Bloody hell," he said. "I know we have to do this, and I understand why, but that woman makes my head want to explode. She's given us homework!"

"It's crazy, isn't it?" Helen said. She turned to him, slung her arms around his neck. No way would she tell him that she thought the timetable was a good idea. "Our future in her hands." She made her eyes go huge. "Imagine it."

"The only thing I'm imagining is my life in your hands," he said. "Can't wait."

"I can't wait, either."

He lowered his head and kissed her, just as she'd hoped he would, three soft pecks with the promise of more. "Shall we get lunch in town when we've done shopping?"

"Oh," Helen said, dropping back onto her heels. "Yes. Sure. Why not?" The why not was the food waiting in the fridge at home. But lunch in town would be good. They could still get their hour in bed. Maybe they could fill in the timetable while they were eating. It wouldn't take that long.

She linked her fingers with his outstretched hand, loving the way his palm was hot and his grip possessive. *Mine*, she thought to herself. *He's mine, and he doesn't care who knows it.*

It felt bloody good to walk through town with a tall, attractive, charming man by her side. They strolled past the boutiques, and he pointed out things he thought would suit her. They went into the big department store, looked at pillows and sheets and lights and chunky mugs with dogs on them. "We should treat ourselves," Tom said. "Get something for our flat."

The way he said "our flat" made her feel all giggly. She'd been on her own for so long, with no one to rely on but herself. She had Mabel and her job, but what Helen craved more than anything was a family. Someone to come home to. Someone who would never leave.

After that they went to a DIY shop and Tom picked out a set of tools that he needed for his college course. It was expensive, so Helen paid. Tom carried their bags. They squeezed around a cozy corner table at their favorite lunch spot. Aware that she'd already spent more than she intended, Helen opted for a ham sandwich and tea. Tom looked over both sides of the menu before ordering a fillet steak with extra fries and a bottle of his favorite beer. When their drinks arrived, he lifted his and angled it toward Helen. "Here's to a successful morning." He smiled. "Only one more session to go." He took a long pull on his drink, the tip of his tongue sneaking out to gather a drop from his upper lip. "Can you believe that? One more session, and we'll finally be living together."

"Can't wait," Helen said. She smiled back. They'd gone overboard that morning, but it didn't matter. It wasn't Tom's fault that he didn't earn as much as she did. Curfew made it difficult for him to work. And she could easily cut back elsewhere for the next couple of weeks. She had enough saved for her escape fund, so she didn't have to worry about that, but babies were expensive, and she already knew that she wouldn't want to go back to work full-time once a baby arrived. All mothers were entitled to claim Childcare Benefit, which they could use to pay nursery fees or keep if they stayed at home with their children, but it wasn't as much as she was earning now and she wanted to be ready for that.

The waiter brought their food to the table and Helen forced herself to relax and enjoy it. She was being silly. Tom was right. They were allowed the occasional treat. After all, she went out with Mabel every week, so why shouldn't she go out with Tom, too?

He caught her staring at him and winked. "I love you so much," he said.

She was lucky he'd chosen her, and no one was going to convince her otherwise. Not Dr. Fearne, and definitely not Mabel.

CHAPTER TEN

Cass

Cass woke early on Saturday morning, though she didn't get out of bed. She pretended to be asleep when her mother opened the door and peered in. She did some fake deep breathing, and Sarah closed the door and left without saying a word. Her slate said it was half eight, which meant that Sarah wanted her to go downstairs for breakfast. But Cass had no interest in sitting on a plastic chair in a communal dining room that smelled of boiled eggs and old women and then being made to clean up afterward. It was bad enough that she'd had to do it the night before. Her hands were still sore from peeling so many potatoes.

After Sarah left, Cass showered and got dressed. She grabbed a handful of chocolate biscuits from the tin in lieu of breakfast. She needed the sugar. She'd had a restless night. Her mind had raced with thoughts of the man at the tagging center, which had somehow veered into thoughts about Bertie, the man at the coffee shop. She'd hidden the tag key inside her pillowcase before she finally fell asleep. She'd felt for it the moment she woke up and when her fingers found it, had felt a thrill of excitement. The urge to tell someone that she had it was almost overwhelming.

She could see the street from the kitchen window. If she moved a little to the left, she could see the corner of Billy's house. She'd messaged him earlier and he hadn't replied. He was probably still in bed. That said, he'd been acting weird with her all week, ever since Miss Taylor had made them arm-wrestle, so maybe he was just ignoring her. Cass didn't like it. He was supposed to be her friend.

She collected her jacket and keys and went out, the tag key safely hidden in the zipped pocket of her bag. She sped down the stairs, one hand on the rail just in case, and clattered out through the front door, sparing a glance at the sign that said PLEASE DO NOT SLAM THE DOOR right before slamming the door.

She crossed the road at a run. The dog in the house next to Billy's jumped up when she walked past and barked at her through the window. Cass ignored it. She stood at the bottom of the steps and pinged Billy on his slate.

Are you awake?

She was still staring at the screen and waiting for a reply when the door opened and she found herself being greeted by the jam-smeared face of Billy's younger brother, Samuel. "Hello!" he said.

Cass pushed her way into the house.

"Shut the bloody door!" came a yell from the living room. She heard Samuel push it closed behind her. The sound of the TV filtered through, as did the smell of an overworked washing machine, and she could see his dad sprawled on the sofa in his pajamas. Cass generally tried to avoid Billy's parents. So did Billy. She headed upstairs, dodging the pile of washing on the bottom step, hoping beyond hope that the ratty orange boxers on top didn't belong to Billy. She banged her fist a couple of times on Billy's door before opening it and walking straight in.

Something moved in the bed and Billy's face appeared. "I said I'd be up in a minute, Mum!"

"I'm not your mother," Cass replied crossly.

"Cass?" Recognition was followed by utter panic. "Oh my god, haven't you heard of privacy?"

"I did knock."

Billy sat up and stretched. "What time is it?"

"Nine." Cass moved away from the door and settled herself into the chair at his desk.

There was some complicated maneuvering with the duvet and a pair of red-checked pajama bottoms, and then Billy shuffled out of the room. Cass heard him go into the bathroom and the flush of the toilet. Then she heard his footsteps on the stairs. There were raised voices at the bottom before things quieted down again.

She spun herself slowly from side to side, looking around Billy's room. There wasn't much in it. The carpet was old and there were scuff marks on the gray walls. There was a wardrobe, but most of his clothes seemed to be discarded on the floor in front of it. And there was a smell. Cass couldn't put her finger on what it was. It wasn't a smell that she encountered at the Motherhouse.

Eventually Billy returned with two mugs in one hand and a plate of toast in the other. He put the mugs down on the desk next to Cass and sat on the bed with the toast. "How was yesterday?"

"Unbelievable," Cass said. "I knew my mother was a bitch, but yesterday was something else."

"Huh," Billy said, eating an entire piece of toast in three bites.

"It was all going fine. Pretty boring, actually. And then this guy in the room next to hers said his tag was too tight." Cass leaned forward. Her toes curled inside her shoes. "We could hear him through the wall, he was shouting that loud. My mother went to see what the problem was, and I followed her, and she shot him with a bloody Taser right in front of me. It was insane. The police came and everything."

Billy stopped chewing and swallowed loudly.

"There was no discussion, nothing," Cass continued. "She didn't even give him a chance to talk about it even though the tag was too tight, even I could see that. Just walked in and boom." She lifted her hand, two fingers stuck out to imitate a gun, and mimed the shot. "There's something wrong with her."

"He shouldn't have kicked off," Billy said evenly. "Everyone knows that."

"So you don't think he had the right to say something?"

"I didn't say that." Billy picked up another piece of toast and looked at it. "But only an idiot would pick a fight with a tagger. You're asking for it if you do that."

"You make it sound like it was his fault."

Billy shrugged, folded the toast in half, and shoved it in his mouth.

"Oh my god!" Cass slumped back in the chair. "You've been off with me ever since Miss Taylor made us arm-wrestle. I wish you'd just stop." She picked up the tea he had brought for her, wishing he'd offered her toast as well.

A door slammed shut and the sound of adult voices drifted up from downstairs. There were a couple of burbles of speech, and then the female voice cranked up a notch, shrill with anger. Billy stared at his plate. "I'm not being off with you."

"Yes, you are," Cass said. She tried to pretend that she couldn't hear his mother. "You've been acting like a pillock all week. But it's fine." She waved a hand in the air to show that she was above his moods. "I just came over to show you something, that's all."

"What?"

She pulled her bag onto her knee and opened it, fingertips resting lightly on the zipped inner pocket that held the tag key. She wondered, very briefly, if she really wanted to show it to Billy, but it was too big to keep to herself. "Don't tell anyone, but I managed to get my hands on this," she told him. She took out the key and held it up, eager to see his reaction.

His eyes went huge. "Is that . . . ?"

Cass nodded. "My mum must have dropped it when she went to deal with that guy I told you about."

Billy went pale. "You've got to take it back."

"It's fine," she told him. "No one knows I have it." She tossed it in the air and tried to catch it, but it slipped through her fingers and bounced across the carpet, disappearing under the bed. "Shit!" She got down on her hands and knees and looked under the bed. "I can't reach it."

Billy sat with his knees bent and his spine pressed against the wall. "I'm not getting it," he said.

"I'm not asking you to."

Cass reached under the bed again and grabbed for it, finding something soft and squishy instead. She threw it away, an automatic reaction to the unexpected dirty sock, and tried again. This time her fingers closed round something small and cold.

She sat back on her heels. "Honestly," she said. "You're such a baby."

"I am not."

"It's not going to hurt you."

"I know that."

The key suddenly felt heavy in her hand, as if the weight of Billy's stare were pressing it into her palm. Cass climbed up onto the bed and sat next to him. "Funny little thing, isn't it?" She turned it over, examining the fingerprint sensor and the protruding silver hook that would slot into a tag lock. "Looking at it, you'd never think it keeps you locked in all night. It should be some big chunky iron thing that you hang off a chain on your belt, like the ones jailers used to have."

"I think we've moved on a bit since then," Billy said.

"The basic principle hasn't changed. It's still a shackle and it's still locked round your leg. You're in irons, Billy."

"Don't be ridiculous." He snorted. "I'm not in prison."

"Not a physical prison, no," Cass agreed. "More like timetabled house arrest. Doesn't it bother you?"

"Of course it bothers me," he said. "But it's not like I can do anything about it. I can't change the law."

"I don't understand how you can sit there and say that." Cass shoved him. His body was sinewy and hard under her hand. It didn't happen often, but sometimes she would stand too close to him or he would accidentally touch her or look at her in a certain way and she would be struck by a deep physical understanding of his body and of hers and what their differences meant. It had happened in class when Miss Taylor had made them arm-wrestle. It irritated her. "Why aren't you angry? I'm angry, and I don't have to wear a tag."

"Because there's no point," Billy said. "And I've got bigger problems than my tag."

Cass knew he meant his parents, who seemed to argue almost constantly. She could see the bump of his tag under the leg of his pajama bottoms. A thought began to form in her mind, one that felt as if it had come from nowhere but hadn't, not really. "Can I see it?"

"What? My tag? Why?"

"Because I want to."

"Didn't you see enough of them yesterday?"

"Come on," Cass replied. "It's not like I'm asking you to show me your dick."

"It wouldn't want to see you anyway," Billy said, flushing. He pulled up the leg of his pajamas and Cass leaned over and looked at the tag. Then she touched it. It was strange, to see this thing that was so important but to have no personal experience of it. "What's it like?" she asked him. "Is it uncomfortable?"

"You get used to it. I barely even notice it anymore."

"Do you ever think about taking it off?"

"I can't take it off," he said. "Stop asking daft questions."

"But do you ever think about it?"

"Sometimes." He reached down and shoved his little finger under the edge of the band, pulling it away from his skin. He couldn't move it far. The fit was too snug.

"What if we could?" The proximity of the key and the slot on the side of Billy's tag made her feel dizzy. "I bet I can get this to work."

"No," Billy said immediately. "Just . . . bloody hell, Cass. We could get in so much trouble."

"Only if we get caught," Cass said. "I'll put it straight back on, I promise."

"They can tell if you've messed with it," Billy said.

"I'm not messing. I've got a key."

The more she thought about it, the more the idea took hold. Cass hated the tags so much. If Greg hadn't been tagged, he would never have gone to prison. He could have come straight back inside, and no one would have known that he'd broken Curfew. There would have been only Sarah's word for it, and if it had come down to it, Cass knew that she would have sided with her dad. No one would have believed Sarah if it were two against one.

Cass rubbed her thumb over the protruding metal end of the key. "Go on. Let's try it. I just want to see if it works."

"What if you break it?"

"I won't. And if I do, we'll make something up. Tell your mum you banged your leg and cracked it or something. It's not a big deal."

"No, Cass. I . . ."

Cass was already moving. She put a hand on his leg to steady him and herself and then slotted the end of the key into the corresponding hole in the tag. She took his stillness as consent.

Nothing happened.

She wiggled the key around a bit, pulled it out, and stuck it back in again, but the tag didn't come off. "Well, that's a piece of shit," she said, trying to hide her embarrassment.

"I told you it wouldn't work."

"It will!" Cass twisted away from him so that he couldn't see what she was doing. She didn't want him to know how little she knew about the tag or how it worked. She wanted him to see that she had a handle on this. "I just need to change the settings, that's all."

The key had a thumbprint scanner and a small touchscreen. Cass swiped it. The screen flashed and a message scrolled across it.

Input code.

Input code? What code? She thought about it for a second, then tapped in her mother's date of birth. Everyone knew that you shouldn't use your date of birth, but everyone did it anyway, and Cass was pretty confident it would work.

Incorrect.

What could it be? She could feel the weight of Billy watching her. She tried her own date of birth.

Incorrect. One attempt remaining.

What would her mum use?

"It's not going to work," Billy said. "It's a terrible idea anyway. Seriously, we could get in a whole world of trouble for this, Cass. Just leave it."

But she didn't. She had one more attempt. If she got it wrong this time, the key would be useless anyway, so she didn't see the harm in trying. She tried the date her father had broken Curfew.

Key unlocked.

"That bloody bitch," Cass muttered. She felt a swell of hatred for her mother, a boiling hot mess of it in her insides. "That bloody man-hating bitch."

Billy let out a nervous laugh. But it didn't escape Cass's notice that he hadn't moved his leg or made any attempt to hide his tag. He wanted this, she realized. He was saying he didn't, but he did. Her hand was unsteady as she slotted the key into his tag.

There was a beep.

She withdrew the key.

And when she pulled at Billy's tag, it came off.

CHAPTER ELEVEN

Pamela

Present Day
9:17 a.m.

The specialist team arrives just as I'm about to go back to the park, intending to walk through it again with the images from the CCTV fresh in my mind. There's a dozen of them, led by a woman called Sue Ferguson, and they sweep into the building in their sharp suits and coats. No uniform for this lot. I can see that Rachel is impressed. She covets their authority and their good shoes. I am called into the office that Sue has taken for her own. I stand in front of her as she sits behind the desk. "What do we know so far?" she asks, though it's more of a demand than a question.

"Very little," I say.

"Identification of the body?"

"Not yet."

"Report from the pathologist?"

"Also not yet," I say. "We have the CCTV footage from the park. But there's not much on it. I was just about to go back there for another walk-through."

She's obviously unimpressed. But I can't give her what I don't have. I wait for her to tell me what she wants me to do. She drums manicured nails on the desktop. "Our first priority is to do something about the media," she says. "There are rumors spreading all over the internet. We have to shut them down. We'll start with a statement. I'd like you to make it."

"Why me?" I ask. Surely Sue or one of her polished team would be better. I've been up all night and it shows. The body was found at the end of my shift. I couldn't clock off after that. And I've got more important things to do with my time. I won't clock off until we know who she is, and who killed her.

"You're local," she says with a shrug. "You've got the accent. You were first on scene. The public will trust you."

The woman in charge of media liaison agrees with Sue. I don't think it's a good idea. I try to talk them through my reasoning. We don't have enough information. I'm a senior officer, and my team needs my direction and support right now. The investigation is more important. Sue doesn't want to hear it. I ask if we can delay it, at least until we know the identity of our victim. I'm told that the worst possible thing we can do is to say nothing.

I get the distinct impression that controlling the flow of information is their main priority. The victim can wait. The press conference will be streamed straight from the steps outside the station.

I run a brush through my hair. I don't have the time or the inclination to do anything else. Inwardly I'm furious. I don't understand why Sue's priority isn't our victim. She's certainly mine. When we were told that a specialist team was being sent in, I thought we'd get more help, more people to search the park, access to faster forensic processing. I didn't expect this. This isn't police work. It's . . . PR.

I'm given a preprepared statement to read out. I skim through it. I don't like it, but I have to admit that Sue is right about one thing. I've had a quick look online. Rumors are spreading and some of them are downright scary. If we don't say something soon, we could have an even bigger problem on our hands. I need people to keep away from the park, not have them flocking to it. I'll make this one statement, and then I'll get on with the job. At least Sue Ferguson hasn't told me to go home. She could if she wanted.

The camera crew is ready for me when I step outside, just one small team, sent by the local TV station. There's a woman with a slate hung around her neck, blond hair tied back in a bun. A man in a blue bobble hat is talking to her. Have they already started filming? I hope not. I introduce myself to the pair of them.

"Is it true?" the woman asks me. "There's a body?"

I've been told I'm allowed to confirm that part of the story, so I do. "Yes."

"Fuck," she whispers, but it's not shock or sadness, it's excitement, and I recoil from it. "Can you give me any details?"

"Not at this stage," I say.

"Have the family been informed?"

I don't answer. I check my watch. "Is this going to take long?"

The woman positions me on the steps, tells me to look at her and not directly at the slate hung around her neck, which she's using to film, as that can be off-putting to viewers. They're going to stream it live, so I can't make any mistakes. Both of them are wearing waterproof jackets, which is just as well, as it's started to spit. I'm out here in my shirtsleeves. I've got goose bumps.

"Right," the man says. "Ready?"

I've got my slate with me, the statement there for me to read so I don't make any mistakes. I lock eyes with the woman, and she gives me a nod. I get a thumbs-up from the man.

I clear my throat. "A body was discovered in Newston Park early this morning. As a result, the park is currently closed, and is likely to remain so for several days. I would like to ask members of the public to stay away from the park, and not to make any attempt to film the officers at work there. I would also like to ask any women who may have been in the town center between the hours of midnight and six a.m. to contact the police, as you may have information that can help us."

I stop. The cameraman moves his head to one side so that he can look at me directly.

"Is that it?" the woman asks.

"That's it," I say.

"No clues as to the identity of the victim? Is it a man or a woman?"

"Thanks for coming," I say, and I go back inside the station. I head into the toilets and splash some cold water on my face.

Then I head back to my desk. Rachel catches me on the way. "It's already being shared online, look." She holds out her slate.

I've got no interest in it. "I haven't got time for that." Rachel shrinks away from me. It makes me wince. I remind myself that we're on the same team. I try to fix it. "A woman has been battered to death and dumped in the park and we have no idea who is responsible. We need to keep our focus on that."

Rachel blinks. "I just thought you might be interested."

Sue walks over to us. "Well done, Pamela," she says. "It's already been picked up by the national news channels, so it's likely that we'll be pushed for more information soon, but we've contained it for now."

"Thank you," I say, ignoring how patronized I feel, how infuriated I am by her presence. She made me give the statement because I'm local, because I have the accent, because I know this town and the people in it, and because we had to say something, because the public is a pet dog that will turn around and bite you if you don't constantly give it a reason not to. But it didn't bring us any closer to knowing what happened to our victim.

"I've got my team looking at the CCTV," Sue says. "They're seeing if they can tidy up the image. You were right, there's some good footage of our killer. She's tall, which should help narrow it down. We should have an accurate assessment of height shortly."

Rachel slides me a sideways look. I ignore it. "Are we completely discounting the possibility that it could be a man?" I ask.

"A man?" Sue says. "What on earth makes you think it's a man?" She sounds utterly bemused. I grit my teeth.

"It's definitely a woman," she continues. "Hopefully the statement you gave will bring someone out of the woodwork. I've assigned some of my officers to handle the calls. Rachel, I want you to assist. I also want to be notified immediately if a woman is reported missing, because she could well be our victim."

"Absolutely," Rachel says. "And I had an idea of something else we could do to help identify the person we saw on the CCTV."

"Which is?" Sue asks.

I pull on my jacket. I'm cold from standing outside. My slate buzzes. It's Michelle, the pathologist. She wants me to call her ASAP. But I want to hear about Rachel's idea first.

"Slates," Rachel says. "We can track those, right? Find out which slates were outside last night?"

"We can," I say. "But they're not the most reliable source of information." When Curfew first came in, we tried to catch men who broke it using their mobile phone data, but they soon figured it out and started leaving their phones at home, and slates are no different in that respect.

"It's a start," Sue says. "Get a complete list of all the slates that were within half a mile of the park between midnight and six."

"On it," Rachel says, and I can tell from the way she rushes off that she's pleased she's been given the go-ahead.

"She seems keen," Sue Ferguson says.

"She is," I reply.

"I like that. We need that sort of proactive thinking. Once she's got the list, I want you to help her go through it. We should have a list of women we need to speak to pretty quickly."

My slate buzzes for the second time. It's Michelle again. I glance at Sue. She can see the screen. She knows who it is. The morgue is at the hospital, a ten-minute drive away. I would prefer to go alone, but Sue insists on coming with me, and I decide that perhaps that's a good thing. Maybe if she sees the body, she'll have the same gut feeling that I did when I first looked at it. She waits for me to refill my travel mug. We take her car. I give directions. I wish I'd added more sugar to my coffee.

When we get to the morgue, we're greeted by Michelle, a plump woman in her fifties. She's wearing tortoiseshell glasses and blue scrubs. She usually has that reassuring, calm quality of someone who has seen the worst and can cope with anything, but today her eyes are red and her hairline is damp. She remains professional regardless. She doesn't tell me how awful it is.

We go into a cold, quiet room. Our victim lies rigid and still on a trolley. As I predicted, Sue is visibly shocked. I'm not. But my chest aches at the sight of her. Michelle talks us through each of the injuries. Cause of death appears to have been strangulation, and she tells us that some of the injuries were probably inflicted postmortem. "Destroyed her face," she says.

"So we couldn't identify her," I say.

"Won't work," Sue says briskly.

"No," I reply. "But it was still a cruel thing to do. Fingerprints?"

"No," Michelle says. "She's not in the system. We don't have a record of them. We'll have to wait for dental records to come back. Should only take a few hours."

It was unlikely that we would have her fingerprints, but I still feel the sting of disappointment.

"Anything else you can tell us?" Sue asks.

We talk through weight, height, hair color, possible age. Her clothes and the sheet have been tested and bagged up so that I can take them with me. Thankfully, these days we can detect and test samples in a matter of hours instead of having to wait weeks for vital information.

"Has she had children?" Sue asks.

"Hard to say," Michelle replies. "No obvious abdominal stretch marks or cesarean scar. Cervical changes were also unclear. Everything has been swabbed and sent for testing. No signs of sexual assault, by the way."

I nod. It's not much. But it's something, knowing that at least she didn't have to go through that before she died.

"It took some strength," Michelle continues. "What was done to her."

"So we're looking for a woman who works out? Someone who lifts weights at the gym, for example?" Sue asks.

It's hard for me to believe that Sue is asking that question, given what she's just seen.

"Perhaps," Michelle says.

It's what she doesn't say that speaks loudest to me. She catches my eye, and I know that she's thinking what I'm thinking. A man is more likely than even the strongest of women. I thank her for her time and she promises to contact us if anything new comes to light, and then we leave, taking the bagged-up clothes and sheet with us. Transfer of evidence has to be done carefully, and Sue records all of it on her slate.

"Sue, can I ask you a question?"

"What is it?"

"Why are you here?"

"This is a murder investigation."

We are almost at her car. "Yes, I know. But why are *you* here?"

"To make sure we get a good result," she says.

I can tell when someone is being evasive, and Sue ticks all the boxes. She unfastens her jacket and gets into the car. I have no choice but to do the same. But she doesn't start the engine. She stares straight ahead, her hands on the steering wheel. "I've dealt with eleven dead women so far this year," she says. "They were accidents, mostly. Falls, a drowning at a lake, an accidental overdose of prescription medication. Only two of them were suspicious. You and I both know how few that is, how many we used to get before Curfew. One woman was killed in a hit-and-run. We were able to gather sufficient evidence to show that the sister was driving. Another was stabbed by her ex-husband's new girlfriend. She was a pathological liar. Kept trying to pin it on the ex-husband."

"I heard about the stabbing. I had no idea there was any suggestion that he was involved."

"Because he wasn't," Sue says sharply. "Curfew, Cohab certificates, escape funds . . . these things make a difference, Pamela. It's not like it used to be, but sometimes the public needs us to reassure them of that, and that's why I'm here. I hope that we can find a way to work together, I really do, but if we can't . . ."

The rest is left unspoken. She starts the car, and we drive back to the station in silence. I've got a difficult decision to make. It's not what she said. It's what she didn't say. It's what was in all the spaces in between. When we get back to the station, I look at the case files for the stabbing she mentioned. I try to call the officer in charge of that investigation.

She refuses to talk to me.

CHAPTER TWELVE

Sarah

When Sarah arrived at work on Monday morning, she found Mabel in the break room, seated at a table with her head in her hands. She looked up when Sarah came in, and blinked huge, stressed eyes at her. "What's up?" Sarah asked.

"Didn't you get the message?"

"What message?" She hadn't checked her slate yet that morning. Cass had been in an obnoxious mood at breakfast, and it had taken all Sarah's willpower not to lose her temper.

"The man you tased on Friday had a heart attack," Mabel said.

"Oh, god," Sarah said. She pulled out the chair next to Mabel's and sat down. "When?"

"Sometime last night, I think."

"No. Oh, no." Sarah opened her bag and pulled out her slate, searching for the message with trembling fingers. "But he survived it, right? So we've got nothing to worry about."

It wasn't until she was in her office and the door was closed that she let herself react to the news. This was bad. This was really bad. Why couldn't men just bloody well behave themselves? Why did they have to put women in that situation? Although she knew that a heart attack was a possible consequence of tasing someone, she had no idea what it would mean for her. Hadiya would want to talk to her again, she was certain of that. She sat down at her desk, pinched the bridge of her nose, then unlocked the top drawer. Checking her keys and tags would give her something to do.

One of the key slots was empty.

Sarah stared at it in disbelief. She was sure that she'd checked the keys on Friday, before she went home. She rummaged through the drawer, shoving everything backward and forward, but there was no sign of the second key. She sat back in her seat and tried to think it through. She'd definitely had both on Friday morning. Her memory of that was clear. She'd remember if one had been missing. Or would she? And now she thought about it, she wasn't sure that she'd checked them both at the end of the day. Although she'd told Hadiya that she was fine to continue working after she'd tased that man, she knew that she'd been distracted. Foggy. She pressed her fingers to her temples, as if she could push the memories into focus, but it didn't help.

Sarah knew the procedure. She knew what she had to do if she found a key missing. It was part seven of basic training, and it was on a poster on the wall of the break room and on a smaller but identical poster on the back of the toilet door. The missing key had to be reported so that it could be deactivated and a new one issued. It would go on Sarah's record. There would be no promotion at the end of the year.

She took a few deep breaths to steady herself. It was important not to rush into anything. It was still likely that the key was here somewhere. Maybe it had fallen down the back of this drawer, or she'd put it in another one by mistake. The tagger who'd trained Sarah had said she knew it was time to retire when she put her key in her coat pocket and took it home.

Sarah was pretty sure she hadn't done that, but she checked her jacket pockets again anyway. No sign. Back to the drawers. Her sense of panic increased with each passing second. It wasn't there. Why wasn't it there?

Where the hell was it?

She turned to her computer, logged in, clicked through to the page that held the information for her keys, then clicked on the Locate Keys button. The first key was shown as being here, at the tagging center, exactly where it should be. The second was at the Motherhouse.

Maybe she had taken it home with her after all.

A sound at the door almost made her jump out of her skin, and her heart pounded inside her chest as the door opened. She quickly closed down the screen. Hadiya came in. Her face was grim. "Mabel told me you were here."

"Is this about Friday?"

"I'm afraid so. His family have already made a formal complaint."

"Really?"

Hadiya closed the door and leaned her weight against it. "Didn't waste a second," she said. "It won't go anywhere because they can't prove the Taser caused the heart attack, and you'll be fine. But it's probably best if you take today off."

"But . . ."

"Go home, Sarah. You'll be distracted, and we all know that's when mistakes happen. I've told Mabel the same thing."

This time it was clear that Hadiya wasn't going to be persuaded to let her stay. There was nothing she could do but lock her drawers, pick up her bag, and do as she'd been told. As she crossed the car park, it occurred to Sarah that there was someone else who could have taken the key to the Motherhouse. Her daughter.

Would Cass have taken the key? Her gut instinct was to say no, of course not, but she knew, if she was honest with herself, that Cass was capable of it, and that she'd had opportunity. Sarah took her slate out of her bag, wondering if she should send her daughter a message. But before she could, her slate buzzed and the New Message icon popped up on the screen. She opened it.

Greg was out of prison. He'd been released a little earlier than expected due to what were described as unforeseen circumstances, and it was hoped this wouldn't cause undue distress.

Sarah quietly swore.

He was out. Free. It was over. She blinked back tears, surprised to find them there. She turned off her slate without messaging Cass and let the news wash over her for several quiet, private minutes, and then she drove home.

She parked in her designated spot and went into the Motherhouse. Mrs. O'Brien was in the hallway watering the ficus with a little silver watering can. "Hello, Sarah," she said. "You're back early. Is something wrong?"

"Everything," Sarah said.

"Want to talk about it?"

"I wouldn't even know where to begin," Sarah said honestly. "First of all, the man I tased at work on Friday had a heart attack over the weekend, and he's in hospital."

Mrs. O'Brien set down the watering can. She walked over to Sarah, put a gentle hand on her arm. "I'm sorry to hear that. Will it cause problems for you at work?"

"I don't know yet. But his family have already made a formal complaint."

"And second?"

"My ex-husband was released from prison this morning. A week early."

"Ah," Mrs. O'Brien said. "Well, we were expecting him to be out soon anyway, so it can't be too much of a shock. Where has he been sent?"

"I don't know," Sarah said. "I didn't check. But it'll be somewhere away from here, thanks to you." Mrs. O'Brien had helped her with the paperwork, tweaking Sarah's clumsily worded request into a brief paragraph that said in plain English exactly what Greg had done. And if Mrs. O'Brien had embellished the truth just a little, it was only to make sure that Sarah got what she wanted.

"Well, you aren't going to bump into him in the street," Mrs. O'Brien said. "There's a lot to be said for that, and even if he has been released a few days early, it's not the end of the world."

"No." Sarah tried to smile. It wasn't as difficult as she'd thought it might be, earlier. "I don't think Cass will be too happy when she finds out, though." She thought of the missing tag key, wondered if she should mention it to Mrs. O'Brien, decided against it. If she could find the tag key and put it back before anyone noticed it was missing, no one would ever have to know that she'd lost it. It didn't matter whether she'd brought it home by accident or Cass had taken it, as long as she found it and put it back ASAP.

She was at the bottom of the stairs when Mrs. O'Brien called to her.

"Sarah?"

"Yes?"

"Even if you decide not to tell Cass that he's been released early, you should tell her the truth about what he did. It will help."

"I can't," Sarah said. "It would destroy her."

CHAPTER THIRTEEN

Cass

Cass lay on her bed, listening to her mother moving around the flat. Her stomach rumbled. But there was no way that she would leave her room and get something to eat until Sarah went to bed. She'd got home from school to find her mother already there, which had ruined her plan to try out the box of hair dye she'd bought on the way home, although that had turned out to be the least of her problems.

After getting through the weekend without any mention of the tag key, during which Cass had begun to believe that she was free and clear, Sarah had asked her if she'd taken it.

Cass had denied it, obviously, but Sarah hadn't believed her, and it had taken a full-blown tantrum to get her to back off. Cass turned over, still watching the door, half hoping her mother would come in so that she could carry on the argument. But Sarah didn't, and that left Cass adrift. The key was hidden in her bra, where she'd hastily pushed it after Sarah had insisted on searching her room.

The obvious answer was to do what she should have done on Friday, which was to get rid of it. The problem was that she'd had to leave Billy's house on Saturday before she could put his tag back on. Billy's mother had kicked her out. She'd told Cass in no uncertain terms that her house had rules, and one of those rules was that Billy wasn't allowed to have girls in his bedroom, and exactly who did she think she was, anyway? Cass had taken one look at Billy and left, intending to go back on Sunday, but Billy hadn't answered her messages and she hadn't wanted to go round unannounced in case Bridget answered the door.

At half eleven, Cass heard Sarah go to bed, but by that point she was too tired to sneak out for something to eat. She fell asleep in her clothes around midnight and then overslept and didn't have time for breakfast, and when she got to school, all they had left at the snack bar was a couple of bruised apples.

So now she was in class, with her stomach growling furiously and a headache that refused to go away, and she'd just noticed that her shirt had a curry stain on the cuff. Amy Hill, sitting one seat in front, kept interrupting the class to complain that she could smell chicken tikka.

Cass tucked the cuff up inside her sleeve, concealing the yellow mark. Maybe she should go to the office and tell them she didn't feel well and was going home. She could always tell them she was on her period and then they definitely wouldn't say anything. All the girls got three days a month period leave if they needed it. But going home meant going back to the Motherhouse. She remembered once walking past the building with Greg and asking him who lived there. He'd told her it was a place for crazy women. The two of them had laughed about it. It wasn't so funny now.

She doodled on her slate. Twenty-eight minutes until break.

She wished that she could tell the other girls that she had a tag key in her pocket, and that she'd taken Billy's tag off. That would give them something to talk about. She'd like to see them try to justify Curfew when they had proof that it was unnecessary right there in front of them. Tossing that thought around kept her occupied for those twenty-eight minutes.

After the lesson, she found Billy in the library. "Hey," she said. "What are you doing?"

"Homework," Billy said. He was scrolling through some
on the suffragettes. More suck-up for Miss Taylor. There was a large
spot brewing on his left cheek. He rubbed a hand over his face and
yawned widely.

"Bad night?" Cass asked him.

"Not the best I've ever had."

She settled into an empty chair. "What time did they start?"

"Early." Billy's hand trembled over the keyboard for a moment,
then he closed the page he was looking at.

His parents argued with predictable regularity. Their rows were
usually alcohol fueled and noisy. No one would be surprised if
Bridget Cobb pushed her husband out the door, and yet she never
did, which made her own domestic situation feel even worse. "What
was it about this time?" she asked him.

"I don't know, and I don't care."

Cass could tell that she wasn't going to get anything good out
of him now. "Do you want to go for a walk round the field?"

It was windy outside and so the path around the football pitch
and the tennis courts was quiet. They saw nothing more exciting
than a squirrel. She didn't mention his tag, or the fact that Sarah
knew the tag key was missing. She'd intended to, but now that she
was here, something held her back. It was the feeling that perhaps
Billy being without his tag wasn't the worst thing in the world. An
idea was forming in her mind. She let it simmer.

"Is your dad out yet?" Billy asked.

"Not yet," Cass said. "But he will be in a couple of days. I'm a bit
worried that he won't know where we are, though."

"Your mum must have told him that you've moved."

"I doubt it."

"Must be weird," Billy said. "Knowing he'll be nearby, but not
being able to contact him."

"Yeah."

Billy gave her a gentle nudge with his elbow. "I'm sorry."

"Yeah, well. I'm sorry about your parents, too." Cass kicked at the leaves on the path. That half-formed idea became real and whole. "At least you can get out of the house when they start now."

He could, if he wanted, break Curfew, and no one would know. She glanced across at him to see if he'd had the same thought. He'd never actually do it, obviously, being Billy, but it was still exciting to think that he could. They had completed a full circuit of the field and were back in front of the main building.

"No," Billy said. "I'm not doing that. It's insane."

"Why?"

"Because it's illegal! I need it back on, Cass. What if I get called for a tag check?"

"Message me straightaway and I'll put it back on for you," Cass told him.

"You could put it on now. You've got the . . . you've got it with you, right?"

The bell went, indicating the start of the next lesson. "Come on," she said. "We'll be late."

They had to rush and Cass was slightly out of breath by the time they reached the classroom. Billy went to an empty seat near the front. Cass found one at the back of the classroom. Her slate buzzed, and she carefully retrieved it from her bag. A little envelope appeared in the top corner of the screen. She sneakily tapped it. It was a message from Amy, who was two seats away.

Cass and Billy, sitting in a tree, s-h-a-g-g-i-n-g.

Cass shut the message down and glanced across at Amy, who was leaning forward, apparently fascinated by what Miss Taylor was saying. Amy was wearing a yellow blouse with a soft open collar and a fine gold necklace. Cass knew that at the front was a tiny locket shaped like a heart, which Amy's dad had given her when she'd turned eighteen. Amy had a habit of hooking her thumb behind it whenever anyone talked to her, rocking it from side to side so that the little diamond embedded in the front would catch the light. She loved nothing more than being asked about it, and why wouldn't she? Her home life was perfect.

The other girls knew that Greg was in prison. There had been no way for Cass to hide it. The whispers had spread around school the morning after his arrest, and by lunchtime, Cass had been cornered by a group of girls in the toilets and was hysterical. A phone call from a worried teacher had brought an ashen-faced Sarah to reception to collect her. Cass had marched out of school and refused to speak to her mother for the rest of the day. She'd never known what it was to truly hate someone until that moment. She understood it now. Sarah had taken her dad away from her, and Cass had no intention of forgiving her for it.

Eventually, the other girls got bored and moved on to other things, but they'd never let Cass forget that they knew. She wasn't one of them anymore. She was tolerated but never included. Billy, who had once been a passing acquaintance, became her best friend and, hard as Cass tried to pretend otherwise, she was secretly a little ashamed of it. Billy, with his thin legs and bad skin, was hardly her first choice. And yet the friendship had stuck. Cass needed Billy. He was all she had.

At the front of the class, Miss Taylor turned expectantly, giving them all the silent signal that said she was ready to start the lesson. Cass flicked back to the messages on her slate and sent a quick reply.

Piss off

She saw Amy's hand move to her own slate, and the quick flash of the screen, and then Amy turned her head and made eye contact with the girl seated next to her, who slid her gaze briefly to Cass before looking away again. There was something dark in her eyes, a gleeful spite.

Cass kept an eye on her slate, but she didn't get another message. Miss Taylor started talking about the introduction of the tags and why they'd been necessary, how it had been assumed that a law change would be enough to keep men in line, how men had frequently broken the law. The police had been overwhelmed, as at that point, most of them were male and obviously couldn't work during Curfew, and there weren't enough female officers available to deal with it. The final straw had been a wild rampage of football fans through the streets after a cup final.

Tags had already been available. It was simply a matter of the government agreeing that it was a necessary step and then rolling out the program. Temporary tagging centers were set up in sports centers and gyms. There were heavy fines for men who refused to comply. But there were concerns that it was taking too long, and so mobile tagging units were sent into workplaces and hospitals and schools. The police were given the power to stop men in the street and ask to see their tag, and to escort them to the nearest tagging center if they didn't have one.

And again, Miss Taylor talked about what had made this necessary. She described a version of men that Cass didn't recognize at all, twisting statistics to prove her point and making Cass itch with anger.

She knew the truth of it. Okay, maybe sometimes men had done bad things to women. She wasn't denying that. But women had done bad things, too. Look at her mother, pushing her dad out of the door. On top of that, Cass wouldn't accept that women had no responsibility for any of it, no control. If things were so bad, why did they stay with the men who they claimed made their lives a misery? And why did they have children with them? That in particular made no sense. Women had total reproductive control. They got to choose if they had children, with the contraceptive pill and abortion. A woman could even have a baby on her own. All she had to do was visit a fertility clinic. Men couldn't do that. They were completely limited by their biology, completely dependent on women if they wanted a family. And Miss Taylor thought that Billy being able to beat her at arm wrestling made him physically superior.

When Cass turned her attention back to the class, Miss Taylor was still on tags. "The thing about tags is that they work," she said. "Nobody likes them. We'd all prefer it if they weren't necessary. For one thing, the tagging program is incredibly expensive. But there was no choice, in the end. It was impossible to enforce Curfew otherwise. Too many men refused to follow it."

Amy put her hand up.

"Yes?" Miss Taylor asked her.

"How often do men break Curfew now?"

"Very rarely," Miss Taylor told her. "According to the Office of National Statistics, twenty-seven men were arrested for it last year, and not one of them got farther than a mile from home."

"What if a man's house caught on fire?" Amy asked innocently.

"The tag would still alert the police and the man would be taken into custody. Once there was confirmation from the fire brigade and suitable temporary accommodation had been found, the man would be free to go."

"That's interesting," Amy said.

No, it isn't, Cass wanted to shout at her. None of this is interesting, and none of this is fair, and why don't you just shut up? But she didn't want to give Amy the satisfaction. She could tell from the way that Miss Taylor kept sneaking glances at her that everyone was expecting her to lose her temper. Everyone was waiting for the girl whose father had broken Curfew to embarrass herself.

"Tags changed everything," Miss Taylor continued. "The law only works if you can enforce it. And they've made life much safer for men as well as women."

Another hand went up. This time, it was Billy's. "How has it made things safer for men?"

At least he'd asked a good question. But Miss Taylor, as always, was ready with an answer. "Lots of ways. You might not know this, but when Curfew was first brought in, we had quite a few cases where women reported men for breaking Curfew when they hadn't. Unfortunately, those men had no way to prove that they hadn't gone outside. It led to some very tricky cases that ended up in court. Some of the men went to prison."

A silence settled over the class as they took that in. Cass could feel the pressure in her head as she clenched her teeth together. How could anyone stand there and say that tags were good for men and keep a straight face? Tags hadn't made it safer for her father. She felt a sudden wave of pleasure at the thought that Billy was sitting at the front of the class with no tag round his ankle and stupid Miss Taylor knew nothing about it. But her joy was short-lived.

Amy turned in her seat. "Didn't your dad go to prison for breaking Curfew, Cass?"

"I don't think that's relevant, Amy," Miss Taylor said sharply, but it was too late. Everyone in the room had heard.

Cass grabbed her bag, got out of her seat, and walked out of the classroom. She knew that she'd be in trouble for it, but she decided that she didn't care. It shocked her to discover that she was crying. She wiped her eyes with the back of her hand to clear her vision. There was a girls' toilet on her left and she ducked into it, locking herself into a cubicle, but even in there, she didn't feel safe.

She didn't go back to class. She didn't think she could cope with the sniggers and the stares from Amy and her friends, or Miss Taylor's grim face, or even Billy. In that moment, Cass felt like she didn't have anyone. There was no one she could turn to. No one who would understand how she was feeling. There was nowhere she could go to escape any of it. She was trapped.

She should have stood up to them. She should have told Amy Hill to get stuffed.

But she hadn't.

She walked out of school and got on the first bus that showed up.

CHAPTER FOURTEEN

Sarah

On Wednesday, Sarah woke to the buzzing of her slate. It was five a.m. She yawned and reached for it, wondering who on earth would be messaging her this early, thinking she would give them a piece of her mind.

It was Hadiya, and it wasn't good news.

Paul Townsend, the man she'd tased, had died.

Sarah sat upright in bed, fully awake now, her heart pounding.

What happened? she messaged back.

It took a couple of minutes for Hadiya to reply. Not sure yet, looks like another heart attack, this one fatal.

Shit.

My thoughts exactly. Need you to come to center ASAP.

Sarah showered and dressed in record time. She hesitated outside Cass's door, then left without knocking. She scribbled a quick note on her slate and pinged it to Cass. She was old enough to get herself to school without help. Hadiya and Mabel were both at the center by the time Sarah got there. Mabel was unbearably pale.

"I've got to formally interview both of you," Hadiya said. "I know we already went through this on Friday, but obviously things are a lot more serious now." Her slate buzzed. "I've got to take this," she said, and strode off in the direction of her office, the slate pressed against her ear.

"This is beyond awful," Mabel said to Sarah. She pushed her hair back from her face. "I just can't get my head round it."

Sarah glanced in the direction of Hadiya's office. The door was half-open, but there was no sound filtering through. She turned back to Mabel. "Look," she said. "The most important thing right now is that we get our stories straight. He kicked off, I heard the disturbance through the wall, I came in to help you."

"You're making it sound like you think they're going to blame us."

"They are," Sarah said. "That's why we have to make sure that there's nothing to blame us for. I'll say that I saw that you were in danger and I acted."

"But I didn't press the alarm."

"Doesn't matter. Tell Hadiya you thought you could calm him down initially. He'd been difficult but manageable. You were happy with the fit of the tag. He wanted you to loosen it, but if you'd done that, in your opinion it would have been too loose and he might have been able to remove it. When you refused, he flipped out. You were about to press the alarm when I came in."

Mabel slowly nodded. "That sounds about right."

"Maybe I heard him call you a name or something, when I came in," Sarah continued. "Did he? Was there any abusive language?"

"I'm not sure," Mabel said. "He might have. He certainly struck me as the type that would."

"So let's say I heard him call you a fucking cunt, which I took as an obvious sign of hostility, I could see that you were in danger, and I tased him."

"Yes. Yes, that works. That makes sense."

Hadiya came striding out of her room. Sarah sat back in her seat. She caught Mabel's gaze, held it for a second, saw the slight nod that Mabel gave her. She didn't doubt for a second that she'd done the right thing, but that had to come across in Hadiya's interviews. It had to be believable.

Mabel went first. It took half an hour, time that Sarah spent toying with a cup of tea. Her own turn took almost as long. At the end, Hadiya sat back in her chair and exhaled. "Okay," she said. "I think I've got what I need. Your stories match up, so that's a good start. Plus, given his age, his general health, they're going to have a hard time proving that the heart attack wouldn't have happened anyway."

But it cast a dark shadow over the rest of the day. Sarah assumed that Hadiya would want her to stay at home until it was all sorted. Instead, she found herself with a full appointment list, because two of the other taggers had called in sick and so it was all hands on deck. All of them were young teenage boys, nervous and easy to manage. Sarah was generous with her lollipops and by lunchtime she'd run out and had to nip to the shop for more. She powered her way through the afternoon with caffeine and sugar. The rhythm and routine of it helped to repair the vicious knock to her confidence that the events of the past few days had caused. She was good at this. She wasn't the sort of person who would tase someone unless completely necessary.

She finished her last appointment on time, tidied her office, and left. It wasn't until she was halfway home that she noticed a silver car driving right up her backside. She slowed down a little, hoping the driver would back off, but they didn't. There was a nondescript youngish man at the wheel, eyes hidden behind dark glasses, thumb tapping in time with music that Sarah couldn't hear. This was why she usually waited until Curfew before she went home, so that she could avoid men like him.

He tailgated her all the way to the Motherhouse, speeding off as she turned into the car park, and she gave him the finger even though she knew he couldn't see. It made her feel better. It had been an awful day, and she couldn't wait for it to be over.

The missing tag key was still a problem, but it was an accident. She decided to wait a couple more days, to let the shock of Paul Townsend's death wear off a bit, and then she'd report it. She still suspected that Cass had taken it, but she couldn't bring herself to ask her about it again. It was easier to tell herself that Cass had given her an answer, and that she had to be satisfied with it. She didn't want to believe that she had the sort of daughter who would lie about something so important.

But with every day that passed, Sarah found herself growing more and more uneasy. She'd no idea when Hadiya would pick her for another random key check. The stress was almost unbearable. She let everyone assume that her mood was due to the situation with Paul Townsend, and perhaps it was, a little, though it was the missing tag key that kept her awake at night. Hadiya repeatedly assured her that she had nothing to worry about.

If only you knew, Sarah thought to herself.

But when Friday rolled around, she still didn't report the key. She wanted to have one more crack at Cass. When Cass got out of bed on Saturday morning, Sarah told her that they were going out. It was going to be a conversation that Cass wouldn't enjoy and she wanted to have it somewhere neutral, away from the Motherhouse. She tempted her out of the flat with the suggestion that they go shopping.

She found a parking space outside the counseling center, and pulled into it in time to see a slim woman in dark jeans heading up the steps that led to the building, followed by a tall, dark-haired man. He seemed vaguely familiar, but since she couldn't see his face, she couldn't be sure. She'd probably changed his tag at some point.

"Isn't that your teacher?" she asked Cass.

"Which one?"

"The young female one. Miss Taylor."

"Dunno," Cass said, sounding utterly disinterested.

"There's a man with her," Sarah said. "I wonder if they're going for counseling."

"Why would any man want to get a Cohab certificate with her?" Cass sneered. "She's awful."

Sarah gripped the wheel tightly. "She seemed pleasant enough to me when I met her at open day."

"Of course she did. She was sucking up to all the parents." It didn't escape Sarah's attention that despite saying she wasn't bothered, Cass craned her neck to get a better look, though it was too late. The two of them had already disappeared inside the building. "He's probably a brother or cousin or something."

"Probably," Sarah replied, although she doubted that the slim and graceful Miss Taylor would have a dark-haired, solidly built brother. But she'd had enough of talking about Miss Taylor. She regretted even pointing her out. She pulled on the handbrake and turned off the engine.

"Right," she said. "Before we go anywhere, you and I are going to talk."

"What about?"

Sarah took a deep breath. She'd rehearsed this. But now that the moment had come, she found that she didn't know where to start. Everything that needed to be said was ugly. All of it would lead to shouting and anger and tears. As Sarah sat there and looked at her daughter, she knew she didn't have the energy for all that. Although she wasn't sorry that Greg was out of her life, solo parenting was exhausting. "About what we should do for lunch. Would you like to go to Puccino's?"

"I suppose," Cass said, and got out of the car.

Sarah watched her through the window. Maybe if she'd been able to spend more time with Cass when she was younger, things would be easier now. But then again, perhaps not. Cass wasn't exactly easy to parent.

She hurried to catch up with her daughter. They spent nearly three hours looking round the shops. Sarah tried to notice every shop that Cass was distracted by, every boy, and she tried not to let her disappointment show when she couldn't see the appeal of any of them. Cass liked skimpy, oversexualized clothing, and men with pumped shoulders and swagger, both of which made Sarah despair.

"Hungry yet?" she asked Cass.

"I guess so," Cass said.

"I think I might have lasagna," Sarah said. "What about you?"

"Calzone," Cass said.

A short response. But it was something. "Good choice," Sarah said. When they arrived at the restaurant, the waiter showed them to a table in the window. Cass checked her reflection in the glass and immediately began to fiddle with her hair. Sarah fought the urge to tell her to stop preening. Fortunately, the waiter reappeared with menus and a jug of water, which gave them something to focus on for the next ten minutes, and the food appeared shortly after that, and as she watched her daughter eat, some of the tension inside Sarah began to settle. Maybe this could still be fixed. After all, Greg was gone, and he was never coming back. It wasn't too late to fix it. Cass was young, her understanding of the world naturally limited, and she'd been spoiled. Horribly spoiled. None of that was her fault. Greg had never been able to say no, and Sarah had felt guilty about how much time she spent at work, had let things slide that she should not have.

Sarah told herself that what happened going forward was what mattered. She had to stop thinking the worst of her daughter and try to see the positives instead. She still hadn't told Cass that her father had been released from prison early, and she decided it was best if Cass didn't know. Let her think he'd been released on schedule. Keep things calm. Make today a good day.

"How's your food?" Sarah asked.

"Good," Cass said.

Sarah tried her own food. The pasta was fresh and the sauce was rich. She didn't want to waste it, so she forced herself to eat, although she didn't have the appetite for it. "Cass," she began.

"What?"

Sarah put down her fork. "Please don't speak to me like that. I don't want to fight with you. I'm tired of fighting. Aren't you tired of it? Don't you wish that we could stop doing it?"

Cass poked at a stray mushroom with the end of her knife.

"I know you're unhappy," Sarah continued. "And I understand why."

"Do you? Do you understand what it's like for me at school, being the girl whose dad went to prison? You made me move to that boring place full of nosy old women, and you never asked me if I wanted to live there. You said you wanted me to go to work with you, and then you made me leave. You don't like any of my clothes; you won't let me wear makeup even though Dad always did. You don't understand anything."

Oh, I do, Sarah thought to herself. *I understand more than you can possibly imagine.*

"I've made mistakes," she said. "I admit that. I wasn't there nearly enough when you were little, and I should have been."

"What for? Dad took good care of me."

"I'm your mother!"

"So?" Cass said. "You were more interested in your job than me. You still are. You made your choice, Mum."

Empty plates were cleared away. The waiter brought the dessert menu, and Cass looked at it. Sarah asked for coffee and the bill.

Cass asked for chocolate cheesecake. Sarah decided not to push it. The things that Cass had said to her had stung. She needed time to lick her wounds before she went for round two.

The waiter brought the coffee and the dessert. Cass had just pushed her fork into the cheesecake when she suddenly froze.

"Cass?" Sarah asked. "What is it?"

Cass wasn't listening. The fork hit the tabletop with a clatter, the chair squealed as it was pushed back, and the door banged as Cass flung it open and rushed outside. Sarah was half out of her seat, ready to follow, when she saw Cass through the window of the restaurant.

Flinging her arms around Greg.

CHAPTER FIFTEEN

Helen

Helen knew that she'd had a bad week at work. Fortunately, because she was the only adult in the classroom, no one else did. Her year nine class had been particularly awful. They'd spent most of Friday's lesson pinging one another on their slates and she hadn't had the energy or the inclination to stop them. She was too busy thinking about her next counseling session with Tom. And there'd been that awful lesson where Cass Johnson had stormed out. She'd spoken to Amy and the other girls afterward and had opted not to report Cass to her head of year, but she couldn't help wondering if she'd done the right thing.

Things would get back to normal next week. She hadn't let them get so far out of hand that it would be impossible to pull them back, but she'd have to really keep her classes in check for at least a fortnight to make sure they got the message. That was kids all over. Give them an inch and they'd take a mile. Sometimes, her job made Helen wonder why she was so desperate for a little girl of her own. Things would be different for her, though. She knew the pitfalls. Her child would have boundaries and rules and she'd know not to break them.

Now it was Saturday morning, and she was sitting with Tom in the waiting room outside Dr. Fearne's office. It was their final session. At the end of it, they'd have their Cohab certificate, and he'd be moving into her flat. Today.

He smiled at her. "Nervous?" he asked.

"A bit." She leaned to the side, putting her head against his shoulder, and breathed in the scent of him. His shirt was lovely, thick and dark and soft, matching his hair. He really was a beautiful man. She wondered if their daughter would take after him. She hoped so.

Dr. Fearne opened the door and stuck her head out. "Come in, come in!" she said, moving out of the way so that the two of them could squeeze past and take their seats opposite her desk. "So, today is the big day. How very exciting!" She took her own seat at the other side of her desk, arranged her skirt, and did the usual fiddling around with her keyboard and slate. "Final session. Goodness. It barely seems like five minutes since you started this journey."

"Twelve weeks," Tom said. "Doesn't feel like five minutes to us."

Dr. Fearne looked at him over the top of her glasses. "Of course not," she said. "You must be excited."

Tom looped his arm around Helen's shoulders. "We're ready," he said. "I can't imagine anyone I'd rather spend my life with than Helen."

"How lovely," Dr. Fearne said, though her expression suggested that she wasn't impressed.

It made Helen feel a little irritated, but she couldn't tell if she was annoyed by Tom or by Dr. Fearne. She wanted to tell Tom not to overdo it, there was so much at stake here, everything had to be perfect, and she wanted to tell Dr. Fearne that their relationship was none of her business and she should just bloody well give them the certificate. She squashed the thoughts down, ashamed of herself for having them.

Curfew was horrible sometimes, though. She wanted to be with

Tom and he wanted to be with her. It irritated her that they had to go through this performance just to be allowed to live together. Helen knew that she was being ridiculous, but she felt like it wasn't just their compatibility that was being judged. She felt, deep down, that what was really being assessed was her ability to pick a suitable partner.

"The final thing we need to discuss is your plans for a family," Dr. Fearne said.

"Well, we'd like to have children, obviously," Tom said.

"How many?"

"Two." He reached out and squeezed Helen's hand. "Maybe even three."

"And when do you think you'd like to have them?"

"When we're ready."

Dr. Fearne clattered at her keyboard. "And when will that be?"

Helen's stomach gave a little quiver. The back of her throat suddenly tasted sour. Ugh. Where had that come from?

"Do we need to decide that now?" Tom asked.

"Well, it can be helpful for a couple to have a specific date that they're working toward. The problem with leaving it to some undefined time in the future is that people can think they're on the same page when they've actually got different ideas about what's going on."

"Two years, then," he said.

Helen glanced across at him. "Two years?" As soon as the words were out of her mouth, she wished she hadn't said them. The look on Dr. Fearne's face spoke volumes. But Tom seemed oblivious.

"Well, yes," he said. "We need time to buy a house, babe, and then we'll probably have to do some work on it. Plus I'm not even thirty yet. We've got loads of time."

"I know that," Helen said. But it was so far away, and thirty-two was old. She couldn't wait that long. She'd thought it would be a few months at the most, and even that had felt unbearable.

Tom smiled. "Stop worrying," he said. He patted her on the knee.

"So I assume that you're using contraception," Dr. Fearne said. "Can I ask what it is?"

"Helen's on the pill," Tom said.

"I see." Dr. Fearne clattered at her keyboard again. "And how do you feel about that, Helen?"

"It's fine."

"Fine?"

"Well, it's easy and it works."

"And has well-known side effects. Tom, how do you feel about the fact that Helen has sole responsibility for this aspect of your lives?"

Helen saw Tom narrow his eyes at that. She could tell he didn't like it. Despite his easygoing manner, he was a very private man. He wouldn't even let her borrow his slate.

"Have you considered alternatives?" Dr. Fearne continued. "If you're not planning on having children for several years, then perhaps something like the male implant could be an option. Have you thought about that, Tom?"

"Not really," he said shortly. "Don't like the idea of it. The pill is much easier. It's only a tablet."

Helen swallowed. Her mouth still tasted horrible. She suddenly felt a bit sick. "Can I get a drink of water?"

Dr. Fearne got out of her seat. "Are you all right?"

"Yes, I'm fine. I just . . . it's quite hot in here."

"Of course." Dr. Fearne left the room, closing the door quietly behind her.

"What's wrong?" Tom asked her.

"Nothing. I just felt a bit off for a minute, that's all. You were getting a bit tense."

"Well, she was getting bloody nosy! Asking me why I don't have an implant. What's it got to do with her?"

"She was just doing her job." Helen took a deep breath. "Anyway, two years?"

"What?"

"You said two years before you want to have children."

"She wanted an answer. I had to give her one," he said. He shoved a hand back through his hair.

"But two years?"

"I don't understand why you're making a big deal out of this. All you had to do was agree with me. It's none of her business anyway. It's not like we have to tell her the truth."

"But . . ."

"For god's sake, get a grip," he muttered sharply.

"Tom!" Helen said, shocked by his tone. "Don't speak to me like that!"

He kept his gaze locked on her face, and there was something in the way he was looking at her, something cold that she hadn't seen before, but before she could say something to make it go away, the door opened and Dr. Fearne came back in, a glass of water in one hand.

"Tom, would you mind waiting outside for a few minutes? I'd like to speak to Helen in private."

The Tom who had spoken to Helen so rudely only moments before had vanished, replaced by the charming, smiling man that she knew. He leaned over and gave Helen a kiss on the cheek before he left, and she found herself wondering if she'd imagined those harsh words.

Helen barely even noticed when Dr. Fearne put the glass of water down in front of her. She'd probably misheard him. She was so wound up this morning that she barely knew which way was up.

"Are you all right?" Dr. Fearne asked her.

"What? Yes. Yes, of course. Just felt a bit dizzy."

"That's understandable," Dr. Fearne said. "It's a big deal, isn't it?"

"It really is," Helen said. "It's like the worst exam I ever sat for. I think I have a bit more sympathy for my students now."

"I think I'd rather apply for a Cohab certificate than try to get through A-level history again." Dr. Fearne smiled. "What a mistake that was."

Helen took a sip of the water. It helped.

"You seemed a little shocked when Tom suggested that he might want to wait two years before having children," Dr. Fearne continued.

"Did I?" Helen took another nervous sip of water. "I didn't mean to. I mean, it's not like there's any rush. We've got a lot to do first. We'd need a house, and obviously Tom wants to be in a better job."

"Sometimes I think men can be a bit ignorant about the female body," Dr. Fearne said, as if Helen hadn't spoken. She settled herself back behind her desk. "They don't understand that we are on a clock and that our body reminds us of it constantly. Sometimes having children isn't something we can be rational about or make long-term plans for. Sometimes your body just tells you that it's time."

"Did that happen to you?" Helen asked, her gaze sliding to the family photo on the windowsill.

"Oh, yes. Very much so."

"What did you do?"

"I had a baby." Dr. Fearne laughed. "Baby fever is a sickness with only one cure, I'm afraid. Are you feeling better?"

"A bit," Helen said. She took another sip of water. "Thanks."

"Good," Dr. Fearne said. She put her elbows on the desk and leaned forward. The move was not lost on Helen; she did it to kids in her class all the time. Dr. Fearne was about to ask a question to which she already knew the answer. "Helen," she began, and then she paused, as if she were trying to figure out the best words to use. "I think things have gone pretty well over the past few weeks. Would you agree?"

"Yes."

"I have to tell you, I like you very much, and I think that we would be friends, if we'd met under different circumstances. I'd also like to think that you trust me."

"Of course. I mean, everything we say in here is confidential. You're not allowed to tell anyone."

"That's true. Helen, how long ago did you stop taking the pill?"

"I haven't!"

Dr. Fearne didn't reply. She sat silently, watching, another technique that Helen knew only too well.

"I haven't," Helen said again, carefully, firmly. "I mean, I've thought about it. I can't deny that. The side effects aren't great and sometimes I get a bit fed up with it. I don't have baby fever, though. I'm not going to do something stupid."

"And if he makes you wait two years?"

"He won't."

"How do you know?"

"I just . . . he wants what's right for both of us. He's the sensible one. That's one of the things I love about him. He doesn't rush. He thinks things through."

"It's interesting that you should say that," Dr. Fearne told her. "Because I would have said it was the other way round."

"No," Helen said. "I know it might seem that way, on the surface, but he's so much better at the important stuff than I am. I guess we balance each other out, in a way."

"I have to be honest with you, Helen," Dr. Fearne said. "At this stage, I would advise you to seriously consider continuing the counseling for a few more weeks. In my opinion the two of you have still got a lot to explore. There's a lot you don't know about each other."

No, Helen thought. *No way*. "Do you think he's a risk to me?"

"I don't believe so, no."

"Then there's no reason not to give us the Cohab certificate now."

"You need more counseling."

Helen could hear the blood pounding in her ears. "If I agree to extend the counseling, can we still have the certificate today?"

Dr. Fearne pursed her lips. "I'm willing to do that on one condition. I want you to think about what will happen if he does make you wait to have a baby. Can you guarantee that you'll wait until he's ready?"

Helen looked down at her hands. She dug her nails into her palms, desperate to hide the lie. "Yes."

"Children deserve to be wanted by both parents, not just one."

"I know."

"You could move on. Find someone else. A man who wants children now, not at some unspecified point in the future. You're healthy, attractive. You've got a good job. It wouldn't be difficult."

A part of Helen wobbled. It was loudly and brashly overridden by the hormone-fueled, animal part of her that refused to take that chance, to wait even a day longer. She took the certificate and moved Tom into her flat within the hour.

CHAPTER SIXTEEN

Pamela

Present Day
10:48 a.m.

By the time Sue and I get back to the station, Rachel has pulled the slate data. She comes rushing straight over to us, proud of her work, wanting to show off to Sue. All of the slates on the list have female owners, and I can tell that Rachel feels that proves something, because it's the first thing she tells us. All it proves to me is that any men who were outside either had a female-registered slate with them or left their own at home.

"Send me the list," Sue tells her, and Rachel does. She pings it to my slate at the same time and the three of us go into Sue's office and go through it. I can sense Rachel's impatience. None of the names mean anything to me, and I already feel that this is a dead end, but we have to explore all possibilities.

"We need to talk to these women," Sue says. "Find out why they were outside, if they saw anything that might be of importance, even if they didn't realize it. But it will have to be done carefully. We don't want to cause alarm."

"I'd like to be part of that," Rachel says.

"Of course," Sue says. "I'll tell my officers you'll be working alongside them on this." Rachel and three of Sue's team set up camp in the room next door and start making calls. It's not the way

I would do it. In my opinion there's no substitute for a face-to-face conversation.

The media liaison officer comes in to tell us that the short message I gave to the local media is being replayed on a loop on all the news channels and it's spreading like wildfire. Everything about it is being dissected online, right down to my haircut. There are people on social media almost frothing at the mouth. They are demanding more information, and they've all got their own pet theory. So far, I've seen references to a drowning, a drug overdose, an abandoned newborn.

"We're going to have to make another statement," the media liaison says.

"Agreed," Sue Ferguson replies. "Pamela, I want you to go next door and work on the slate list with the others. I'll let you know when we need you."

I leave Sue's office and join Rachel and the others. Over the next hour I speak to fifteen different women. I quickly rule most of them out, as they're nurses and delivery drivers and postal workers, and it's easy enough to verify their stories.

I'm left with three women who give me what I like to call "the feeling." I've checked their details and it's clear they had no good reason to be outside at three in the morning. A phone call isn't enough; I need to see them in person.

"Where are you going?" Rachel asks me, as I get to my feet, patting my pocket for my car keys.

"Out."

But that's not good enough for Rachel. "Sue wants us to work on this from here."

I don't like the way she's looking at me. "That's not going to work."

I head out. Rachel follows me. "Pamela!" she says. "Don't you think you ought to at least clear it with Sue first?"

"I don't need permission to do my job."

"But . . ."

I catch sight of one of Sue's team watching us. I hustle Rachel downstairs before we draw any more attention to ourselves. When we get to reception, a crowd has gathered on the pavement outside, so we use the rear exit instead. Fortunately, they don't seem to have found their way round there yet. I might not rank as highly as Sue, but I certainly rank higher than Rachel, although she seems to have forgotten that. "You're coming with me," I tell Rachel. "That's an order."

She sits in the passenger seat in cool silence, listening as I update her on the three women I want to see, and why I want to see them. "Technology can only do so much," I say. "Sometimes you've got to speak to someone face-to-face."

"Have you given up on the idea that it might have been a man?" Rachel asks me as I pull out of the car park.

I concentrate on my driving. The first address is on the far side of town. The woman who answers the door has long hair tied back in a ponytail, and gym-toned arms. "Yes?" she says, eyeing our uniforms.

"Scarlett Caldwell?"

"Yes."

"I just want to ask you a couple of quick questions. Can we come in?"

"What's this about?"

"We need to know where you were last night," Rachel tells her.

Scarlett Caldwell is good, I have to give her that. She hides her reaction well. But not well enough. She closes the door quietly behind her. A curtain twitches in the house next door.

"It really would be better to do this inside," I say gently. But she's having none of it. She folds her arms across her chest, a sentry in front of the door. We are not getting in. I wonder what's in there that she doesn't want us to see.

"What business is it of yours where I was last night?"

"Mrs. Caldwell," I say. "I assume you've seen the news this morning. We know you left your house last night because we tracked your slate. We just want to know where you were."

She pales a little. "I didn't have anything to do with that!"

I wait, giving her space.

She exhales. She's visibly twitching. "My partner doesn't know." She glances behind her, but the door is still closed. "Do I need to spell it out?"

"If you wouldn't mind," I say.

"I've got . . . there's someone else. I went to see him."

"We'll need to speak to him," Rachel says. "I assume you can provide contact details."

"Is that really necessary?" Scarlett Caldwell asks. She squares her shoulders. She reminds me of a bulldog.

"I'm afraid so." I hand her my slate, and she taps in a name and address. I can't help but wonder why she'd be interested in a man who lives in that particular location, but each to their own. "Thank you," I tell her.

She goes back inside, slamming the door behind her.

"Lovely woman," Rachel says.

"Hmm," I say, but to me, Scarlett Caldwell is already forgotten.

The second woman is quickly ruled out, too, because she lent her slate to her daughter, a locksmith who was called out in the middle of the night. Again, we get contacts, and we're able to confirm all of it.

That just leaves one.

Rachel works at her slate as we head over there. I can feel the pressure of every minute that passes without an answer to any of our questions. I ask her to ping Michelle, and she does. We get a quick response. There's still no match on dental records. I knew there wouldn't be, but my frustration is still a heavy weight around my neck. I know, logically, that it's only been a few hours, and it can

take weeks, months even, to solve cases like this. I know that improvements in DNA testing have helped to cut that time down. But
we are still held back by other things. Privacy laws that mean we
can't have everyone's DNA sample and fingerprints on file, despite
how easy it would be to get them. CCTV that doesn't work properly
anymore because we've pumped all our money into tags.

I press my hands against my face.

"Are you okay?" Rachel asks me.

"Not really," I say. I feel like our victim is in the car with us, sitting in the back, breathing down my neck. I'm letting her down.
"This feels like shooting in the dark. In the wrong bloody room."

"I think we're making progress," Rachel says. "We've already
ruled out most of the women who were outside last night."

I can sense that there's a rift growing between Rachel and me.
It opened when we watched the CCTV of the park, and she saw a
woman and I saw a man, and it got bigger when Sue Ferguson turned
up. We've always worked well together before. I've always thought
that Rachel respected me, that I'd managed to rub the edges off the
training that tells young women like her that the world works a certain way. I thought she was listening when I told her about policing
before Curfew, and the fact that no system is infallible. I'm beginning to wonder if I was wrong about that.

I wonder if I should tell her about the cases that Sue mentioned
earlier, the hit-and-run and the stabbing. But I don't want anything
to be reported back to Sue.

The third address leads us to a woman in her early thirties.
She's pale and twitchy, but she lets us into the house. There's a man
there, too, a bit younger than her, but definitely related. Flowers fill
the living room, and the mantelpiece is lined with cards that read
Sorry for Your Loss and variations on that theme.

"Are you here about Dad?" the man asks us, and there's definite
hope in his voice. "Have you arrested that woman who tased him?"

"I'm afraid not," I say.

His shoulders slump. "No," he says. "I don't suppose you would have. You lot protect your own, don't you? Police, taggers, you're all the same."

There's something going on here that we know nothing about. We're going to have to tread carefully. I glance across at Rachel, but I can tell from her expression that she doesn't know, either. Her fingers work her slate. Mine pings. I unlock it, glance at the message she's sent me, and immediately I know there's something of interest here, in this house.

I look the woman over. She's very slim, but she's tall.

Maybe I was wrong about the CCTV.

Maybe.

CHAPTER SEVENTEEN

Helen

By the end of school on Monday evening, Helen was shattered and hungry. She'd had to stay late for parents' evening, which had included ten minutes with a foul-tempered Cass Johnson and her mother. Cass weighed heavily on her mind. There was much she could have said. More she should have said. She strongly suspected that Cass, despite her bluster and bravado, was deeply unhappy.

Helen thought that much of it probably had to do with Cass's father. There had been an emergency meeting for all staff the day after he'd broken Curfew. It was the first time their school had had to deal with that particular situation, but they had a plan already in place. The head had told them exactly how they were to respond to the inevitable questions from pupils and other parents. Cass hadn't been one of Helen's students at that point and she hadn't paid as much attention as she probably should have. Helen had assumed it was over and done with, until the lesson the previous week when Amy had asked all those questions about what happened to men who broke Curfew and Cass had walked out.

She hadn't mentioned Cass leaving the lesson to Sarah Wallace, and she couldn't help wondering if she should have. Should she phone Sarah now and tell her what had happened? Would it make things better, or worse? Her mind spun those thoughts around, over and over. She drove home in a daze. All she wanted was a warm bath and a soft bed and Tom. He'd make everything okay.

By the time that she reached her front door, she was exhausted. Even her clothes felt too heavy for her body to carry. Her skirt chafed against her legs. She dropped her bag to the floor, nestling it between her feet, and found her keys. She pushed the door open. "Tom?" she called out as she toed off her shoes and placed them neatly on the rack.

"In here!"

His voice came from the kitchen.

Wearily, Helen followed the sound. At least she wouldn't have to cook. He'd already said that he'd have something ready for her when she got home.

"Hello, love . . ." she began, but the rest of the words stuck in her throat as she took in the mess. The sink was full of dirty pots. A baked bean tin with the lid stuck up at a right angle had dripped sauce all over the worktop. There was a pile of used tea bags next to the kettle, and a large cardboard box sat on the kitchen table. It had been opened. An iceberg of polystyrene lay next to it. Tom had his head in the fridge.

There was no sign of dinner.

Voices trailed in from the living room as Helen walked over to the sink and turned on the tap. Strange, male voices. "Who's that?" she asked. She tried not to sound snappish, but she wasn't sure if she succeeded. She added a squirt of washing-up liquid to the bowl.

"Just a couple of mates," Tom said, closing the fridge door. There was milk on his upper lip and he wiped it off with the back of his hand.

"Oh," Helen said. "And what's this?" She gestured to the box.

Tom shifted his weight from one foot to the other. "Thought I might upgrade my game system," he said. "This one was on offer. It was a good deal, too good to turn down, really."

Helen swallowed. A game system? That was a big-ticket item.

She hadn't agreed to anything like that. He hadn't even asked her if it was okay. "How much was it?"

"Does it matter? We can afford it now that I'm not paying rent for my flat. Seriously, babe, lighten up a little. It's just a game console." He moved in a little closer, slid his arms around her waist. "Don't be mad," he whispered. "You know how much I adore you. I don't like it when you're mad at me."

Shouts of victory came from the living room, and Tom glanced toward the door. "Tell you what," he said. "Give me a minute to get rid of those two, and then we can clean up in here and order a take-out. Have an early night."

He grinned down at her, gave her waist a squeeze, then wandered off into the living room. She heard male voices mingling together, laughing, though she couldn't make out the words. Her anger had faded, but she could still feel the weight of it in her chest and it frightened her. What frightened her even more was the possibility that Tom might notice and question her feelings for him. She wouldn't let that happen. Their relationship was one of the good ones. They weren't a couple that had fights. That wasn't them.

Helen looked round the kitchen once more and sighed. She picked the box off the worktop and set it on the floor then piled the polystyrene inside it, the pieces squeaking as they rubbed against one another. She washed the dishes, stacking them carefully on the draining board. She swept the floor. She told herself that she'd over-reacted. This was Tom's home, too. She had to stop thinking of it as hers.

Then she went through into the living room. Two men she'd never seen before were in there with Tom. Neither of them looked like they were intending to leave anytime soon. One of them was lounging in her armchair, dirty trainers resting on top of her coffee table. The other was standing in the corner with Tom, arms straining as they lifted her sofa.

"Fucking thing weighs a ton," he muttered.

"Stop whining, you big girl," Tom told him as they shifted the sofa three feet to the left. The man, whoever he was, let go of his end of the sofa. It hit the floor with a bang. Helen winced. Tom let go of his end in the same fashion. It sounded like a bomb going off inside her usually quiet flat.

Helen felt invisible, faced with all this shouting. She thought about retreating into the kitchen, maybe all the way outside and into her car, but Tom had said that he would ask them to leave.

"Hello," she said. She stood with her hands clasped loosely in front of her, not wanting to be rude to his friends in case they decided they didn't like her, but desperate to ask exactly what they were doing to her living room. She wondered why she'd never met either of them before.

"Hi," said the one by the sofa, and she got a similar grunt from the one seated in her armchair. He must have felt her gaze on his feet, because he moved them off her coffee table, albeit slowly.

"Sorry, guys. That's going to have to be it for today," Tom said. He tucked his hands in his pockets. "Guess I'll catch up with you on Sunday."

"What's on Sunday?" Helen asked.

"Football practice."

"Oh," she said. "Of course."

The one in the armchair got to his feet. "It was nice to finally meet you," he said.

"Yes," she said faintly as the other one acknowledged her with a nod and followed his friend out. She heard the door open and close, and then it was just her and Tom in the flat. She stood, looking at the sofa wedged in under the window, and the dirt smeared across the coffee table. Her precious hand-knitted blanket, which had been neatly folded on the sofa, now lay in a heap in the corner. The TV had been moved, too, with the new black console given plenty of space beside it, and her armchair was lined up to give whoever sat in it a perfect view of the screen.

Tom dropped into the armchair. "What do you fancy for dinner? Pizza? Chinese?"

"Pizza," Helen said, because there was a place just around the corner so it would at least be quick. She checked her watch. It was just after six.

"Are you going to call, or do you want me to do it?" he asked. "Probably best if you collect it. If we wait for delivery, god knows what time it'll get here."

"I'll do it," she said. She went back into the kitchen to find her slate, pulled up the site, sent the order, then returned to the living room. She picked the blanket up off the floor and folded it neatly, looking longingly at her armchair. Tom had a game controller in one hand and the TV remote in the other. Helen was relegated to the sofa under the window, from which she could see the kitchen doorway and through that, the overflowing kitchen bin.

"Oh, that reminds me," he said. "I think there's something wrong with my tag."

"What?"

He set his ankle on top of his knee, pulled up his jeans, and showed it to her. "The light is flashing, look."

A properly functioning tag had a constant red light on the side, showing that it was active. But as Tom had said, the light on his was blinking away. "What happened?" Helen asked him.

"No idea," he said. "I just noticed it was doing it this afternoon."

"You should have called me," she told him. "I'd have come back sooner, taken you to the tagging center. If we go now, we might not get back before Curfew."

"We can do it in the morning," he said. He clicked the buttons on the controller. "You'll give me a lift, won't you?"

"Yes, of course," Helen said. She had a free period in the morning, which she'd intended to use for marking and lesson prep, but she could take him to the tagging center instead. But for the rest of the evening she couldn't shake the feeling that she didn't really want to.

CHAPTER EIGHTEEN

Sarah

Sarah had barely slept on Saturday night and had spent the Sunday evening drinking white wine from a box with Mrs. O'Brien and a couple of the other women, partly to avoid Cass, and partly because she'd needed to talk to women who would understand how awful she was feeling, how shocked and disappointed and frightened. She still couldn't believe what had happened. Not only had Greg been released earlier than he should have, he'd been sent back home.

She'd spent Monday lunchtime on the phone, trying to find out why. The answer was that there had been a fire in one of the wings at the prison, causing the early release of Greg and several other prisoners, and in the confusion, her request had been overlooked. The woman on the phone had listened to Sarah with astonishing patience, but the end result still hadn't changed. Moving Greg now wasn't high priority unless he did something stupid, like breaking Curfew, or assaulting someone. She'd ended the call with a headache and the feeling that she'd aged ten years. She was bitterly frustrated. To think that Greg was the past, something she could leave behind, and then find out that he wasn't . . .

After all that, Sarah had completely forgotten that it was parents' evening on the Monday night, until Cass had reminded her half an hour before they were supposed to attend and they'd had to rush over to the school.

On Tuesday morning, she got up to find a massive scratch across the bonnet of her car. She stood there, looking at it, her mind and body frozen. How had that happened? Her mind flicked back to the young man in the silver car who had followed her home from work. She told herself she was being paranoid. Cars got scratched. For all she knew, it had happened at the school the previous evening and she simply hadn't noticed.

She didn't mention it to anyone at work. Things had finally calmed down there, and she didn't want to stir them up again. They were waiting for the coroner's report on Paul Townsend. Hadiya didn't seem concerned. "Doctor's report said he smoked and he was overweight," she'd said. "And Mabel confirmed what you said, that he was verbally abusive. You did the right thing, Sarah. The coroner will see that. Trust me."

All Sarah needed now was the right moment to report the missing tag key. But that morning, Hadiya caught her on the way into her office, a grabby hand to her sleeve, and said the thing that Sarah had been dreading hearing for days. "I need to check your keys and tags at some point today, Sarah."

"Okay," Sarah said, although it obviously wasn't. "I'll just get my room set up and check my list for today." She hurried away before Hadiya could say anything else, although she had no idea what she was going to do. Shit. Shit. Why hadn't she reported the key when she first realized it was missing? It would have been a blip on her record, yes, but she could have blamed it on the man she'd tased, said that it had gone missing in the chaos afterward. She'd have got a slap on the wrist, and yes, it might have delayed a promotion, but it would have been fine.

It wasn't bloody well going to be fine now.

She was in her room with the door closed trying to figure out what she was going to do when there was a knock and Hadiya came in. Sarah felt sick.

Hadiya had her slate in her hand, and she crouched down next to the drawers. She went for the bottom one and the tags first, as Sarah expected. She checked each open box, counted the number in it, compared that to the numbers Sarah had inputted, found them to be correct. She closed that drawer and reached for the top one.

Sarah knew she had to say something about the key. But just as she was about to, Mabel appeared in the doorway. "Hadiya?" she said. "We've got a broken tag, needs an emergency appointment. Can we fit it in?"

Hadiya sighed and got to her feet. "We're full today. He'll have to ring round some of the other centers."

"I know," Mabel said. "But his girlfriend is a friend of mine and I said we'd do it. Please?"

"Add him to my list," Sarah said quickly. "I'll do him first."

"Are you sure?" Hadiya asked.

"Yes. It's not a problem."

"Thanks," Hadiya said. "That's all fine, by the way." She waved a hand at the drawers, turned on her heel, and went out into the waiting room.

Sarah almost collapsed into her chair. That had been a far, far closer call than she would have liked.

"Is everything all right?" Mabel asked.

"Yes," Sarah said. "Just having one of those weeks."

When the man with the broken tag strolled in, Sarah recognized him immediately. It was Tom Roberts. The boyfriend that Mabel didn't like. Sarah didn't like him, either, especially not when he smiled at her like his presence in her office was a gift, but he had saved her from a very difficult conversation with Hadiya, so she didn't feel too much ill will toward him.

"We'll have to stop meeting like this," he said.

"Indeed," Sarah said as he settled himself into the chair and tugged up the leg of his jeans. There wasn't anything obviously wrong with the tag, no cracks or scratches or signs that it had been damaged or otherwise tampered with. They were designed to be tough. They could withstand an hour in the bath or the swimming pool, a kick on the ankle at football, a good poke with a screwdriver. She'd seen men try all of the above. It had come as something of a shock, when she'd first started working as a tagger, that a small minority of men tried to mess with their tags. Greg had never done it, as far as she knew, and it had never occurred to her that other men might.

This one was something of a puzzle, however. The red light was flashing on the side, which usually indicated that an attempt had been made to remove it, but there were no scratch marks to show that it had been tampered with. Maybe the battery wasn't working properly or there was a loose connection inside somewhere. But it had been working perfectly when she'd checked it. *Must be faulty*, she thought to herself, making a note of it on his record. "I'll have to fit a new one."

"I assumed as much," he said.

"Any idea how it happened?"

"No. I just noticed the light was flashing. Weird, really. It's never happened before."

"What time was this?"

"Yesterday afternoon. I know, I should have come over straightaway, but my girlfriend had the car so I had to wait for her to get back from work, and then she'd had a rough day and didn't want to go out again. She's a teacher, you see, and it was parents' evening last night."

"I see," she said, as she pulled out her tape measure and measured his ankle. She glanced at him now, studied him a little more closely. Dark eyes. Sharp cheekbones. She mentally compared him to the man she'd seen walking into the counseling center with Miss Taylor. "Which school does she work at?"

"Burnside High."

Cass went to Burnside. Sarah could have told him that, asked the name of his girlfriend, but she knew better than to share anything personal with the men she dealt with. She double-checked the measurement on the tape, opened her drawer, and selected a new tag, size medium. Then she took updated headshots and verified his date of birth before fastening the tag around his ankle. She went through the motions of checking the fit and asking him if it was comfortable. He said that it was. He thanked her and smiled again, bigger this time. It had no effect on Sarah. Perhaps it was her experience with Greg. Perhaps it was this job and the hundreds of men she'd come into contact with since she'd started it. It didn't really matter. The end result was the same. She saw men as they truly were now. She knew the games they played. He'd turned on the charm because he knew that he should have found a way to get to the center the previous afternoon and he didn't want her to make a fuss. She decided that she'd let him get away with it, this time.

"Okay," she said. "That's done. Hopefully there won't be any problems with this one."

"Thanks," he said. He got to his feet, tugging the leg of his jeans back down over his new tag, and Sarah followed him out, intending to nip to the toilet before the next man came in. She spotted Helen Taylor immediately, sitting on a chair at the far side of the waiting room and chatting to Mabel. The pair of them got to their feet when they saw Tom. So she'd been right. He was the man she'd seen walking into the counseling center.

He went straight over and took Helen's hand.

Sarah noted Tom's closeness to Helen, the tight grip he had on her hand, the way he looked at Mabel. Once, she'd have seen his behavior as evidence of caring. Now it just made her want to roll her eyes. She lingered, watching the three of them, acknowledging Helen with a quick smile when the other woman glanced in her direction.

"Where do you want to go for dinner tonight?" Mabel asked Helen.

"I can't do tonight," Helen said.

"Why not?"

"This week is tricky," Helen said. "There's loads to do in the flat. But we can go next week, I promise."

"Sure," Mabel said, and she turned and went back into her room.

Sarah had never heard anyone load so much meaning into one syllable. But again, not her problem. She quickly went to the toilet, then went back into her own room, tidied her desk, and called in her next appointment. She wasn't at all surprised when Mabel wanted to talk about it over lunch.

"Take my advice," Sarah said. "Don't fall out with her over it."

"I'm not going to," Mabel said. "But she doesn't seem to have much time for me right now."

"She will," Sarah said. "Keep the door open for her, Mabel. She's in a strange phase right now and she's not thinking. New love is weird. It makes people behave like idiots. But it will pass, I promise you."

"I don't know about that," Mabel said. "She's besotted with him. She's got no room, no energy for anything or anyone else."

"Things change," Sarah said, though she wasn't sure that Mabel believed her. "Whatever is happening right now, it won't last forever."

Just as beautiful infants became bitter teenagers, domestic bliss became domestic drudge, and husbands who had broken Curfew came home, men always showed their true colors eventually.

They couldn't help themselves.

CHAPTER NINETEEN

Cass

C ass got home to an empty flat that afternoon. She was more than pleased that her mother wasn't there. It had been horrible, going back to school after walking out of class. Nobody had said anything, but she knew that they were all talking about her behind her back.

It was lovely to have the flat to herself for a couple of hours, where she could relax in front of the TV without Sarah breathing down her neck. She wondered what her dad was doing. She wished that she had a way to get in touch with him. She'd managed to tell him that they were living at the Motherhouse, but then Sarah had come out of the restaurant and Greg had told her he had to go.

She still didn't know exactly where he was living, but it had to be at Riverside. Everyone knew that was where men who'd been released from prison were sent, and everyone avoided that part of town as a result. She'd seen the sort of men who got on the bus that went there, in their cheap clothes and old trainers, and always found them gross. She hated the thought of her dad being with them.

Fortunately she would be eighteen in a few days, and then she'd be able to access all the information she needed online, whether Sarah wanted her to or not. It made her feel better about the fact that she'd walked out after Amy Hill had said all that stuff about her dad being in prison. Well, he wasn't in prison now, and even if he was at Riverside, it wouldn't be for long, she was sure of it. He'd get a job and move out of there as soon as he could.

Cass went into her room and flopped down on the bed. She reached into her bag and retrieved the tag key, then lay on her back, fiddling with it. It shifted her thoughts to Billy. They were no longer two people who were friends because no one else would have them, but two people with a shared secret, a bond built on something real, and by removing his tag, Cass knew she'd done something that actually mattered. She wasn't like the other girls at school, gossiping in the toilets at lunchtime, worrying about petty, stupid stuff.

And she liked knowing that Billy needed her. All she had to do was refuse to put the tag back on, and he'd be totally screwed. She'd never do it, obviously, but the thought of it left her slightly breathless, and it went a long way toward soothing the anger she still felt over that other embarrassing lesson when Miss Taylor had made them arm-wrestle.

She heard the front door open and close. She shoved the key back in her bag. Her mother, when she stuck her head round the door, wanted to talk about Cass's birthday. Cass was surprised. Given that Sarah had knocked back her earlier attempts to discuss it, Cass had assumed that Sarah intended to ignore it.

"I thought we could go out for dinner," Sarah said. "Get dressed up. Go somewhere nice."

"Can Dad come?" Cass asked.

"No," Sarah said.

"Why not?"

It all went predictably downhill after that. Not only would Sarah not agree to invite him to the meal, she also wouldn't give Cass his address. So by the time her birthday rolled round, she wasn't expecting Sarah to do anything. She was almost looking forward to the disappointment.

The first thing Cass did when she woke up was to register with the data portal that tracked all the men released from prison. It took only a few minutes to verify her identity and age and pull up Greg's record. She scrolled through it, reading every word, letting each one fuel the little cauldron of hate she'd kept burning inside over the past year.

Their old house was listed as his previous address. His new one was listed to the right of it. Cass wrinkled her nose when she saw it. He was at Riverside, exactly as she'd predicted, in flat 4C.

The second thing she did was to join iDate, the government-approved dating app that everyone used. It had strict rules. You had to be eighteen to join, although you could join at seventeen with parental permission. She'd tried to persuade Sarah to let her join a few months back, just after her dad went to prison. Sarah had refused, obviously. Cass couldn't see what the problem was. iDate was perfectly safe. Only women were allowed to make first contact, and sending nudes would result in a lifelong ban, as would asking for them. That particular rule always made Cass giggle. Why would anyone send a naked photo to a stranger?

She'd been planning an iDate account as her birthday present to herself for months and would have done it first if her mother's refusal to invite Greg to her birthday meal hadn't been so fresh in her mind. She chose a headshot, making sure it was a good one, and she wrote and rewrote her bio three times before uploading it. She had to go through the whole rigmarole of verifying her identity before she could use the account and that wasted several annoying minutes. Then it was done.

She started her search with great enthusiasm. Five minutes in, she couldn't believe how awful most of the men on the site were and went back to the search screen and narrowed her parameters. No one over thirty, no one under five foot ten. Good taste in music. Someone that other girls would be jealous of. The options it gave her were still pretty poor.

She didn't understand why they were all so rubbish. Where were the young, attractive, interesting men? There had to be some.

Her slate pinged and she flicked to her messages. It was Billy.

Happy Birthday! How does it feel to be 18?

Better than being 17

Lollolololol

Be better if we didn't have school. Wanna skip?

She waited, but he didn't respond. Cass turned her slate off and shoved it under her pillow. She pushed her hair back from her face and swung her feet to the floor. Time to face her mother, and the inevitable disappointment of what was guaranteed to be a shitty birthday.

Her toes curled against the carpet as she padded down the hallway and into the bathroom. "Eighteen," she said to herself. "I'm eighteen, and I can do whatever the fuck I want." She'd thought it would feel bigger than it did.

She took a few minutes to look at her face in the mirror, turning her head this way and that, pressing her lips together to make them pinker, pulling up her hair to see how it would look if she wore it that way, thought about changing her iDate photo and decided she'd do it later when she had more time. Then she shuffled her way into the kitchen. Sarah was seated at the table, hands wrapped around a fat white mug. Her hair was still damp from the shower. Since their argument about the birthday dinner, they'd barely spoken, and Cass wasn't too sure what to expect.

"Morning, love," Sarah said. "Happy birthday!" She held out a small rectangle wrapped in shiny gold paper. A silver ribbon had been wrapped around it and tied in a skinny bow.

Cass took it. The edges of whatever was inside were sharp and firm, some sort of box, and the wrapping suggested it was expensive. "What's this?"

"Open it," Sarah said. "Go on!"

Cass tore the paper carefully. She tore a little more, then faster when she realized what it was. She could feel herself teetering on the edge between excitement and disappointment and didn't know which way to go. Her mother wasn't supposed to do this. She was supposed to screw up.

"It's a new slate," Sarah said. "I know yours is getting old, and I thought you might like a better one."

Cass could feel how desperately her mother wanted her to like it, and that enabled her to school her expression into something flat and cold. "These are really expensive."

Sarah shrugged. "Yes, well, we're doing a bit better now, aren't we? And you're only eighteen once." She got up from her seat, emptied the rest of her coffee down the sink, and rinsed out the mug. There was a gray tint to her skin, caught for a moment by the light as she leaned over the sink and held the mug under the fall of water. Her body seemed suddenly tired and lumpen under her dressing gown. "Look, Cassie," she said, her face turned to the window so that Cass couldn't see it. "I know you and I haven't been getting on very well recently and I think it's time we tried to do something about it. We can't carry on like this. It's not healthy for either of us. We argue all the time. We go days without speaking. We don't even give each other a hug. Don't you wish that we could be nicer to each other?"

Cass felt a flash of something, a feeling she hadn't had in a long time, one she'd forgotten. Once she would have welcomed a hug from her mother. Now she couldn't remember the last time she'd let Sarah touch her at all. She didn't know how to. Just the thought of it was unnatural. It wasn't going to happen. But she could sense that she had to give her mother something. She didn't want Sarah to take the slate away. "Thanks for the slate," she said. "It's really thoughtful."

"Good," Sarah said. She turned back to Cass. "I'm glad you like it. And you know, Cass, you can tell me anything. I don't ever want you to feel like you need to keep secrets from me."

The two of them stood there, looking at each other, and there was a second moment, one where something could have been said and something might have changed, but Cass saw the wet gleam in her mother's eyes and it frightened her. She didn't want to see her mother's feelings. She didn't want to hear them, to know them, to be close to them. She thought about her father, living at Riverside, and about the tag key, buried at the bottom of her school bag. She backed away. "I've got to get ready for school."

"What about breakfast?"

"I'm not hungry," Cass said, but she was already halfway out of the room and then in the safety of her own, behind the blessed barrier of the closed door. She looked at the slate. It was a lovely shade of petrol blue with a glossy touchscreen, far nicer than the one she currently had. She turned on her old slate, tapped it against the side of the new one, and waited for all her stuff to transfer. It happened almost immediately. She messaged Billy.

Got a new slate

Nice

It was very pretty. Sarah never bought her anything pretty.

"Oh my god," Cass whispered. "She's trying to buy me."

You can tell me anything. All of a sudden, it unraveled in her mind. She'd let herself think that Sarah had given her the slate because she cared, when in fact the expensive gift proved the opposite.

Her mother didn't care. She just wanted Cass to stop asking questions about her dad and play nice with the women in their building. Maybe . . . maybe she even thought that she could bribe Cass into admitting that she'd taken the tag key.

Cass got dressed, picked up her bag, and headed back into the kitchen. Sarah was still sitting there, staring out of the window as the kettle boiled. Usually she left early. She certainly didn't hang around in the kitchen in her dressing gown at this time.

"Aren't you going to work today?" Cass asked her.

"I'm going in a bit later," Sarah said. "I had hoped we could have breakfast together."

Cass slipped her hand into her pocket, feeling the smooth surface of the new slate against her fingertips, reminding herself of what was really happening here. "Like I said, I'm not hungry. I don't have time now anyway. And I'll probably be late home, too."

"Why?"

"I've got Dad's address. Thought I might go and see him."

She saw her mother's expression darken, and knew she'd been right about all of it. "I don't think that's a good idea."

"Why not?"

"He just got out of prison, Cass. He's dealing with a lot right now. He needs some time to sort himself out first."

"So you're saying he's too busy for me?"

"I didn't mean it like that," Sarah said.

"Then what did you mean?"

Her mother's eyes turned sharp. "Stop it, Cass."

"Stop what? Asking about Dad?"

"You know exactly what," Sarah told her.

"I can see him if I want. It's not up to you."

"Maybe not," Sarah said slowly. "But that doesn't mean that I should encourage you to make stupid decisions, either. Leave it alone, Cass. You don't know . . ."

But whatever it was that Cass didn't know was lost. She could see her mother's mouth moving, forming the words, but Cass's anger was so loud that it drowned out everything else. She welcomed it. "Everything was fine!" she yelled. "We were happy! We were a family! And you ruined it!"

The toaster popped and the smell of warm, cooked bread permeated through their little kitchen. Cass couldn't bear it. She couldn't stand this room, this flat, or her mother for a moment longer. She grabbed her bag and stormed out. She was sick of living like this. It made her feel like she couldn't breathe.

She thundered down the stairs.

The other women who lived in the building were gathered in front of the main door. Someone had strung up a homemade banner that said HAPPY BIRTHDAY, CASS in huge gold letters. Someone thrust a bunch of flowers at her. Her arm was squeezed. "Get off me!" she shouted furiously. A couple of the women were holding presents, but she couldn't deal with them right now, she just couldn't.

She burst out onto the street and ran across the road, narrowly dodging a car. The driver honked their horn at her. Cass gave them the finger and walked on. She hated the Motherhouse and the nosy, shriveled old women who lived in it. They thought they knew everything. Well, they didn't. They didn't know anything about what Cass wanted, how she felt. She knew they laughed at her when she wore a short skirt or makeup. Each and every single one of them was bitter and jealous. Cass would never let herself go the way they had.

And now Sarah was turning into a bitter old woman, too. Cass had given her mother a chance to be reasonable, to acknowledge that Cass was now an adult and show her some respect, and Sarah had chosen not to. At least Cass knew where she stood. Sarah still thought she was a child, someone who could be pushed around and controlled.

Well, Cass would show her.

CHAPTER TWENTY

Sarah

Sarah rested her hands on the edge of the sink, her shoulders hunched, and allowed herself a brief moment of self-pity. She could see Cass through the window, head down, arms swinging. She saw a car pull to a halt as Cass stepped out in front of it without looking, heard the horn, saw Cass turn and give the driver the finger, felt a jolt of disgust. She watched until Cass was out of sight, and then buried her head in her hands, wondering how on earth they had ended up here. This was not at all how she'd wanted Cass's eighteenth birthday to go.

Greg wasn't even here. He shouldn't have been able to dominate this birthday as he had so many others, and yet she couldn't shake the feeling that he had. It felt like she would never be rid of him, never, and she found herself thinking about what Mrs. O'Brien had said, that she should tell Cass the truth about that awful final day, about the video call she'd walked in on. But even now, she didn't want Cass to know. It was too horrible, too embarrassing, and in some ways, it was better if Cass carried on thinking that her father was a decent person. Finding out that a person you thought was one thing was something else entirely was a hard and painful lesson. She didn't want Cass to have to go through that.

Maybe it was simply time that she accepted that this was how things were going to be from now on. Cass would leave home and head off to university soon anyway. Perhaps things would improve once they had a little distance.

Sarah dropped her hands from her face, blinked back tears, and found herself looking at the street again. Things were a little blurry, but she was sure that she could see . . . no. It couldn't be.

But it was.

She bolted out of the flat, barefooted and in her dressing gown, but she wasn't quick enough. The breakfast room was still full as Mrs. O'Brien opened the front door of the building and an all-too-familiar male voice broke through. The female chatter paused as if a switch had been flicked.

"I'm looking for Cass Johnson," he said.

"You need to leave," Mrs. O'Brien told him.

"I told you, I'm here to see Cass Johnson. I've got something for her."

"You can leave it by the gate."

Sarah ran to the door, her dressing gown flapping round her legs. She tugged it into position, trying to keep everything covered. "Sorry, Liz," she said. "I'll deal with this."

Mrs. O'Brien stepped back, leaving Sarah face-to-face with her ex-husband on the doorstep of her precious home, where men were not allowed to be. She pulled the door closed behind her, wanting to block his view inside the building. "You've got no right to be here," she told him.

He looked at her like she was something he'd stepped in. "I've got the right to see my daughter on her birthday."

"No, you don't."

"Excuse me?"

"She's eighteen. You've got no rights at all."

"Let's just ask Cass about that, shall we?" He started to reach past her for the door handle.

Sarah blocked his way. "She's not here. And you need to leave.

You shouldn't even have come to the door. This is a Motherhouse. Men aren't welcome here."

He took a step backward, and with it, his entire demeanor seemed to change. "Right," he said. He glanced up at the building. "You'll have to forgive me. I assumed, given the occasion, that I'd be allowed to drop off a present." He set the package down on the ground. "I trust you'll give this to Cassie? I don't want her to think that I've forgotten about her on her birthday."

Sarah watched him go with a tight, angry knot in her stomach. All of a sudden, she was the unreasonable one, not him. She snatched up the package, took it inside the Motherhouse, slamming the door behind her, and then ran up the stairs to her flat, not wanting to look at the women in the breakfast room, feeling the weight of their stares on her back as she went.

By the time she got there she was crying, the mixture of fury and adrenaline too much to bear. She set the package down on the kitchen table and ripped it open. No way was she going to let him give a present to Cass that she hadn't seen. Inside the thin, cheap paper, she found a pair of earrings and a bottle of nasty perfume. She didn't want Cass to have either of them. She dumped them both in the bin, then went to get ready for work. She was glad of her plain clothes, her easy-to-manage hair, her routine.

She was startled out of it by a knock at the door. She answered it to find Mrs. O'Brien standing in the hallway, arms folded, a grim look on her face. "We need to talk," she said.

Sarah's heart sank. "I know. I'm sorry. I had no idea . . ."

"A couple of the women are very upset. Men are not allowed to come here. They don't go beyond the gate. That's the rule."

"I'll talk to them."

"Good. We like you, Sarah. We want you to carry on living here. But this can't happen again. The rules of the building are very clear. If you're intending to have some sort of relationship with your ex-husband, you'll have to find somewhere else to live."

"I know," Sarah said. "I didn't tell him he could come here, I swear. And I have absolutely no intention of having any sort of relationship with him."

"I believe you," Mrs. O'Brien told her. "I want you to know that. But it's my job to make sure everyone understands. We've had women move into the building before who thought the rules didn't apply to them." She hugged Sarah. "Happy birthing day, by the way. Make sure you treat yourself to something. You deserve it."

"Thank you," Sarah said.

It was both painful and deeply embarrassing for Sarah, and not at all the start to the day that she'd been hoping for. Cass's birthday had always been bittersweet. She couldn't help wondering if other women found their children's birthdays difficult, if they, too, spent them immersed not just in feelings of celebration, but in memories of labor and birth. Sarah's most vivid memory was of the shock that had hit her immediately afterward, when she lay on the hospital bed, empty and alone, all attention turned to the baby, as if the baby was the only thing that mattered. She remembered her anger over the fact that no one had told her what it would really be like. But at the same time, how could they have? How could you describe that experience in a way that someone who had never been through it would understand?

She got to the tagging center at the same time as Mabel. As she got out of her car, someone shouted something at her from the other side of the car park, but she couldn't make it out, and when she turned her head to see who it was, the woman turned on her heels and scurried away, a little dog trailing after her on a long lead.

"How's your morning going?" Mabel asked.

"Terrible. My ex-husband turned up at the Motherhouse."

"He did what?"

"Waltzed right up to the front door with a birthday present for Cass. I couldn't believe it."

"These Curfew sentences are too short," Mabel said. "Seriously, they should get a year. Minimum. Three months doesn't teach them anything."

"The funny thing is, I thought I'd feel better when he was released," Sarah told her. "I felt awful when he was inside. I mean, it's not a nice thought, is it? Your husband being in prison. Having to admit to people that's where he was. But now . . ." She groaned. "I asked for him to be rehomed somewhere else, but there was a fire and he's here."

"Oh, god. Where's he been placed? Riverside Court?"

"Yep."

"Does Cass know?"

"Yes," Sarah said. "She told me this morning that she would be late back from school because she's going to see him."

Mabel reached out and rested her hand briefly on Sarah's wrist. "Oh, Sarah."

"I can't bear the thought of her seeing him again. You probably think I'm being foolish."

"Not at all."

"He was just . . ."

"Male," Mabel said, and with that single word, Sarah knew that she understood. She didn't have to explain the rest of it. "At least you've got a daughter and not a son."

"That's true," Sarah said. "I can't imagine anything worse than getting pregnant and then finding out that you're having a boy."

CHAPTER TWENTY-ONE

Cass

After leaving the Motherhouse, Cass headed over to the bus stop. Billy was already there. She asked him again if he wanted to skip school with her. She was only half joking. She wasn't sure that she had the nerve to do it alone, even though she was feeling far less inclined to follow the rules since she'd walked out of that Curfew class. He said no and gave her a hand-drawn card and a secondhand book about Henry VIII.

"It's just one day," Cass pointed out. "No one's going to care if you miss one day."

"No, Cass."

"But it's my birthday!"

"I know," he said. "Will you come round after school?"

"What for?"

He gestured to his ankle. "That."

"I don't know," Cass said, irritated with him. "I don't know what time I'll be home."

When their usual bus arrived, she didn't get on it. Billy asked her where she was going. She told him it was none of his business. She got on the next bus on her own. It took her straight to the town center. She had a half-formed idea that she could get the bus across to the other side of town, where Riverside Court was, but when she saw it at the bus station, she lost her nerve.

She spent an hour wandering around the shops, desperately hoping that someone would ask her why she wasn't at school so that she could tell them she was eighteen and see the look on their face as they flinched with embarrassment and slunk away. But no one did, and with little money to spend, she quickly got bored. There were only so many lovely blouses and skirts you could admire when you couldn't have any of them. But there were still some things she could have, like hot chocolate at her favorite coffee shop.

Her head was all over the place. She'd woken up so confident, so sure that this was the day when things would start to fix themselves, but so far there was no sign of that happening at all. If anything, the opposite was true. She was angry with Sarah for buying her a new slate, and at the same time, angry with her for only buying a slate and not making more of a fuss. She was angry with Billy for making her skip school alone. And she was angry with herself for chickening out of getting on the bus that would take her over to Riverside Court.

But when she got to Coffee Stop, Bertie was there, and she began to feel that maybe the day wasn't a total loss after all. It was almost as if fate had arranged it. She was here, he was here, the coffee shop was quiet, she didn't have Billy hanging round her neck. Bertie was standing behind the counter and wiping the machine with a white cloth. He gave her that same smile he'd given her before, and something inside Cass went all squirmy and she wanted to giggle. She had to bite her tongue hard to force it back. He was wearing his usual short-sleeved T-shirt that clung to his chest and biceps, with his hair falling across his forehead. How could she have forgotten how good-looking he was? She bet he was a really good kisser. With that cushiony lower lip, he couldn't possibly be bad.

"What'll it be?" he asked as she approached the counter.

"Caramel mocha, extra shot," she said. She didn't bother pretending she wanted chai tea this time.

"Coming right up," he said. "Take a seat. I'll bring it over."

"Thanks."

Her favorite table was empty and she headed straight for it, arranging herself carefully in her seat, flicking her hair forward over her shoulders and then tucking it back behind her ears. She pulled out her slate and busied herself scrolling through her messages. He brought her drink over and they went through the payment performance.

"Nice slate," he commented.

"Thanks," Cass said. "It's new. Birthday present, actually."

"From your boyfriend?"

"I don't have a boyfriend."

He flashed her another one of those killer smiles but went back to the counter before she could say anything else. She told herself to be patient, that he was at work and he was busy, but she felt on edge. He kept sneaking glances her way as she tapped her nails on the table, needing to move, to do something to drain some of the energy she felt. She wondered what her mother would say if she knew that this gorgeous guy was looking at her.

Something was happening between them. She could feel it. They had a connection. Why else would he keep looking at her? But before he could come over again, the place started to get busy, and it soon became obvious that he wasn't going to be able to talk to her again. A couple of women waiting at the counter started giving her dirty looks and Cass could tell they wanted her table. She ignored them. She'd sit as long as she wanted, and there was nothing they could do about it.

But then another member of staff appeared and started to collect empty mugs. She took Cass's with a polite "Is this finished?"

Cass knew what she was really saying. She put her jacket back on and slowly picked up her bag, but he still hadn't come back over. She'd really hoped he would talk to her again before she left.

Right before she was about to go, she had a brain wave. She had an iDate account now—why didn't she just look for him on it? She opened the site, tapped his name into the search box, and let out a little squeak when it returned the information she'd been looking for. His profile came up straightaway. He was twenty-seven, and he liked long bike rides and going to the cinema.

She tried to catch his eye one last time before she left, but the shop was too busy, so she left without saying good-bye, and then as she sat on the bus heading back in the direction of the Mother-house, she sent him a friend request. She'd decided to go to see her father another time. A weekend would be better. More chance that he'd be in.

Her friend request was accepted almost immediately.

"Ohmygod," she muttered.

The man seated in front of her turned round to see who she was talking to. Cass slid a little lower into her seat. A notification popped up alerting her to a new message. It was Bertie.

Hey, thanks for the friend request

You're welcome. You make great coffee

He didn't respond immediately to that one, which made Cass panic and wish that she hadn't sent it. Then a smiley face appeared on her screen.

Was just looking at your profile. You're very pretty

Thanks

Are you a model?

Cass squeaked. No

You could be. You photograph really well. Are you sure you haven't got a boyfriend?

No! OMG, would I be on iDate if I did?
I'm not a slut!!!

She hesitated before using that word. But she didn't want him to think that she was a prude, the sort of woman who was afraid of a little bad language.

Oh, I can tell, he replied. You're definitely a bit of a princess.

I am not!

It's OK. I like a woman who knows what she wants and doesn't take any crap.

Her skin tingled. They messaged each other for the rest of the day.

Maybe this wasn't the worst birthday after all.

CHAPTER TWENTY-TWO

Pamela

Present Day
11:27 a.m.

tread carefully, but within fifteen minutes I have the information I need. Kate's father, Paul Townsend, was tased by a woman at the tagging center and died of a heart attack several days later. The reports from the tagger and the police officers who went to the station to deal with it describe a verbally abusive, aggressive man who kicked off and was dealt with accordingly. There's no suggestion that the use of the Taser was inappropriate. Tragic for the two people in front of me but nothing sinister.

The problem is that these two obviously don't agree with that. The brother, David, spends several minutes raging about a cover-up, and how he's getting legal advice and he's going to sue, although who he's going to sue, and for what, he doesn't seem to know. More interesting is Kate's refusal to explain why she was out in the middle of the night. She's clammed up completely. She keeps shooting nervous glances at her brother and picking at her cuticles. I know nerves when I see them. She's hiding something. They both are. His noise is as much of a cover as her silence.

"Can I speak to you outside?" Rachel says to me quietly.

I'm not sure that I want to leave Kate and her brother alone, but I don't want to argue with Rachel in front of them. We head outside and stand next to the car.

"I think we should take them down to the station," Rachel says.

"On what grounds?" I ask, though I suspect I already know.

Rachel counts the points off on her fingers. "She won't tell us where she was. She fits the person we saw on the CCTV. And she's got motive. You heard what he said. They blame that tagger for the death of their father. What if she's our victim?"

"I agree that there's something odd going on here, but you need to slow down a little," I say. "You're getting ahead of yourself. Let's start by checking if the tagger is missing first."

But Rachel is already on her slate, and it doesn't take a genius to work out who she's calling. She speaks quickly, with Sue Ferguson on speakerphone, pulling me into the conversation whether I want to join it or not.

"Bring them in," Sue orders us. "Both of them. Do you need support?"

"Yes," Rachel says. "It would be easier if we could put them in separate cars."

We're closing the stable door after the horse has bolted, if you ask me, but neither of them does.

"I'll send someone now," Sue says. "What's the name of the tagger?"

"Sarah Wallace," Rachel tells her.

"Do we know where she is?"

"Not yet," I say.

"Bloody well find out!" Sue's voice booms through the slate. "If she's missing, then that puts us well on our way to identifying our victim and clearing up this mess."

Rachel starts making further calls as we wait for the other car to turn up. Two arrive, both unmarked, with Sue Ferguson's officers inside. Rachel and I are swept aside. We stay long enough to watch Kate and David be marched out of the house and ushered into the backs of those cars and driven away.

I don't like it.

I'm sure that I could have got the truth out of Kate Townsend with a little gentle pushing. It didn't need any of this, or the twitching curtains of the neighbors. There'll be videos of this streaming online within a matter of minutes. I'd bet money on it.

"Sarah Wallace isn't at work and she's not answering her slate," Rachel says. Her excitement is palpable. "No one seems to know where she is."

"Keep trying," I say. Maybe Rachel will turn out to be right, and Kate Townsend is guilty of murder, but I don't believe it, perhaps because I don't want to believe it and I'm letting my feelings color my judgement. If only I'd had five more minutes with Kate.

We head back to the station. The crowd outside has grown threefold, and I have to be careful as I ease forward and into the car park. Someone bangs on the window. I tell Rachel not to say anything, not to answer any questions, and we rush into the building with our heads down.

When I get upstairs, I look for Sue. I'm told she's already in an interview with Kate Townsend. The media liaison is frantically rushing all over the place, speaking to different people, tapping at her slate as if her life depends on it. Technically neither Kate nor David is under arrest. They are, as we like to say, "helping us with our inquiries."

I can't get anywhere near Kate, but that doesn't mean I can't get a few minutes with David. His tag tells us he was indoors, exactly where he was supposed to be, but as I told Rachel, we cannot make assumptions.

He sits, slouched in a chair, picking at his thumbnail.

"Why was your sister outside?" I ask.

"I don't know."

"Come on, David," I say. "The two of you live in the same house. We've got the data from her slate. You and I both know it didn't take itself out for a drive. You need to stop messing me around and take this seriously. We found a body in the park this morning and there are officers in this building desperately looking for a way to prove that Kate had something to do with it. Tell me the truth. Give me something to hold them back with."

If that doesn't frighten him into telling me what I need to know, nothing will. His cheeks flush. He tugs the sleeve of his sweatshirt down over his hand and wipes his nose with it. A muscle tics in his cheek. "She went out."

"Why?"

"She felt like going for a drive. It's not illegal."

"No," I say. "Does she often go out for a drive at that time?"

"Does it matter?"

"I just want to know if this is a regular thing."

There's a knock at the door. I pause the interview, step outside. It's Rachel. "We got a bit more data from her slate," she says. "Messages to David. And we've got a clearer map of where she went."

I flick through the messages and check the map, and my heart sinks. "Any sign of Sarah Wallace yet?"

"No," Rachel says. "She's not at home, and wherever she's gone, she didn't take her slate with her."

We go back into the interview room. I'm not kind this time.

"Kate went to the Motherhouse," I say. "Care to explain that?"

"How could I possibly explain it? It was Curfew. I was at home!"

"I see." I make a note on my own slate. Everything he says is being recorded, but writing things down buys time, not that I need it. I already know what my next moves are going to be.

"Do the two of you know anyone at the Motherhouse?"

He's visibly twitching. "No."

"Are you sure?" I ask him.

"I said no, didn't I?"

"The woman who tased your father lives there," I say. I set down my slate. "Look, David. I've read the messages you sent to Kate. I know what the two of you have been up to. You wanted to get your own back on Sarah Wallace. I can understand that. What I need to know is how far it went."

He starts to cry. "Sarah Wallace killed my dad."

Before I can say anything further, there's a knock at the door. I go out to find Sue Ferguson in the corridor. She's taken her jacket off, and her shirtsleeves are rolled up to the elbow. She looks like she means business.

"It's coming together," she tells me. "You've done good work here, Pamela. Very good. At this rate we'll have this wrapped up by the end of the day. It's going to be a good result. I want you to keep pushing him. As soon as you think he's ready to tell us what we need to know, bring me in. Once we've got him on record confirming that Kate Townsend is our killer, she'll confess, I've no doubt about that."

My slate buzzes. I take it out and check it. "It's Michelle. The pathologist," I tell Sue Ferguson. I take the call.

When I end it, I know that Sue isn't going to like what I have to say. "There's male DNA on the body," I say.

Even though I already know that Sue has come here to make sure we find a female killer and not a male one, I'm still surprised by her reaction.

"It doesn't matter," she says.

She goes back into the room with Kate Townsend.

I am shut out.

CHAPTER TWENTY-THREE

Helen

Things returned to a state of relative calm after Tom's tag was replaced. Helen was proud of the way that they'd handled their first major incident. It had been challenging, but they'd survived it. They'd proved that they weren't one of those couples that would crack at the first sign of trouble, and why should they be? They'd passed their Cohab certificate. Their relationship was a strong one. It wasn't about how long you'd been together but how compatible you were. A six-month relationship between people who were meant to be together was better and stronger than a twenty-year one between people who weren't.

But she had a new problem now. The dizzy spells and the odd, sick feeling in her stomach were getting worse. It had crossed Helen's mind when it first started that what she was experiencing might be something more than just a virus, but she'd shoved the thought aside. No one got pregnant that quickly. Women on the pregnancy forum she'd been secretly reading said that it could take up to a year, and she'd been okay with that. A year would give her time to talk Tom round. She couldn't face the thought that it might have happened already, especially in light of what Dr. Fearne had said to her in that final counseling session.

Two years.

What will I do?

She hadn't told Tom. She hadn't told anyone, not even Mabel. She'd feel like a fool if it turned out to be nothing. But when her period didn't show, she knew that she had to stop kidding herself. She bought a pregnancy test in the supermarket, hiding it in her basket under shampoo and apples in case any of the kids from school happened to see her. Now she was locked in the supermarket toilet with it, her bag of shopping wedged between her feet.

She played out both scenarios in her head, trying to rehearse how she'd feel, how she'd react, what would need to be done.

Pregnant.

Or not pregnant.

Everything.

Or nothing.

After all the months of longing and trying to hold back the rising swell of baby fever that had consumed every waking moment and had burned through her dreams until she'd felt like she was going mad, it seemed absurd that it all boiled down to peeing on a stick. It wasn't as if the stick had any influence on the outcome. She could not pee on it, and a baby would still either arrive in nine months or it wouldn't.

And yet it felt as if this were the point at which her life would change.

It wasn't the first time she'd taken a test. She'd secretly bought one before she stopped taking the pill, just to try, even knowing that her chances of being pregnant were zero. She'd stared anxiously at the test window, waiting for an impossible line to appear, and had been embarrassed by the depths of her disappointment when it inevitably hadn't. She'd stopped taking the pill the next day. She'd felt the side effects of the artificial hormones quickly fade away, had felt her own long-forgotten rhythm return, and now here she was.

Helen took a deep breath as she looked down at the test. Her hand was shaking.

The screen flashed.

Testing . . .

It started to count down.

5 . . . 4 . . . 3 . . .

She held her breath.

The screen flashed again.

Helen let out a squeak. She quickly suppressed it.

Pregnant.

Ohmygodohmygodohmygod

She felt hot and then cold. The cubicle seemed to spin. It had happened. It wasn't a virus. It was a baby.

The screen flashed again, and another message appeared, one she hadn't seen on the test she'd taken before, because that had been a cheap, bottom-shelf one and this was the most expensive one you could buy. She'd wanted to be sure.

Boy/Girl?

Helen hesitated. Did she want to know? Something that had been a murmur in the background of her thoughts suddenly became very loud. A girl would mean freedom. Opportunity. Her life wouldn't be caged at the age of ten. Helen was a teacher. She knew what it meant to have a boy. She saw the mothers rushing to bring their sons to early slots at parents' evening, how their careers were limited by the restrictions placed on their children. When she pictured herself with a child, she always saw a girl.

A boy was an entirely different proposition.

And yet just as possible.

Her insides went cold at the thought of it.

She pressed a hand to her belly. A girl, she told herself. Definitely a girl.

She pressed the button.

Congratulations! It's a BOY!

"Fuck," she muttered. "No. No!" She pressed the button again as if she could make it give her a different result, but it didn't. That awful three-letter word stayed stubbornly on the screen, refusing to budge, refusing to change. She set down the test stick and grabbed the box, turning it over, tracing the small print on the back with the tip of her finger. It could be wrong, right? Nothing was 100 percent accurate.

`Sex identification 99.9% accurate in a study of 10,000 pregnancies.`

"Fuck," Helen whispered again. She could feel the back of her throat starting to burn. She screwed her eyes shut and bit her bottom lip and just about managed to get it under control. She threw the test into the toilet and flushed. Then she opened the door. She went to the sink and washed her hands, then went back to her car.

A boy might be all right. Lots of women managed with sons. It didn't have to mean that her life was over. Yes, things would have to change, and she wouldn't have the same freedom for a while at least. But she'd make sure he got a good education, so that he would be able to get a job. Maybe he'd move abroad when he grew up, like her parents had, leaving her to take care of herself. Or maybe he'd stay here and live within the limits of Curfew, like Tom was doing. Maybe Tom would leave both of them and she'd end up a little old lady with an unmarried forty-year-old son taking his hatred out on her because he couldn't afford to leave home.

Oh, god.

A wave of nausea hit her, making her stomach heave and her eyes feel too big for her head. She thought that she was going to be sick, but she wouldn't, she wouldn't. She swallowed again, a fierce, determined contraction of muscles. It worked long enough to get her home.

When she walked in, she could see Tom in the living room, sitting in her armchair, his gaze fixed on the TV. "Grab me a beer, will you?" he called.

"All right," Helen said. She went into the kitchen and did as he had asked. She carried the bottle through to him and set it gently down on the coffee table. "How was your day?"

"Good." He caught hold of her wrist and pulled her onto his lap.

"What's up with you? You've got a face like a wet weekend," he said. "Cheer up. What have you got to be miserable about, anyway?"

Helen tried to fix on a smile. "I'm just tired," she said. "Busy day."

He turned his attention back to the TV. He didn't ask her more about her day. Perhaps it was just as well. It saved her from having to lie. She moved to the sofa and they watched television in silence for almost an hour before Tom got up and disappeared into the bathroom, leaving Helen alone. She stared at the screen, her thoughts racing.

What was she going to do?

She could hear Tom running the shower, the water thundering against the tray. It would continue for at least another twenty minutes. She'd quickly learned that he didn't understand the concept of saving water. She scribbled a message on the whiteboard in the kitchen, then grabbed her bag, shoved her feet into her shoes, and headed out.

Mabel would know what to do.

Helen held it together until her friend opened her front door, and then fell completely apart. "I'm pregnant," she said, and saw Mabel flinch. "The test said it's a boy. I can't have a boy, Mabel. I can't. I won't be stuck with a child that can't get a decent job."

Mabel took her through to the living room and sat her down on the sofa. "Are you sure?"

"Yes."

"Well, you know what the options are," Mabel said. "You've got a choice, Helen. You don't have to have it if you don't want to."

"I know," Helen said. "But abortion . . . I don't know if I can do that."

"How far along are you?"

"I'm not sure. Not very."

"Then you've got time. Take a few days to think it over. You don't have to rush into anything."

"Maybe it'll be all right," Helen said. She tried to smile. "A boy wouldn't be that bad, would it?"

Mabel didn't answer.

CHAPTER TWENTY-FOUR

Cass

The next day, Cass skipped school again. She'd dithered and delayed until it was impossible to get there on time and then told herself that there was no point in going as she'd only be late. The truth was that she didn't want to face the other girls. She didn't have the energy for it. Things were still difficult after the Curfew lesson the previous week, when Amy had asked all those questions about men in prison and Cass had walked out.

She'd reminded them that they could get to her if they wanted, that she had a weak spot that they could poke at. She didn't want to face their fake interested questions about her birthday. She didn't want to tell them what presents she'd got, if she'd been out for dinner. The new slate was good but not good enough for them.

Anyway, her birthday had not ended well, despite the chain of messages from Bertie. She'd returned to the Motherhouse just before lunch and had managed to sneak into the flat without being seen. Sarah had come home at the usual time and lectured her about being polite to the other women in the building. Then they'd gone downstairs to the communal dining room. Cass was expecting the usual midweek meal, but instead there was a pile of presents laid out for her, and the tables had been decorated, and someone had made a banner with the number "18" painted on it in sparkly blue.

The food had been lovely. There had been a big chocolate cake with candles on it. In the middle of it all Cass had realized that she was enjoying herself, and that had ruined the entire evening, and then she'd realized that she hadn't had even so much as a card from her dad. When she'd asked Sarah if Greg had sent her anything, Sarah had gone very red in the face and then rooted in the bin and fished out a torn bundle of brightly colored paper, wrapped around a bottle of perfume and a pair of earrings. Sarah spent the rest of the evening shut in Mrs. O'Brien's flat, leaving Cass to her own devices, which Cass thought was a pretty crappy thing for her mother to do to her on her birthday.

She hadn't seen Billy at the bus stop this morning because she had deliberately waited around the corner until their usual bus had been and gone. She didn't want to talk to him. She got the next bus but didn't go to the town center, getting off at the park instead. The geese rushed over to shout at her as she circled the lake. Cass hissed right back, and the geese opened their wings and then backed off. It put a little bounce into her step.

When her slate buzzed, she checked it, hoping for a message from Bertie. But it was a message from Billy.

Where are you? Are you sick?

It buzzed again.

Please come over tonight and sort out my you know what.

The empty text box stared up at her, waiting for a response.

She shoved the slate back into her pocket. It was strange. Until a few days before, Billy had been her best friend. She'd spoken to him every day, had messaged him multiple times. He'd been the first person she'd wanted to tell when she'd taken the tag key. Probably because he was the only person that she could tell. Now, as she looked at her slate, she found herself with nothing to say. She didn't want to tell him she was skipping school again or tell him about Bertie. She didn't want to tell him anything.

But no messages from Bertie left her at a loose end. She decided, therefore, to do what she'd been too afraid to do the day before and visit her dad instead. Sarah had said that Greg wouldn't want to see her. Cass refused to believe that. She took a left along the main road, walked down to the bus station, and jumped on a bus heading in the direction of Riverside just before it pulled out.

There were empty seats at the back. Cass swung her way toward them, landing hard as the bus turned a corner, and peered anxiously out of the window. She wasn't sure exactly which stop was the right one. Tapping the address into her slate brought up a map and she was soon able to track the bus, and that helped her to relax. There was a possibility that her dad might not be in. She decided that was okay. At least she'd know where the place was and how to get there.

She played a couple of games on her slate to pass the time and stared at the awful haircut of the woman sitting three seats in front and wondered if she knew that it looked like crispy noodles from the back. Went back to her slate, played another game, and then rummaged in her bag for the half-empty packet of mints she was sure was in there. She found the mints, as well as a vivid orange lipstick she'd forgotten buying. Then, for the lack of anything better to do, she went back to obsessively checking iDate.

Every time she looked at Bertie's photos, she felt a rush of heat to her cheeks. She desperately wanted to send him a message, but the *Cosmo* Ten-Step Guide to Dating a Hot Guy had been very clear that it was important not to appear too keen.

She tapped back to the map and pinged for the next stop to let the driver know she wanted to get off. The bus came smoothly to a halt. "Are you sure this is the stop you want?" the driver asked her.

"Yes," Cass said, and quickly got off. She stepped up onto the curb as the doors hissed shut behind her, then slowly and carefully pulled her bag to the front of her body and wrapped a protective hand around it as the bus moved off, leaving her alone and regretting that answer.

Rubbish lay strewn in the gutter and in the verge; beer cans squashed flat after being driven over multiple times, wrappers from take-out food, and that thick silver tape that was used to bind cardboard boxes and stop them from splitting. There was a solitary shoe. A dingy block of flats squatted next to the road, and the fence that divided them was broken in places. She could smell the river, an old, boggy stink.

The thought of her dad living here was awful. Even prison couldn't have been as bad as this, not that Sarah had ever allowed her to visit, selfish bitch. Cass scurried along the pavement, looking for a way in. Eventually a gap in the fence appeared that looked deliberate rather than unfortunate, and she turned through it, stumbling on the uneven, potholed tarmac. The entrance to the building was under a narrow porch with a sagging roof and smelled like a toilet.

There was a row of buttons on a panel on the wall, but none of them were labeled and the door was ajar, so Cass pushed it all the way open and went inside. A pile of flyers for a pizza place moved under her feet. They were covered in muddy footprints and it was easy to ignore them. Everyone else had.

To the right was a lift. To the left was a staircase. The lighting was harsh and yellow, the paint a dingy shade of gray, or maybe pale blue, it was hard to tell. There were scuff marks along the bottom of the wall, and someone had scratched the name DAVE over and over.

It was hard to believe that people had to live like this. It shouldn't be allowed to happen.

The lift was broken. Cass climbed the stairs quickly. Three flights up, she found herself on the top floor, facing a lonely corridor with a single light in the middle. Most of the doors had their numbers written on the outside with marker pen. She already knew Greg's number, but she took out her slate and double-checked it anyway, and even then, when she found herself in front of his door, she hesitated.

What if her mother was right? What if this was a mistake? A little thought pricked at her conscience, that a decent man would never find himself here, because this wasn't the sort of place that decent people ended up in. She took a step back. Maybe she should just go. This place was giving her the creeps anyway.

But something kept her where she was. This was her dad, stuck in this shithole. If the shoe were on the other foot, he'd do something to help her out. She lifted her hand and was about to knock on the door when the one next to it swung open, and a strange man stuck his head out.

"Who the fuck are you?"

"I'm . . . that's none of your business," Cass snapped at him. His head was shaved completely bald, and he had a blobby blue tattoo on the side of his neck. What she could see of his body looked like it was sculpted from lard. She banged again on her father's door, harder and more urgently this time. She would give him to the count of five and then she was leaving.

The door jerked open, and her father's face was right there in front of her, beetroot red and twisted into a scowl. "What . . ." he began, and then his face shifted into confusion. "Cass?"

"Hello, Dad," she said nervously.

He leaned out a little farther, saw the man at the other doorway. "Come in," he said. He waited until Cass was inside, and then closed the door and locked it.

"Thanks for my presents," she told him. "They're lovely." She angled her head so that he could see that she was wearing the earrings. She didn't really like them and they were already making her ears sore, but that was beside the point.

"You're welcome," he said. "I'm glad to see that your mother gave them to you. I wasn't sure that she would."

"She nearly didn't," Cass told him. She looked around. The flat consisted of a single room, with a small kitchen section in one corner and a bathroom off to the right, screened by a limp curtain instead of a door. The window was streaked with condensation, making it impossible to see outside.

"Sorry about the mess," he said. He moved past her, started picking up blankets and pillows from the sofa, and turned this way and that with the pile in his arms before tossing it into the bathroom and tugging the curtain as far across as it would go, which was not far enough to hide it. "Have a seat."

It was awful. It was absolutely bloody awful. But Cass was determined to make the best of it. "Thanks." She carefully positioned herself on the edge of the sofa. The cushion collapsed down to nothing under her bum.

Greg busied himself at the kitchen section, rinsing mugs and boiling the kettle. After a minute or so he plonked a mug of very thin, very pale tea down in front of Cass and she picked it up and tried to smile. But three months' worth of unsaid things was an impossible load for her to carry cheerfully. "I know what happened. I know what Mum did. You should never have gone to prison. I wanted to visit you, I did, but Mum wouldn't let me, she's such a cow, you wouldn't believe what it's been like, the place she's moved us into, it's full of these old women and they all hate men and I'm sick of it, I'm so sick of all of it." She was breathing hard, as if she'd just run up a flight of stairs.

Greg slowly stirred his tea. "Thanks for saying that. It means a lot to me, knowing that you don't believe I did anything wrong."

"Of course you didn't do anything wrong! I was there, Dad. I know that she pushed you."

"Did she tell you why?"

"No." Cass laughed. "I'm not interested in her excuses, anyway."

"How's school?"

"It's fine. It's school."

"They sent me your report."

"Oh," she said. "Good. I asked them to do that." She smiled. Greg had always been pleased with her reports.

"It seems that you're doing okay. There was just one teacher who gave you a low grade. Miss Taylor?"

"She teaches Curfew class. She doesn't like me because I've pointed out the flaws in the system so many times."

Greg laughed. "I bet you have. Good for you."

Something settled inside Cass. This was what she'd needed. What she'd missed. He understood. She shifted a little in her seat. The sofa was so uncomfortable.

"Why aren't you at school today?" he asked.

"I came to see you!"

She thought he might push the issue further, and was ready to argue her case, but he didn't. He took a long sip of his tea. "How's your mother?"

"She's fine," Cass said.

"She's working?"

"Yes. At the tagging center in town."

"She's a tagger?"

There was a definite note of surprise in his voice at that.

Cass nodded. "Started there after . . . after . . ."

"After she had me arrested." He walked the three steps it took to put himself in front of her, sat down on the edge of the sofa, and turned to Cass. "I'm sorry that I had to leave you with her. If there'd been anything I could do . . . but they wouldn't even let me make a phone call when I was inside. Nothing. I tried to write, but I didn't get a reply."

"I never got the letters," Cass said.

"Your mother must have thrown them away."

"Did you know that we moved?"

"Not until you told me. I went to the old house, but obviously you weren't there. I couldn't believe it when you said you were living at the Motherhouse. What happens if you get a boyfriend? Are you supposed to move out?"

Cass hadn't thought about that. Billy couldn't visit her at the Motherhouse, but as she saw him at school and they usually went somewhere if they met up at the weekend, she'd never seen it as a major problem. Her mind slid to Bertie. She imagined his face if he found out where she lived and decided she'd never tell him. *Though it isn't as bad as this place*, she thought to herself as she noticed a huge brown stain on the ceiling just above the door. She tried not to stare at it, but her gaze was drawn there anyway. *What is that?* Probably best not to think about it too much.

They talked for another half an hour or so, or rather Cass talked, and Greg asked the odd question, which she found herself more than willing to answer. He seemed interested in everything she had to say, particularly if it was to do with her mother, and having had no one to spill these thoughts to other than Billy, who wasn't a particularly good listener anyway, it was difficult to stop, although she did manage to keep the tag key in her pocket to herself.

He checked his watch. Cass stopped in the middle of what she was saying when she saw the movement.

"Sorry, Cass," he said, "but they're coming to check my tag soon, and it's probably best if you go."

"Can you give me your number?" she asked him.

"I'm afraid not. I don't have a slate. I can't afford one."

"Not at all? That's crazy! What if you need to contact someone?"

"I can ask my probation officer to pass on a message for me."

Cass stared at him in disbelief. "I can't believe they don't even give you a slate. How are you supposed to talk to your family? What if there's an emergency?" She opened her bag and rummaged through it. Her hand closed over the tag key and she squeezed it, then opened her hand and felt around for something else. She found what she was looking for.

"What's this?" Greg asked.

"A slate," Cass told him. "My slate. My old one." She held it up. "It should still work for the next couple of weeks." She hoped that was true and that it hadn't already been cut off.

Greg took it. "Thanks," he said.

"'Bye, then," Cass said, and threw her arms around him. The embrace didn't last long, but it was long enough, and when she got downstairs, she found that she had a message from Bertie at last.

She left with a spring in her step and a smile on her face.

CHAPTER TWENTY-FIVE

Sarah

S arah had learned of Cass's second absence from school thanks to a short phone call from one of the women in the school office. She was at work at the time, which left her in a tricky spot.

"I need to go," she'd said to Hadiya. "Family emergency."

Fortunately, Hadiya was in a charitable mood. The coroner's report had arrived that morning. Sarah wasn't responsible for Paul Townsend's heart attack. Case closed.

"Will you be able to come back later?" Hadiya asked.

"I'm not sure. I don't think so. I'm sorry to be a pain in the backside."

"It's fine," Hadiya said, and Sarah didn't hang around. She locked up her office and her solitary tag key, promising herself yet again that she'd report it the following day, and sprinted across the car park to her car. As she unlocked it, she had the strangest feeling that she was being watched.

She looked around. It was lunchtime, and it was busy. But there, at the edge of the car park, was the same woman she'd seen before, with the same little dog. The woman broke into a run when she saw Sarah, although this time she was moving toward her, not away.

"You're not going to get away with it," she screamed breathlessly when she was within striking distance. She was tall, almost as tall as Mabel, and her tearstained face was surrounded by a halo of frizz. "We're going to prove it! I don't care what the fucking coroner said!" This was followed up by a series of full-body shudders that left her gasping for air, unable to speak.

Sarah got in and drove away, regularly checking her rearview mirror to see if she was being followed. She wasn't. She felt oddly calm. She knew who the woman was now, and why she was there. It could be dealt with. She shifted her thoughts back to more important things. Cass was in for it when she got back. Skipping school not once but twice was unacceptable.

Perhaps the other women in the Motherhouse were right. Maybe she'd been too easy on Cass over the past three months. But she'd felt so guilty about Greg, and she'd been so busy trying to figure out her own mess and sort out her own life that there hadn't been much energy left for her daughter. She'd behaved as if the freedom from her marriage had also been freedom from motherhood, and she had told herself it was all right because Cass was almost an adult, and because Cass had fought so hard to push her away that it hadn't been hard to let her. But almost an adult was not an adult. Cass had proved that. What she needed was guidance and boundaries. It would be difficult to put them in place now. Cass would resist. But it had to be done.

Sarah regretted buying Cass a new slate, too. It had been an impulse purchase, a decision made on the spur of the moment after an hour wandering around the shops, knowing she had to buy something but shackled by the fact that she didn't want to buy any of the things that Cass liked. She'd looked at clothes, makeup, bags. She'd found a pile of the magazines that Cass was obsessed with in a secondhand bookshop and nearly bought those. But the pouting model on the cover had put her off. Sarah had never liked those magazines. She hadn't really been able to analyze why, until one of the other women at the Motherhouse had pointed out that all they did was tell young women that the secret to happiness was looking like something men would want to masturbate over.

She'd tried to explain that to Cass once, but Cass had refused to see it. She'd said that wasn't the point at all, that feminism was about choice, and that a woman could wear lip gloss and a push-up bra for herself. It was empowering. Men had nothing to do with it. Anything Sarah said about the way Cass looked was met with tears and outrage until she stopped saying anything at all. She had told herself that Cass would grow out of it and had left her to it.

That had been a mistake. She knew that now. Left to her own devices, Cass had become rude and lazy and the sort of teenager who thought truanting was okay.

Sarah sat on the bed in Cass's room and waited.

Cass arrived home at half past two.

She held her breath and listened as her daughter dropped her keys into the copper bowl by the door and kicked off her trainers. Cass muttered something to herself, then went into the kitchen. There was the sound of the microwave door being opened and closed, the beeps as it was programmed and turned on.

Sarah got to her feet. She waited in the doorway of Cass's room with her arms folded, gripping her elbows tightly. She felt like she would explode if she let go. She didn't think that she'd ever been so angry. Cass came out of the kitchen with a steaming mug in one hand and a teaspoon in the other.

"Hello, Cass," Sarah said, and Cass let out a screech and almost dropped her drink. Some of it sloshed over the edge of the cup and onto the pink carpet. Sarah watched in disgust as Cass put the mug down on the hall table and sucked the spillage off her fingers.

"Aren't you supposed to be at work?" Cass asked her.

"I decided to take the afternoon off," Sarah said. "Why are you here?"

"I didn't feel well, so I got sent home."

"Liar." Sarah took a step toward her daughter. "I know you haven't been to school. You didn't go yesterday, either. Care to tell me why not?"

"It's none of your business."

"I'm your mother, and it is my bloody business, especially when I've got the school receptionist ringing me at work to ask why you aren't there. So I'll ask you again. What's the reason?"

"I felt like a day off."

"That's not how school works, Cass. You don't get days off. You go, you pass your exams, and you go to university."

"Why?"

"What do you mean, why? So that you can make the most of the opportunities available to you, that's why. You're not a boy. Don't screw this up."

"What's that supposed to mean? That if I were a boy, it wouldn't matter if I bunked school?"

Oh, no. She was not having that argument. Not today. "You don't take any more days off, and that's the end of it."

"I'm eighteen. That means that it's up to me whether I go to school or not. They had no right to ring you." Fury burned bright in her daughter's eyes. "I'm so sick of this," she yelled. "I'm sick of this place and I'm sick of school. Why do we have to live here, anyway? What happens if I get a boyfriend? Do you expect me to move out?"

"Keep your voice down!" Sarah hissed at her.

"Why? Worried the miserable old bats might hear me?"

Sarah got hold of Cass's arm and shoved her against the wall. Cass hit it hard. Sarah kept going until she had her pinned in position. She put her face in so close that she could see the pores on Cass's nose and the tiny blond hairs on her upper lip. "You're going to stop this, Cass. Right now. You're going to be polite to the other women who live here. You're going to apologize to them for the way you behaved yesterday morning. You're going to go to every breakfast, every evening meal. You're going to help with laundry. You're going to help with shopping and cleaning. And you're going to do it until you learn how to be bloody grateful for what we have here. Boyfriends can wait."

Cass stared directly at her with tears in her eyes and a hurt, frightened look on her face. Her cheeks flushed vivid pink. The mascara she'd put on that morning got caught in a tear and trickled blackly down the side of her nose. "No," she said. "I won't. You're a bully, and I'm not going to do anything you say. If I want a boyfriend, I'll get one, and there's nothing you can do to stop me."

Sarah looked at her daughter, with her big brown eyes and soft wavy hair and round cheeks.

She saw Greg.

And she did to Cass what she'd wanted to do to her ex-husband for a long time.

She slapped her across the face.

CHAPTER TWENTY-SIX

Pamela

Present Day
12:37 p.m.

The station is abuzz. Everyone seems sure that we're onto something. The frantic movement among desks and tapping of slates has stopped. Everyone is waiting. Kate Townsend admitted that she was harassing Sarah Wallace, then asked for a solicitor and refused to answer any more questions. David Townsend has done the same.

Sue has called all of us into a meeting room for an update. I'm expecting to be told that she wants me to make another statement to the increasingly large crowd waiting outside the station. We can hear them chanting faintly in the background.

"We believe our victim to be a woman called Sarah Wallace," Sue tells us. A photo of Sarah flashes up on the screen. It's been taken from her work ID. Does it match the body? I can't say that it doesn't. "She didn't turn up for work this morning, and no one seems to know where she is."

Then the screen changes, and she flashes up a photograph of Kate Townsend, side by side with a still image taken from the CCTV. "We believe this woman to be our killer. Kate Townsend. Sarah Wallace tased her father at the tagging center and he died of a heart attack a few days later. The coroner ruled that the two were not connected, but it seems that Kate Townsend thought otherwise. At the moment, she's refusing to talk. Find me the thing that will make her change her mind."

"I think we should compare the male DNA found on the body with the samples in the database," I say to Sue. "And with the brother."

"To what end?" Sue asks me.

"We at least have to try and find out who it belongs to. Sarah Wallace—assuming she is our victim—lives in the Motherhouse, which means that she doesn't have any close relationships with men, so where did the DNA come from? How did it get on the body?"

Sue Ferguson stares at me with a look of utter disdain. I can feel my face starting to burn. None of the other officers back me up. I'm fully aware that over the past few weeks, since I announced my decision to retire, I've been gradually eased out, that the other officers have started to move away from me. None of them wants to be associated with a woman who won't be here in a month.

That's not all it is, though. I am the past. There aren't many of us left, women like me with years of pre-Curfew experience. This job tends to wear you out. And the job is different now. Sue is the future. They want to impress her. I can't blame them for that. I can't say I'd do anything different if I were twenty years younger.

But that male DNA on the body . . .

"It might help us to confirm the identity of our victim," I say. "If it is Sarah Wallace, and the DNA belongs to a man we know she had contact with, say at work, then we're a step closer to confirming it's her."

It's only a half-truth. It doesn't matter what Sue and the others think. I still can't see Kate Townsend as our killer. She looks like a stiff breeze would blow her over, thin with grief and exhaustion. But the brother is an entirely different proposition; he has the same motive and he also fits the image on the CCTV. The only reason we're not looking at him is because of his tag. I'm not sure that's enough.

"All right," Sue says. "Run it."

Everyone drifts back to their desks. Sue's officers are searching the Townsends' house and Kate Townsend's car. My officers have been left to deal with background inquiries into both of them, trawling through years' worth of social media posts, speaking to people Kate Townsend works with, looking at her medical history and bank transactions, seeing what shakes loose.

Sue catches me as I'm heading back to my desk, a firm hand on my arm. "Pamela, a word, if you don't mind."

We go into her office. She closes the door behind us. "Don't do that again," she says.

I feign innocence. "I'm not sure what you're talking about."

Sue sighs and sits down behind the desk. "You're a smart woman, Pamela. Stop pretending otherwise. I agreed that we should run the DNA through the database because you're right, it might help to speed up the identification of the body. But that's not the reason you asked me to do it."

"You saw the body," I say. "Do you really believe that Kate Townsend is physically capable of doing that?"

"It doesn't matter what I believe," Sue says.

"So you don't think she did it?"

"Like I just said, it doesn't matter. My job is to get a good result." She taps at her keyboard, her eyes on her slate. She doesn't look at me at all. "Your job is to get me what I need in order to do that. Do I make myself clear?"

"Crystal," I say, and I leave her office. I don't slam the door behind me, but I want to. As I walk back to my desk I can sense everyone looking at me, although they're all pretending to be busy.

Rachel is searching through Kate Townsend's online photos. I organize the cheek swab for David Townsend and decide to invest my time in Sarah Wallace as I wait for the result to come back. There isn't much to go on. She doesn't have any social media. I am able to access what's known about her officially—her address, her work history, her parental status (one child, a girl, aged eighteen), her marital status (recently divorced, husband was just released from prison for breaking Curfew). I make a mental note of the husband as a potential person of interest.

"Has anyone tracked down Sarah Wallace's daughter? Cass Johnson?"

"Not yet," Rachel says.

"Do we know where she is now? Is she at school?"

"She didn't turn up for school this morning, but apparently she's been off a lot recently and no one seems too concerned."

"Off for what reason?"

"I didn't ask," Rachel says. "The receptionist was busy."

I ping Michelle and ask her to pull the dental records for Cass Johnson as well as Sarah Wallace.

Something about Cass Johnson's name jumps out at me, but before I can dig into that any further, another six people turn up, expanding the media liaison from one person to an entire press team. I'm quickly drafted in to help put together what will be our next statement. The feeling seems to be that pinning this on Kate Townsend is the best possible outcome, allowing us to build a picture of the doting daughter driven crazy by grief and attacking the tagger who she blames for the death of her father. They'll dig up something on her and probably David as well, paint them as a violent family, offer additional protections to the women who work at the tagging centers, let it all fade away.

I don't like how desperate everyone is for this to be the answer, how convinced they are that Sarah Wallace is the victim, as if the dental records, the confirmation, is merely a box-ticking exercise. They've abandoned all other lines of inquiry without a moment's hesitation.

Surely, the truth is the most important thing. It certainly is for me. But this is the time of Curfew. The women here are blinkered.

Kate Townsend makes sense to them. The situation makes sense to them. It reflects society as they understand it. Women do kill, that has never been denied. But they do it accidentally; or as a result of mental ill health; or postpartum psychosis, depression, grief, the fallout from abuse. Kate fits that. And it's rare. Women have considered themselves safe from male violence for years now. I don't know what will happen if it turns out that they're wrong. But I refuse to think too deeply about that. It's not my problem. Sue might not think that the truth is important, but I do.

From my desk, I can see the office in the corner where a conversation that I'm not a part of is taking place. Rachel is in there, as is Sue and a couple of other officers, plus an assortment of civil servants on video call. We've made national news. Our victim is now all anyone can talk about on the news channels. I can still hear shouting outside the building. Through the window, I can see that the crowd is rapidly swelling. This has already become bigger than just one dead woman. It's on the verge of exploding into something that we can't control. My fear is that we'll give them an answer because it's acceptable, not because it's true. The Townsends may well be that answer. That they're guilty, I have no doubt, but of what?

I can't concentrate. I can't sit here and watch as Sue Ferguson and her team plot a potential miscarriage of justice. I grab my stuff and head out, keeping my head down. I take my own car, rather than an official one, hoping the crowd will see me as an officer heading home. It still takes me a long time to get out of the car park. I haven't told anyone where I'm going. Something is nagging at me. It's a question that has been asked many times before. It's been answered many times as well, but this time I want to hear it from someone who knows what they're talking about.

Could a man break Curfew without anyone knowing about it?

When I get to the tagging center, it's busy. The men in the waiting room look up at me as I walk in. Whatever is happening elsewhere, it's business as usual here. It's been a long time since I last came to the tagging center, as usually more junior officers deal with incidents here, and I don't know the staff. I introduce myself to the woman on reception and ask to speak to the center manager.

Soon after that, I'm sitting across from her in the break room. Her name is Hadiya. "Is this about Sarah?" she asks. "I already told the officer who called earlier that she hasn't turned up today. Honestly, I'm having a real run of it. I'm down two taggers, Sarah and Mabel Bright. At least Mabel had the decency to message and tell me she's sick. I've no idea what's going on with Sarah." The words come fast, too fast, and they're driven by a panic she's trying to tell herself she doesn't feel. "Is it her? The body in the park? Is it Sarah Wallace?"

"I'm afraid I can't talk about that," I say.

"Oh, god," she says, and closes her eyes. "Is there anything I can do to help?"

I can tell that she's translated my refusal to answer as bad news, but there's nothing I can do about that. I can't give her information I don't have. "What can you tell me about Sarah?" I ask. "What is she like?"

"She's good at her job," Hadiya said. "New, but a fast learner."

"I understand that there was an incident with a man recently and that she used a Taser."

"She did. He'd had a new tag fitted by another tagger, Mabel Bright. He said it was too tight and kicked off. Sarah heard the noise, went in to assist Mabel, and used her Taser."

"Should she have?"

"Absolutely," she says, although she doesn't meet my gaze, and a hint of color rises in her cheeks. *You're lying*, I think to myself.

I tap my own slate, letting her know that all of this is being written down, that what she says is important, that none of it will be forgotten.

"Sarah has good judgment," she continues. "She wouldn't use the Taser unless she had to. But there were problems for her afterward. She'd brought her daughter here for work experience, and Cass saw the whole thing. It was a lot for a teenage girl to take in. I think it caused some difficulties at home. The impression I get is that Cass is a bit of a handful. Sarah's husband went to prison, you know. Broke Curfew. That's why Sarah retrained as a tagger. She wanted a new start."

"Right," I say, and make a note of that, too. To be honest, she's not told me anything I didn't already know, although it's been useful to hear it from someone who works here. But it isn't really what I came for. "Can I ask you a question about the tags themselves?"

"Of course."

I turn my slate off. "I want to know if it's possible for a man to break Curfew without anyone knowing about it."

Her eyes open, but she doesn't ask me why I want to know, and I like her for it. She mulls it over. "I'd like to say no. But honestly? It's possible. He'd have to remove his tag, though, and that's the difficult part. Men try to break their tags all the time. But it's almost impossible to stop one from working, and they can't be cut off without cutting yourself very badly in the process. And we monitor the men we think have attempted to remove it, call them in for extra tag checks, that sort of thing. Really the only way to take one off is with a tag key, and they're all kept here and they're checked regularly."

"I see."

"Sometimes keys go missing," she says. "We've got procedures in place for that, too, but it does happen. I suppose there's a chance that one could be used. Or that a man could figure out a way to make his own key. That's not beyond the realm of possibility. Or that a tagger would remove a tag."

My spine tingles. "So a man could, in theory, be walking around right now without a tag on, if a tagger had removed it for him."

"Not in this town," Hadiya says immediately. "I trust my team. I know these women, and none of them would do something like that. They understand the importance of Curfew. They believe in it. I'm very careful in my choice of staff. We don't make mistakes here."

Another lie. I can see it in her face. There's a lot to unpack there. I thank Hadiya for her time and leave to the sound of my slate buzzing. It's Michelle. I rush outside. I hold my breath as I answer. Have the dental records come back yet? Is she about to tell me that our victim is Sarah Wallace?

"Still no ID on the body," she says. "But I have got something. The male DNA on the body doesn't belong to David Townsend, and there are no traces of DNA from Kate Townsend, either. It is very, very unlikely that either of them had any contact with our victim."

I can't deny that I'm disappointed, but not nearly as disappointed as I suspect Sue Ferguson is going to be.

CHAPTER TWENTY-SEVEN

Helen

Helen left the school early on Friday, too. A wave of dizziness and nausea had hit her right in the middle of her year thirteen lesson. She'd picked up her bag, told the class someone else would be along to supervise them shortly, and left the building with a quick detour to the office to tell them that she wasn't feeling well and was going home.

She knew exactly what was causing it. She could no longer pretend that the symptoms weren't real, that they were due to tiredness or a virus or her imagination. This was the pregnancy making itself felt. She sat in her car with the doors locked and waited for the shaking to subside before she started the engine. She'd spent the past few days alternating between panicking about the pregnancy and trying to ignore it. Neither had worked.

There was only one way to fix this.

She stopped at a pharmacy on the way home. She waited until it was empty before she went in, and then she asked to speak to the pharmacist in private. Fifteen minutes later she walked out with a small white box containing the drugs she would need to end the pregnancy. The pharmacist hadn't blinked an eye and the medication had been free.

The flat was empty when she got home. It would be hours before Tom got back from work. Surely that would be long enough. She swallowed the first tablet and the painkiller that the pharmacist had also pressed on her, then distracted herself with laundry. She cleaned the kitchen and the bathroom. But nothing happened. When Tom came home, she cooked spaghetti Bolognese for tea and told him she was tired and went to bed early, although she couldn't sleep. She lay perfectly still when he climbed into bed just after midnight, and thankfully he left her alone.

Saturday passed in a daze. She was alone for most of it, as Tom had arranged to meet up with his friends. There was still no sign of anything happening. Helen didn't know what to do. When she'd taken the first tablet the day before, she'd been expecting something rapid and dramatic. She'd thought it would be over and done within a couple of hours. But nothing had happened apart from a creeping sense of unease and a faint discomfort in her belly that could easily have been imaginary.

The pharmacist had told her to wait forty-eight hours before taking the second tablet, and to take it only if the first didn't work. On Saturday night, sleep was almost impossible, and she spent most of it sitting in her armchair, watching rubbish on television with the volume turned low. Tom didn't get up and ask her if she was all right. In fact, when he got up on Sunday morning, he gave no sign of having noticed that she'd spent most of the night awake. He got dressed and went to football practice as normal.

As Helen was wondering if she should take the second pill now or wait the remaining three hours, she felt something, and when she went to the toilet, there was blood. She stared at it in shock and relief. She cleaned herself up, found her bag, pulled out her slate, and sent a message to Mabel. She had a sudden urge not to do this at home, for it to happen somewhere else.

Not feeling great. Coming to yours. Hope that's OK.

She drove over to Mabel's without waiting for a reply. It felt like she was traveling through water. Every move, every decision took far more effort than it should, but she got there in one piece, somehow. She let herself in, glad that Mabel had trusted her with a spare key. The house was empty.

Mabel lived in a pretty little terrace that she'd inherited from her grandmother. She'd kept much of the old woman's stuff. A pink velvet sofa draped with a crocheted blanket was pushed up against one wall and a mismatched rug with a huge flower on it covered the floor. The kitchen was painted various shades of green. It was familiar and comforting. Helen was waiting for the kettle to boil when the pain started again.

She sensed immediately that it felt different this time, more intense, as if what she had experienced before had been merely a rehearsal. The kettle hissed a plume of steam and flicked off. Helen barely noticed. All her attention was focused on the cramping in her womb. It eased a little and then came back even worse than before, exploding into her backside and down her legs. She grabbed the edge of the worktop, light-headed and more than a little frightened, focusing on breathing in and out. She wished, desperately, that she hadn't taken the painkiller on Friday. She'd thought at the time that it would be sensible to get ahead of the pain. Now she realized how foolish she'd been. She should have waited until she was sure that she needed it.

For the next hour, she lay on the sofa with the TV on and an untouched cup of tea on the floor next to her. The pain raged on, squeezing her organs down to nothing and then releasing them, only to repeat the process all over again. It was impossible to get comfortable. It didn't seem to matter what position she lay in. Nothing helped.

She managed to drag herself upstairs and ran the bath very deep and very hot. That at least offered some respite. Helen wallowed in the water. Each new round of pain felt like a small war taking place in her body.

It peaked just as the water was starting to cool. The pain became continuous. She could hear herself making an awful low sound like an animal. It was impossible to stop. She clung to the side of the bath. Her insides contracted, a fierce spasm, once and then again. Then the pain disappeared. It was over.

Alone and in shock, it took Helen a while to move. Eventually, she climbed out of the bath and drained the water. She dried herself and wrapped herself in one of Mabel's dressing gowns, faded purple with a starburst embroidered on the pocket; then she cleaned out the bath.

After that, she crawled into Mabel's bed and lay there, clutching the duvet, nestling deep into a soft pillow that smelled comfortingly of her friend. Her legs felt incredibly heavy. Every muscle in her body ached. She curled her knees up against her chest and lay there without moving, staring blankly at the clock on the bedside table, watching as the minutes slowly slid by.

She was still in the same position when Mabel arrived home.

"Helen?" Mabel asked from the doorway. She came hurrying into the room. "Sorry, I was visiting my parents. Are you okay?"

"It's done," Helen told her, managing a weak smile. "The tablets worked. It's over."

"How are you feeling?"

"I don't know," Helen said honestly. "Tired."

"Stay here tonight," Mabel said. "I'll make you something to eat. We'll sit in bed and watch cheesy films in our pajamas."

"That sounds perfect," Helen said. She forced a smile. "Thank you, Mabel. For all of this."

"I'm your best friend," Mabel said. "It's my job." She leaned in and stroked the hair back from Helen's face, her fingers soft and incredibly gentle. Maybe everything would be all right after all. The worst was done and she'd survived it. "Was it horrible?"

"Yes," Helen admitted. She buried her face in her hands, and Mabel hugged her as she cried. Later, she brought Helen toast and chicken soup and her slate, and Helen sent Tom a message telling him where she was.

At Mabel's

What time will you be back?

Don't know. Late. Might stay here tonight.

He made her wait for a reply. She sat up in bed, knees bent, slate held in both hands, desperately refreshing the screen. She'd felt nothing earlier. Now every muscle in her body was tight with tension. She typed in three new messages and deleted them. She didn't want to do anything that would make him think that something was up. But he didn't usually make her wait for a response. Mabel tried to distract her by painting her toenails with a new polish she'd bought.

Finally, her slate buzzed, and his message popped up on the screen.

Have fun

That was it.

Love you, Helen messaged back. She followed it with a series of hearts.

Another heart-stopping wait for a response, thankfully this time not as long as the previous one. Love you too, he said, and with that, all was right in the world, and Helen could breathe again.

"Are you going to tell him?" Mabel asked her.

"No," Helen said. She pulled the duvet up a little higher. She wanted to sleep. She didn't want to talk about Tom.

But Mabel persisted. "I understand why you don't want to, Helen. I'd probably do the same if I were in your shoes. It's just . . ."

"Just what?"

"It really worries me that you're with someone you can't talk to about stuff like this, someone you have to keep secrets from. A relationship shouldn't be like that."

Helen sat up. "What would you know? You're hardly an expert. You haven't even been on a date in a year." She knew, even as she said these things, that what she was really afraid of wasn't that Mabel was wrong, but that she was right. Helen should be able to talk to Tom about this. She should be able to tell him that she didn't like the way he'd rearranged the furniture in her living room, or the fact that he didn't cook when he'd said he would, or that he spent his evenings playing video games. But that would mean admitting that maybe he was a mistake, and that was unbearable. She flung back the duvet and got out of bed, staggering a little as she got to her feet. "You're jealous. That's what's really going on here, isn't it? You're jealous of Tom and me."

"No! Helen, it's not like that at all . . ."

But Helen didn't want to hear it. She found her bag and her shoes and she went home.

CHAPTER TWENTY-EIGHT

Cass

C ass had never been smacked as a child. She'd known that other children had, because they'd talked about it at school, and the teachers had told them that a parent who hit you could go to prison if the hitting was bad enough. There had been no explanation of how bad was bad enough, leaving a young Cass terrified that minor contact could see her parents taken away from her. She'd lost her dad anyway, despite everything, and it hadn't been a smack that had stolen him from her. It had been her mum.

But now, sitting alone in her room with her bedside table wedged against the door to keep Sarah out, she found herself utterly terrified that she would lose her mum, too. The fear was so overwhelming that she put it aside and focused instead on the burn in her cheek. It had faded within seconds, because Sarah hadn't hit her that hard, but Cass easily convinced herself it was still there. She pressed light fingers to her face, moved her jaw from side to side, testing the joint, looking for pain, relieved when she found it, needing the proof that her mother had well and truly crossed the line.

Later, Cass would divide her life into before and after. She would wonder if she'd have made different choices if it hadn't happened. For now, she replayed the minutes leading up to it and wondered if her mother had always had a violent streak. Had it been there all the time, simmering away, waiting for an opportunity to show itself?

Cass dredged up old childhood memories, digging them out and mining them for information, trying to see what she'd missed. She remembered Sarah always being halfway out the door, rushing out to work or rushing in from work, furiously ironing her blouse in the kitchen as Cass ate her cornflakes, snapping at requests for lip gloss and highlights. She remembered sitting in her room, the duvet pulled up to her chin, listening to the sound of voices rumbling up from the kitchen, wishing her father would stop shouting.

Cass grabbed her duvet and pulled it closer. Where had that memory come from? It wasn't real. It was her mind playing tricks. She shook her head violently, hair swinging this way and that, catching the moist inner edge of her lip and sticking to it. She pushed those strands away with her tongue, spitting them out. Her father wasn't the angry one. That had been her mother. Always her mother. Hadn't Sarah proved that? What she'd done today. Pushing Greg out of the door. Tasing that man. Three violent, angry acts. As she'd once overheard Mrs. O'Brien say, when someone shows you who they are, believe them.

There was a sharp tap at the door. "Cass? I'm going out. I'll be back shortly. Then we're going to talk."

"Fine," Cass shouted back. But she'd no intention of being there when Sarah got home. As soon as the front door shut, Cass scrambled out of bed. She grabbed her slate and wrote a message, pinging it to her old slate, hoping her dad would read it.

Mum hit me. She didn't bother with any sort of preamble. This was too serious and too important for niceties.

Greg replied almost immediately. What? Have you called the police?

No. I don't want to do that.

Then I'll do it.

No, Cass typed hurriedly. Don't. Can we meet up?

Outside the bus station in an hour.

OK.

She grabbed her jacket and her bag, got as far as putting her hand on the door handle, then froze. What if Sarah hadn't really left and it was a trick to draw her out? She leaned forward and pressed her ear to the door and listened. Nothing.

It still took all her courage to move the table away from the door and open it. She did it slowly, just in case, but the flat was silent. Sarah had gone. Cass lingered in the hallway, checking her face in the mirror. It was definitely a bit swollen on one side. She could smell a hint of her mother's perfume in the air, soft and rosy, and it turned her stomach.

She hurried to the door. She arrived at the bus station with twenty minutes to spare, and spent that time sitting on the wall outside, watching the world go by as she waited for her father to arrive. She was beginning to think that he wasn't coming when she spotted him walking in her direction. He was wearing that same thin gray jacket with his hands buried deep in the pockets, and his jeans had a hole in the knee. Cass jumped down from the wall and ran toward him.

"Dad!"

"She hit you?" he asked.

Cass tilted her head to the side, showing her cheek. "Right across the face."

Greg took his hand out of his pocket and took hold of her chin with hot fingers. He angled her head further to the side, examining her cheek closely, and his expression darkened. "Make sure you take pictures."

"What for?"

"Evidence," Greg said. "You're going to report it to the police, aren't you?"

"I'm not sure," Cass said. This was the second time that Greg had mentioned the police, and it made her uneasy. The thought of telling them what Sarah had done frightened her. What if they took Sarah away? Cass didn't think she'd be allowed to live in the Motherhouse on her own and, although she didn't like it there, she didn't have anywhere else to go. Thoughts of moving in with Greg had vanished as soon as she'd seen his flat at Riverside.

"Why not?" Greg asked. "She assaulted you, Cass. You've got to take this seriously."

"I am taking it seriously. That's why I told you about it."

"And you did the right thing."

"Thanks, Dad," she said, and smiled at him. That was all she'd wanted, to see that look on her dad's face, to know that she'd pleased him. Stories about Sarah had always worked before, and she was glad to know they still did.

It started to rain, so they nipped into a nearby café. The door squeaked as Greg pushed it open. "Grab a table," he said, so Cass picked one close to the back and far away from the window and sat down. There was a smear of dried ketchup on the table. A sticky menu was propped up between a saltshaker and a bottle of malt vinegar. Her father stood at the counter, counting out the coins from his pocket. All around her were other men, mostly old and gray, eating baked beans and pale bacon from cheap plates. She was the only female in the place.

Her gut reaction was to get up and leave. She didn't like this greasy place, not the way it looked, the way it smelled, the hunched, miserable shapes of the men around her, but she forced herself to stay.

Greg came over to the table with two mugs of tea. Each was a milky brown with its tea bag still floating in it. Cass looked down at hers unenthusiastically. She longed for a large mug of hot chocolate with a swirl of cream on top rather than this sad concoction.

"I don't suppose your mother brings you to places like this," Greg said. "She'll be making a good wage as a tagger. Pity she didn't decide to take it up before. But then I suppose that would have meant that she'd have to stop blaming me for the fact that money was always tight." He laughed. "Still bloody is."

"It's not your fault, Dad. Things will get better."

"I hope so," Greg told her. "But to be honest, Cassie, I'm not sure that they will. I got turned down for three different jobs this week. They wouldn't even give me an interview. The moment they see that you've been in prison, they don't want to know, and it doesn't help that I haven't got a lot of recent work experience. Apparently looking after your own child doesn't count, not if you're a man, anyway."

"That's awful," Cass told him. "It's not even like you did anything wrong. Mum is the one who . . ."

He reached out and put his hand on hers. "It's all right. You don't have to say it."

She said it anyway. "You don't know what it's like, living with her. Since she became a tagger . . . it's like she really hates men, you know?"

"I think she always did," Greg said. "She just hid it."

"She took me to work with her a couple of weeks ago."

"She did? What was that like?"

"Not great," Cass admitted. "I was only there until lunchtime and then she made me go home. Some work experience day that was. She tased a man while I was there, just because he said that his tag was too tight."

"I guess anger management still isn't her strong point. It sounds like you're pretty unhappy."

Finally, someone who understood. "She doesn't listen," Cass said. "She treats me like I'm five years old. She makes decisions and I'm expected to go along with them whether I want to or not. I didn't even want to do work experience with her in the first place, but she decided that's what I should do and that was it. End of discussion. I'm not a child anymore. I'm eighteen. I don't understand why she can't accept that."

"It's because she's selfish," Greg said. "She always has to have things her own way. I tried to hide it from you when you were little, to make excuses for her. I didn't want you to see it. But I guess I failed." He sighed. "I should have left her years ago, when I had the chance, but you were so young and I didn't want to split up our family. Every time I thought of doing something about it, she talked me out of it."

"You and Mum nearly split up?" Cass couldn't believe it. She'd always known things were bad between her parents, but she'd never realized they were that bad.

"Several times," he admitted. "I was a fool. I stayed because I always believed that things would get better. And I was scared that she'd take you away from me."

"I wouldn't have let her," Cass said boldly. Now the flash of memory she'd had recently made sense. It hadn't been rage that she'd heard in the penetrating rumble of her father's voice. It had been hurt, and fear, completely reasonable given what he'd just said.

Greg smiled. His perfectly white teeth weren't so white anymore. "You're a good girl, Cassie," he said. "I only wish that I'd protected you more. I never thought that she'd turn on you like she has."

With his encouragement, Cass told him more and more about her new life with Sarah. He made it easy because he was interested in all of it, and Cass basked in the glow of his undivided attention.

She'd missed this. She'd moaned about her mother to Billy, but it wasn't the same.

Greg started to ask her questions, not just about the Motherhouse but about Sarah's job and her routine and what she did in her free time, where she shopped, what car she drove, and Cass ignored the little alarm bell ringing somewhere in her subconscious, because it was her and her dad against the world, just like it had been before he went to prison, the world being her mother.

She was left almost breathless by the desperate need to tell him. The more she said, the more details she gave, the happier he seemed to become. A particular spark would appear in his eyes whenever she told him about the things Sarah did that annoyed her, and Cass found that now she thought about it, there were all sorts of things that she hadn't realized she hated, like her mother's new hairstyle and her clunky shoes.

"Her job is so dumb," Cass heard herself say. "They all sit there with their noses in the air, feeling superior, bullying the men who come in. She once told me that they keep a tally chart of how many men they can get to kick off so that they can call the police. They think it's funny."

Nothing of the sort had really happened, of course, but by this point Cass found it incredibly easy to convince herself that it had.

"Awful," her father said. "But it doesn't surprise me, after listening to the stories of some of the other men in prison."

"God," Cass said. "Really?" She paused, hoping he would offer more information, but disappointingly, he didn't. He drained the last of his tea instead. She leaned forward. All that mattered now was keeping his attention. She'd been deprived of it for so long. "They're not as clever as they think, though."

"Of course not," Greg said. "Bullies never are."

They got up to leave. *This is your dad,* she told herself. *You owe him this.* As soon as they were outside, she put a hand to his arm.

"Do you know how stupid they are? When I was there, I took a tag key."

He froze. "What?"

"When I did my work experience. I took one." Cass could feel saliva flooding into her mouth. She swallowed. "And it works."

"Fucking hell, Cass," he said.

She barely had time to react before he grabbed her arm and dragged her away from the café. "Let go! You're hurting me!"

But he didn't. He pulled her round to the rear of the bus station to a lonely, dirty bit of road with broken pavement and a burger van that looked like it hadn't been open in quite some time. Finally he let go, and Cass took a step back, rubbing at her arm. She was confused and more than a little scared.

Greg started to pace, four steps this way, four steps back, before he whirled round and came right up to Cass, their feet only a couple of inches apart. "Have you told anyone about this?"

"No," she lied. She could feel her bottom lip starting to wobble.

"Good," he said. "Bloody well make sure you keep it that way."

"I'm not stupid, Dad." After everything she had told him, she couldn't believe that he was reacting like this. "I thought you'd be pleased."

"Why would I be pleased? Do you have any idea what could happen to me if anyone finds out you've got it? They'll send me straight back to prison. And it won't be three months this time. It'll be five years."

"Why would they send you to prison? It's got nothing to do with you!"

"Because that's how it works. Once you've broken Curfew, they'll use any excuse to cause trouble for you. That's why so many men end up back inside."

"You're not going to end up back in prison," Cass promised him. "Like I said, no one knows I've got it."

"Yes, well," her father said. "It better stay that way. Because I am not going back there for anyone." He glared at Cass. "Not even for you."

He stormed off, leaving Cass alone and in tears. She scrubbed at her face with the sleeve of her jacket. His anger had frightened her, too, and that same memory from earlier filled her head again, and there was another one now, of a morning the previous year, when there had been another argument, something about a credit card bill. She remembered Greg saying that she had needed a new pair of shoes for school and so he had bought them for her, and yes, they'd been expensive, but didn't he have the right to treat his daughter? He hadn't given Cass any new shoes at that point, and so she'd been expecting them, and she'd been disappointed when they hadn't materialized. When she'd asked her dad about them later he'd said that her mother had made him return them. He'd said that he hadn't meant to lose his temper, and he was sorry that she'd had to hear it, but Sarah was so unreasonable sometimes.

Cass had taken comfort in knowing that he would never turn on her that way. She didn't know what to do now that he had. He was her dad, and she couldn't bear the fact that she'd disappointed him.

CHAPTER TWENTY-NINE

Sarah

Sarah had only meant to go out for an hour. She'd needed some space from the flat and from Cass. The air in there had been stifling. She'd felt like she couldn't breathe. What was happening to her? When had she become this person, someone who had so little control over herself that she could raise her hand to her own daughter?

The sound of her palm hitting the soft flesh of her daughter's cheek rang through Sarah's head. She felt sick. She'd never hit Cass, never. It went against everything that she believed as a mother. And she'd continued to hold that line, even as Cass pushed against it, throwing everything she had at Sarah's patience.

But in the end, Cass had found her weak point.

And the weak point was Greg.

Sitting in her car in the supermarket car park, Sarah did something she hadn't done in a long time. She cried. The tears fell hot and fast down her cheeks, running over the back of her hand when she tried to wipe them away. The tip of her tongue caught the salty taste. She reached over to the glove box and rummaged for tissues, but there weren't any, so in the end she was reduced to wiping her face with the hem of her T-shirt. The crying jag was fierce and it wore itself out quickly. Afterward she felt as drained as if she'd been going for an hour. She leaned her head back against the headrest, muscles limp and exhausted, and watched other people going peacefully about their business. They all looked so calm and at ease.

Sarah had always thought of herself as a fundamentally decent person. Now that belief had a massive crack in it. She wished that her life could return to how it had been a month before. She'd known that Greg would be released from prison. Nothing could have prevented that. Nor did she really want anything to. Once he was out, whatever happened to him was his responsibility, not hers. She simply wanted him too far away to cause any trouble. She wanted to be able to walk across town, knowing that the chance of bumping into him was zero. She wanted to sleep easily in her bed at night without sparing him a single thought. He belonged in the past and should have remained there, and yet here he was, back in their lives, ruining everything simply by existing.

It fleetingly occurred to Sarah how much easier life would be if he were back inside. But she couldn't make that happen. She wasn't going to be able to push him out of the door again. It felt as if all the work she'd done to build a new life for herself and Cass had been for nothing.

The sides of the car seemed to close in around her. She could feel them squeezing the air, compressing her lungs and making each breath difficult. She grabbed her bag and her keys and pushed open the door.

She wandered aimlessly around the town for a good twenty minutes, though she put purpose into her steps, trying to make it look like she had somewhere to go and something to do. She fingered clothes that she had no interest in and browsed the shelves of the bookshop, but her mind was elsewhere.

When Greg had been pushed into the back of that police car,

leaving their lives for what she hoped was forever, it had felt like a new beginning. She'd gone to bed that evening charged with an energy that she hadn't felt in years and had lain awake for most of the night unpacking the events that had led up to it, playing them over and over again, wondering how she hadn't been able to see it when it was as plain as the nose on her face. The video call she'd walked in on. The volcanic eruption of temper that had followed. The dawning realization that the problem wasn't her, it was him.

After she'd moved into the Motherhouse, late-night conversations with the other older, wiser women had helped her to unravel the lies. And Greg had lied. Worse than that, she'd believed him, even when her gut had told her not to, because it had been the easier option, because she'd been so busy and so tired. She put down the book she'd been looking at and walked out of the bookshop, intending to go straight home, needing the comfort of the other women in the Motherhouse.

And then she saw him.

Her entire body reacted. It was a shiver from the top of her head to the tips of her toes. It happened even before she could process the information that her eyes were feeding to her brain. Somehow it didn't matter. There was something about being within fifty meters of the man she'd spent the best part of eighteen years married to that triggered something within her, a deep physical reaction that stirred just as quickly as if she'd seen a snake.

She froze, her body icicle stiff, but it only lasted for a moment and then it was gone and she was marching forward, not away from Greg but toward him. He was the cause of all of this. He was the reason that Cass wouldn't talk to her, that she'd become this raging, twisted, shrieking shrew, a woman with no patience and no trust when it came to men, who had so much anger contained within her that she'd hit her daughter when all Cass had really done wrong was to be related to him.

She could see nothing else apart from him. "What are you doing here?" she screamed at him.

He turned and stared at her. "Sarah?" he said, his voice low. His shoulders seemed to hunch, and his cheeks darkened.

"All this is your fault," she continued. "All of it. Why couldn't you have stayed in prison? Everything was fine when you were there. Things were getting better. Now you're back and you're ruining everything. You weren't even supposed to come back here. I told you that. But you did it anyway."

Her mind began to sift through the events of the past few days, shuffling things into a new and deeply disturbing sequence, and something occurred to her that stole the breath from her lungs. But once thought, the idea refused to go away, taking root deeply in her mind. Greg had been there when she'd taken Cass out for lunch. And here he was now, just as inconveniently, putting himself in her path.

"Are you following me?" she screeched at him.

"For god's sake, keep your voice down," Greg hissed back.

"Why? Are you worried that someone might hear?"

"You're insane." The light was bouncing off his head, highlighting the thin patches at his temples, and a new deep crease between his brows that pulled them down in a mean and angry vee. "Honestly, Sarah. I think there's something very wrong with you. I just got out of prison. Do you really think that I'd spend my time stalking you across the town center and risk going back there?"

She'd been so sure, so completely and utterly positive, but when he put it in those words her certainty wobbled. She looked around. People were staring. She only realized that she'd sunk her teeth into her bottom lip when she tasted blood. "Well, what are you doing here?"

"Getting on with my life," he said. "At least, what's left of it now, which isn't a lot, thanks to you. Get help, Sarah. You need it." He walked off, shaking his head and muttering something to himself that she couldn't make out.

Maybe he was right. They were divorced now. He was no longer her problem, even if he was living in the same town. She should be able to let this go. She wanted to let it go. And yet she couldn't. She was still so angry, so ashamed. She wanted to hurt him the way that he had hurt her. She wanted him to feel the same confusion and uncertainty that she had for all those months before she'd finally discovered the truth.

Maybe she was going crazy.

But if she was, it was only because he had made her that way.

CHAPTER THIRTY

Cass

Bertie started messaging Cass again on the Sunday evening. She stayed awake until well past midnight, reading and re-reading his messages to her, obsessively looking at his iDate profile. She didn't think about anything else. Not school, not her mother, none of it. Even Greg was pushed aside. It wasn't that she no longer cared or no longer wanted to help her father, but he'd faded into the background, eclipsed by the glow of a young and sexually attractive man.

But in the early hours of Monday morning, she stumbled across part of Bertie's iDate profile that she hadn't noticed before, and found something that couldn't possibly be true. It said that he had a valid Cohab certificate. She messaged him about it immediately, and Bertie admitted that he had a girlfriend. This revelation both upset and confused Cass. The words felt like a knife to the gut. She stared at them in disbelief.

> It's complicated. Our relationship is over. Has been for ages. It's just difficult for me right now b/c we're still living together.

She didn't respond to that. It didn't matter. He filled in the gap.

Please don't be mad at me

But she was. He kept going.

She just doesn't understand me. Not like you.
I feel like I can tell you anything.

Cass weakened. You can

No. It's not your problem. I need to
sort this out on my own.

            You don't have to. And friends tell each other stuff.

God, you're amazing.

Cass snuggled deeper under the duvet. She was still tapping in her reply when he sent another message.

Do you want to meet up?

We shouldn't, she replied.

I know, but I really want to see you.

They went round like this for another hour before Cass finally let him persuade her to meet him. She fell asleep with the slate still in her hand and had bright, wild dreams in which she and Bertie were on the run from a nameless, faceless woman, and woke up feeling almost drunk with excitement.

When she went into the kitchen to make herself a coffee her mother was there, dressed in black trousers and a gray shirt that

Cass hated. "We're having breakfast downstairs," Sarah said. "And that's not up for discussion. Get dressed, please. I don't want to be late."

No apology, then. Not that Cass had really been expecting one. She wanted to argue about the breakfast, but her late night had made her hungry, and although she wouldn't have admitted it, she felt a little frightened of her mother. She didn't want to make Sarah lose her temper again, especially not now. She didn't want to meet Bertie with a slap mark on her cheek. She spent five minutes in the shower and ten picking through her clothes and wondering what to wear.

She got dressed as if she were going to school, stuffing a change of top, a lipstick, and some jewelry into her bag, then went downstairs as instructed. She sat next to Sarah at the table in the communal dining room and rushed her way through croissants and jam. With her stomach full, she took her plate to the hatch and stupidly managed to get herself hooked into washing-up duty. Twenty-five minutes of plunging her hands in and out of soapy water and rinsing away other people's dried-on porridge. Yuck.

Sarah worked alongside her, drying the pots and putting them away. Neither of them spoke. After that, they went back upstairs. Sarah closed the door behind them; then she turned to Cass, and Cass knew that the earlier silence had been only a reprieve. Her mouth went dry.

"Cass, sit down."

"I've got to get the bus or I'll be late for school."

"It will only take a minute."

It didn't, though. Sarah went on and on about Greg and her job and how she hadn't meant to lose her temper, and about how much she loved Cass and hoped that she knew that. She stood, hands twisted together, in her black work trousers and that baggy gray shirt, with her feet buried inside a pair of furry slippers that looked like wet dogs were sitting on her feet. Her legs were still thin, but she'd started to thicken around the middle and the shirt only made it look worse.

Sarah held out her hands. "Hug and make up?"

If this had been any other day, if Cass hadn't known that she had to do everything in her power to get out of the flat without a fuss, she'd have said no. But she didn't want to risk it. She let Sarah hug her. She felt the stomach-turning squish of her mother's breasts against her own, the bony dig of Sarah's chin into her shoulder, caught an unpleasant whiff of coffee breath.

Sarah patted her on the back, then leaned back and brushed Cass's hair away from her face. "I thought we could get a takeout later, watch a film together. Like a girls' night in."

"Okay."

Sarah's face broke into a smile that was obviously fake. "Great. I'll see you later, then."

There was an awkward moment when Sarah seemed unaware that she was still holding on to Cass, leaving Cass no choice but to push her away. She grabbed her keys and made a run for it before Sarah could say anything else.

Ugh. It was all so fucked up. Why was her mother being so clingy and weird? Did she really think that making her eat breakfast downstairs was the way to make up for what she'd done? If she did, she was very much mistaken. Cass was buried so deep in this train of thought that she didn't realize that she'd gone straight to the bus stop and got on the bus heading into town rather than walking around the corner to pretend to catch the one to school until she'd done it.

She anxiously checked and rechecked her slate for the next five minutes, but when she had no message from Sarah, decided that her mother hadn't seen her do it and she was worrying over nothing. She turned the slate onto mirror mode and did her lipstick, but the movement of the bus made it impossible to get the edges straight, so she wiped it off with a tissue and decided to wait until she got to town. She got changed in the toilets in the shopping center and had another go at her makeup, then she walked through the perfume section of the department store and sprayed herself with Chanel N°5. After that, she made a call to the school, pretending to be her mother, and said she was sick and wouldn't be in. She didn't know why she hadn't thought to do that on the other days. She'd have saved herself a lot of trouble.

Bertie had suggested that they meet at ten near the library. Cass played with her slate as she waited for him. She wondered if she should message her dad and tell him about the conversation she'd had with Sarah. She decided against it.

There had been something in the things Sarah had said that morning, a sense of genuine remorse, and at the same time, something in the fury that Greg had displayed when Cass had told him about the tag key that had left Cass feeling deeply uneasy. She flicked to iDate and read through Bertie's profile again.

If only the other girls at school could see her now. Though maybe she liked it better that they didn't know, stuck-up bitches. This was hers and hers alone. The thought was lost in a wave of fiercely hormonal excitement as Bertie walked round the corner. His gaze fell straight on her as if pulled by an invisible magnetic force. He acknowledged her with a slight jerk of his chin that made Cass feel all wobbly and strange. "Hi," she said.

"Hello, you."

They walked together down by the canal, not as pretty as the park but pleasant enough in the crisp autumn air. Cass couldn't help taking in the broad line of his shoulders and the long, lean line of his legs. She loved the way his hair curled down over his collar a little and the way he kept glancing toward her, as if he were checking that she was still there.

She'd wanted to act cool, play a little hard to get; that was what the magazines had said to do, but now that he was here, she found that an idiotic smile pasted itself on her face and refused to go away. She also seemed to forget how to talk. It didn't seem to matter. Bertie talked enough for both of them.

"I wasn't sure you were going to show up," he said.

"Why not?"

He shrugged. He was so gorgeous. "Because whenever I think my life is about to get better, something always comes along and tells me that no, I was wrong."

He thought she was going to make his life better. OMG. O.M.G. "Well, here I am." She giggled; she couldn't help it, it just slipped out. She blushed, realizing how immature she must have sounded. He was telling her something important and she was saying dumb shit like that. "How are you, though? You sounded really depressed last night. I was worried about you."

He sighed. "Yeah, I'm fine. Sometimes it's just . . . it's all such a mess, you know?"

"Yeah," Cass said, although she had no idea.

"God, how did I get myself in this position? What was I thinking? She didn't even come home the other night. God knows where she was."

"Do you think she's cheating on you?"

"I just . . . I don't know. It's possible, I guess."

Cass couldn't believe that anyone would cheat on Bertie. "She must be crazy."

"You're just being kind," he said.

Seriously, did he not know? Did he really not know? His girlfriend must have done a number on him. Cass already knew she had to be awful, a controlling, manipulative shrew. She'd obviously battered his confidence down into nothing.

They talked for an hour, and with every shared word, they

moved a little closer together, their voices dropped a little lower, until they were talking in an intimate whisper. Bertie fascinated Cass. She was completely aware of his body and its proximity to hers. When his slate pinged and he checked the message and said he had to go, the disappointment was almost overwhelming. "Are you sure you have to?"

"Yeah," he said. "Sorry."

He walked away quickly, leaving Cass staring after him like an idiot. She had to run to catch up with him. "Bertie!" she called. "Bertie, wait!"

He turned his head, saw her, spun around so that he was walking slowly backward. "What's up?"

"Nothing, I just . . ." Cass had to take a moment to catch her breath. He walked very fast. "Do you really have to go?"

"Got to do something for a mate of mine."

"Oh." She tried to think of something else to say, anything to prolong the time she spent with him. She hoped that he would say something more, but he didn't. "I guess I'll message you later, then," she told him, repeating what he'd already said to her.

"You are so cute," he said. He stopped walking, gave her one of those smiles that made her feel all funny inside.

"I am? Why?"

"No reason."

"There must be a reason."

He shrugged. "You just are."

He stopped walking, and Cass took a step closer to him, then another. "Are you laughing at me?" she asked, and gave him a playful shove. He didn't budge an inch.

"Not at all," he said.

She was very close to him now, and she found herself staring at his mouth, and a thought overtook her, that she wanted to kiss him, but she'd never kissed anyone before, not that way, and she didn't know how to make it happen.

"Good," she said, adjusting her face into a scowl, planting one hand on her hip, wanting to hide her uncertainty.

"'Bye, Cass," he said, and he turned, still laughing.

She was overtaken by a rush of longing that drove her to chase after him again. She caught hold of his sleeve, pulled on it, and when he stopped, she moved in front of him, lifted onto her tiptoes, and aimed her mouth at his. She made contact. Then she dropped back onto her heels, feeling her face start to burn with delicious excitement. "'Bye, Bertie," she said, and she started to walk as fast as she could, her mouth twisting into a grin that she couldn't hold back.

She didn't have anywhere to go after that. She didn't want to go back to the Motherhouse and risk Mrs. O'Brien catching her and telling Sarah that she'd come home early again. Her only option was to go to school. She told the receptionist that she felt better and sailed into class as if nothing had happened, even though it had. Unfortunately, she had Curfew class that afternoon, but even that seemed manageable.

Bertie messaged her ten minutes after she sat down.

CHAPTER THIRTY-ONE

Helen

Helen was also starting to question her sanity. She'd been so sure about everything, about Tom and their future, about motherhood. She'd even been sure about the abortion. She'd thought that it would be a little thing, a bit of bellyache and then done with. She'd been wrong. She knew that now. Nothing she'd read had prepared her for the reality of it.

After fleeing Mabel's, she'd driven around for a while, but she wasn't fit to be behind the wheel and she knew it. She got home a little after midnight and slept on the sofa. She didn't see Tom. The bedroom door was closed, but his shoes were inside the front door, his discarded jumper lying on the sofa, the kitchen cluttered. He was there.

If she was a little tired and a little slow on Monday morning, if she shut herself in her classroom at lunchtime and claimed that she was behind on her marking so she wouldn't have to talk to anyone, it was no big deal. Physically she was fine. No one would ever know what she'd done unless she chose to tell them.

But she couldn't shake the fear that she would do or say something that would give it away, that someone would somehow guess that she was one of the many thousands of women who'd secretly ended a pregnancy because the test had said it was a boy. The issue was raised in Parliament a couple of times a year, and the press published articles about it when news was slow and there wasn't much else to report, but no one really took any notice.

The bell rang for the end of lunchtime. It was with great reluctance that Helen got up from her desk and unlocked the door. The class turned up in dribs and drabs. She saw Billy come in and thought, not for the first time, what an odd sort of boy he was. He always blended into the background, having no noticeable impact on the room. It was one of the reasons why Helen had always tried to push him a little in class, to ask his opinion, to draw him out rather than let him fade entirely.

When she saw him today, wearing a tired T-shirt and in desperate need of a haircut, she found that she couldn't be bothered. It wouldn't make any difference in the end. She turned on her laptop and loaded the PowerPoint for the lesson just as Cass Johnson walked in. "Sorry," she said, not sounding it in the slightest, pushing her way among the desks and sitting down next to Billy. She took out her slate and turned it on. She didn't look at Helen.

Her mood wasn't anything that Helen couldn't manage. But a new feeling crept in as Helen looked at Cass, and it was an overwhelming sense that she didn't care about that, either.

In the lesson today, they were due to discuss the introduction of the Cohab certificate. Helen wasn't looking forward to it. She didn't want to examine the reason for that too closely. "The certificates were introduced in 2026," she began, "as part of a wider examination of our marriage laws, which were generally considered out of date. There were laws to protect women from violence in the home, which was at the time a major issue, but many women felt it wasn't enough, and it's easy to see why. If you're prosecuting a man for battery or coercive control, the damage has already been done. We needed to prevent these things from happening in the first place.

Simply making them illegal hadn't worked, although it was an important step."

She picked up her slate and turned on the video, which went through the process of applying for a Cohab certificate. The wall screen showed an attractive young couple walking into a counseling center, talking to a smiling counselor. It was all very cheery and nice.

When it ended, Helen turned her attention back to the class. She had watched it so many times before, and it had always made her feel a little teary, such was her excitement at the thought that one day it would be her. She had never thought beyond the moment that the Cohab certificate would be granted. The future after that had been fuzzy. She hadn't thought for a minute that it would be such an anticlimax.

Because that was how she felt now. Flat. Disappointed. Let down. Perhaps she should ring Dr. Fearne after work and arrange another session for that weekend, although she wasn't sure that Tom would be happy about it. She could always go alone, she supposed. Yes. She would do it. All she needed was for Dr. Fearne to tell her this feeling was normal, and that it would get better in time. It was inevitable that you'd come back down to earth with a bump after you'd built something up so much.

"Do you think a Cohab certificate would have helped Susan Lang?" she asked the class.

"Definitely," Amy Hill said. "She'd never have got into a serious relationship with him if she'd known what he was really like."

Then there was Cass. It took a brave soul to argue against the certainty of the other girls. Either that, or a fool. Was it possible to be both? Cass did it anyway. Even Helen found herself breathless and shocked as Cass poured forth. "Cohab certificates are a terrible idea," she said. "For one thing, it implies that women aren't intelligent enough to make their own decisions, like we're children who can't do anything without supervision."

Helen would never have admitted that she'd had that exact thought when she and Tom were going through their Cohab counseling. Hearing it from Cass Johnson made her realize what a naive, petty thought it was.

"And for another thing," Cass said, "it's hardly infallible. Couples who get Cohab certificates still break up."

"The counseling doesn't mean a couple are perfect for each other," Helen pointed out. "That's not what it's for. It's simply meant to identify couples with an increased risk of interpersonal violence and prevent them from living together."

And that had seemed like enough. Now she wasn't so sure. Before Tom had moved into her flat, cohabitation had been an intellectual exercise, just like motherhood. Not anymore. It wasn't that she thought that she and Tom would break up, and she knew she was safe with him. But she wished that Dr. Fearne had been more open with her, and that she'd been better prepared for the realities of living with a man.

"I still don't see how a Cohab certificate would have helped Susan Lang," Cass said. "They never lived together, and they'd broken up when she was killed."

"She might have ended the relationship sooner, before they became as deeply involved, had they had the counseling. Couples usually break up if a certificate is refused. If they've got no future together, people tend to drift apart. If that had happened to Susan, and she'd been able to move on from him sooner, maybe that would have made a difference."

"She hardly needed a counselor to point out that he was bad news! He'd been reported to the police for stalking a previous girlfriend."

"Susan didn't know that at the time."

"But she kept seeing him after she found out."

"It's a bit more complicated than that. He wouldn't leave her alone," Helen said. "He would turn up uninvited at her home, at her place of work. He threatened to put intimate photographs of her online. She was trying her best to manage his behavior. Sometimes women find themselves in a position where it's easier and safer to say yes even when they want to say no."

"Fine," Cass said angrily. "Let's agree he was dreadful. Why didn't Susan Lang go to the police? His other girlfriend did."

"The police had a long history of ignoring women." Helen folded her arms and sat on the edge of her desk. "Of not listening to them. Of not taking them seriously. Susan was a public figure. She had her image and her job to think about. She was worried that if she went to the police, the press would find out, and that could harm her career."

"Then you can't say that none of it was her fault." Cass's face burned hot pink. "I don't understand why men get all the blame."

The rest of the room seemed to fade away. Helen could see only Cass. She felt as if they were having a completely different conversation, that there was something going on that she didn't fully understand. There was a furious yet somehow smug subtext to every word that Cass uttered. The girl was leaning forward, her skinny teenage shoulders hard inside her T-shirt. She'd ringed her eyes with black, making them look huge and wild and her skin pale and even younger in contrast. "That's enough, Cass."

Fortunately, the bell went at that moment, signaling the end of the lesson. Cass grabbed her bag and shoved past, bumping into Helen with surprising force. Helen stumbled back against her desk, knocking her own bag to the floor, where it landed with a thump and spewed its contents all over the floor. The door was opened with a squeak and closed with a bang.

The rest of the class quickly followed suit. Helen crouched down next to her desk and began shoveling stuff into her bag. Feet moved past her, mostly clad in scruffy trainers and Converse. Within minutes, the school was empty. It always surprised her how quickly teen-agers could move at the end of the day. Normally she would stay for another hour or so to prep for the next morning, but not today. She didn't feel like it. Even though she wasn't pregnant anymore, her body felt heavy as she headed out to her car and drove home. All she wanted now was a hot bath and then to curl up in bed. It didn't seem too much to ask. She told herself things would be better tomorrow.

But when she got to her front door, she couldn't find her house key. She checked her pockets, her bag, her car, her bag for a second time. No sign. She contemplated driving back to the school to look for it, but even the thought of it made her feel like bursting into tears, so she gently banged her head against the door a couple of times to knock some sense into herself and pinged Tom. Monday was his day at college, though he should be back soon.

Locked myself out.

Do you need me to come home?

Yes please

Be there in 15 minutes. Love you

Fifteen minutes wasn't too long to wait, although it stretched out to almost forty before he got home, by which time Helen was cold and hungry and pissed off. She was sitting in her car, bored and close to tears, when he came walking along the road. She opened the door and got out.

His gaze moved to her, and for a second Helen found herself holding her breath, suddenly unsure of how this was going to go, wanting to berate him for taking so long but knowing somehow, instinctively, that it was the wrong thing to do.

"I couldn't find my house key," she said.

"I lent it to a mate of mine because he wanted to drop some stuff off this morning. I'm sure I told you. Don't you have a spare in the car?"

"No," Helen said. Had he told her that? He must have done.

"Come here," he said. He opened his arms and she stepped into them. He held her close for a moment. "I'm here now," he said. "Let's get you inside."

He shoved a hand into his pocket and pulled out the new set of keys that she'd had cut for him. He unlocked the door with practiced ease and went in ahead of her, tossing the keys onto the table just inside the door. They landed with a clatter, missing the bowl. Helen stooped down to pick them up. She set them gently into the bowl, and if her fingers lingered for a moment on his door key, and if she thought about taking it off the ring and putting it in her pocket, it was only a thought. It didn't mean anything.

Now that he was here, and she was inside, the forty minutes on the doorstep were swiftly forgotten. She joined him in the kitchen, taking mugs from the cupboard as he filled the kettle, and reminded herself how nice it was to be able to do things together, even small things like this, how much she had wanted it. Yes, she was annoyed about the key, but it wasn't worth starting a fight about it.

Maybe it was a good thing that the baby had been a boy. It had been too much, too soon. She'd been in such a rush, not thinking straight, not thinking at all, if she were honest. Helen had been on her own for a long time. Her parents were strangers on the other end of a video call. She craved family. But she and Tom needed time to get to know each other better first. Dr. Fearne had tried to tell her that.

Well, there was time for that now, and she could do it with a clear head.

"What's for dinner?" Tom asked as he set the kettle down and turned it on.

"There's chicken in the fridge. I thought you might want to make that chicken curry you told me about."

He pulled a face. "Tonight?"

Helen put one hand on the worktop and leaned her weight against it. She was so tired, and sitting outside for almost an hour hadn't helped. "Yes."

"I cooked last night."

"But I wasn't here last night." She'd been at Mabel's instead, in pain and then in shock.

"No," he said. "But that's hardly my fault. What did you expect me to do? Starve?"

Helen didn't know. She hadn't thought about it. Her mind and her body had been consumed with something far bigger than Tom. As she looked at him, the urge to tell him the truth was almost overwhelming. But she didn't. "I'm just a bit surprised that you'd cook when I wasn't here," she said. "You haven't cooked for the two of us yet."

"Oh my god," he said, slamming both hands down on the worktop. "I don't know what's up with you at the moment, but I wish you'd get over it. I'm not cooking tonight because I've got an online game arranged with the boys. I told you that as well."

Had he? She didn't remember it. But she didn't want to challenge him. She wanted a nice evening, not a fight. There were plates from breakfast still in the sink, so she turned on the tap and waited for the water to run hot. "Sorry. I forgot."

He opened the tin with the tea bags in it and pulled one out. "You've been like this all week," he said.

"Like what?"

"A complete miserable bitch. I love you, Helen, but you're seriously hard work sometimes."

Helen felt like the floor was moving under her feet, such was her distress at hearing him speak about her in that way. She knew she'd been distracted, but had she really been that bad? She went over to the fridge and started pulling out ingredients for dinner, trying to figure out what she could throw together with minimal time and effort, desperate to please him, to bring back the positive feelings they'd had for each other only a few days before.

"Now what are you doing? Why are you rummaging through the fridge like a lunatic?"

Helen paused, a red pepper in one hand. "I'm making dinner."

A muscle twitched in his cheek. "You can do that without making a big fuss about it."

"I'm not making a fuss."

"Yes, you are. Look at you. You're practically hysterical. Bloody hell, Helen." He moved in, pushing her firmly to the side with his arm. He retrieved a chopping board and knife with the same impatient fury. "All I wanted was to have a nice evening in, a couple of hours gaming with the boys, and now I've got to deal with this shit."

Shocked, her heart racing, Helen retreated as far as the doorway.

"You wanted me to move in, Helen. I would've been happy to wait a bit longer, but you were so keen and I didn't want to disappoint you."

Was that true? Would he rather have waited? Had she forced him into it? "Why didn't you say?"

"I've tried so hard to make you happy." Bang bang bang went the knife. "I just don't know what I'm supposed to do. I don't know what you want. You know that I adore you. I'd do anything for you. But it's not enough, is it?"

Helen desperately wanted to tell him the truth. That yes, she'd been strange and distant, because she'd aborted their baby and she knew it was the right thing to have done, but it felt wrong regardless, and did it make her a bad person, did he think she was a bad person, but she was too afraid of the answer to ask him. But she had to give him something, anything to take the look of anger from his face and the weight of it from her body.

"I am happy," she told him. "It's just . . ."

"Just what, Helen? Seriously. Just what?"

Anything to make his anger go away. "Mabel and I had a fight." She didn't mean to throw Mabel under the bus, but it was the one thing that she knew would work.

The atmosphere in the room changed immediately.

"What about?"

"Nothing, really," Helen said. "Just . . . she was annoyed because I didn't go out for dinner with her last week."

"That fucking cow," he said. He stopped chopping, but the point of the knife trembled in midair. "She's jealous of you. Of us. You know that, don't you?"

"That's what I told her."

"You're not to see her again," he said. "That's it. You and her are done."

"But . . ."

"No, Helen. She's trouble. All I care about is you. I won't have her upsetting you again. And if she does, I will deal with her myself."

CHAPTER THIRTY-TWO

Pamela

Present Day
1:30 p.m.

get back to the station to find that the mood there is sober. Try as she might, Sue hasn't been able to get anything even close to a confession out of Kate Townsend, and she's got no other evidence. Everything else we have is circumstantial, and so both Kate and her brother have been released without charge.

I walk in to find Sue Ferguson standing in the middle of the room. "We're not ruling Kate out," she says. "I want to be clear on that. She remains a person of interest. We've got motive. We know she was in the area at the time. We know she fits the description. As soon as we get confirmation that the body is that of Sarah Wallace, we'll bring her back in."

There's a definite air of dejection in the slumped shoulders and folded arms. Coffee cups litter desks. The artificial light in here feels overly bright.

"Back to work, all of you," Sue orders them, but I am taken into her office.

"Where have you been?" she asks me.

"Headache," I lie. "Popped out to get painkillers. What did I miss?"

Sue looks at me. She takes a swig from a cup of coffee, licks her lips. I wonder if she knows that I'm lying. "There are no traces of DNA on the body from either of the Townsends. We've had to let the two of them go, for now. The media team have prepared another statement. I need you to give it. Ten minutes."

I nod my understanding, and then I walk over to my desk and sit down. I hate this place, the open plan, the sprawl of desks. I can't think here. I can't think. And yet I've got to. I've got pieces of something, parts of a jigsaw that don't fit together, but they have to, they must. I didn't tell Sue the truth about where I've been because I knew she'd take those pieces from me and refuse to let me look at them. Because I looked at the face of our victim and I saw the mark of a man, and Sue saw only a problem to be managed.

I quickly pull up Sarah Wallace's information again. A picture flashes up on a screen in the background, a headshot of an unsmiling woman. I think of the body. I try to merge the two faces, the broken one with this. It could be. I can't say that it isn't. And yet . . . "Any sign of the daughter?"

"No," Rachel says quietly. "We've ruled out it being her on the CCTV. She's not tall enough. We checked her medical records."

I wait for her to say it. I wait for her to ask me if I think Cass Johnson could be our victim. She doesn't.

"What about the ex-husband?"

"What about him?" Rachel asks me, and turns back to her screen.

I delve into the prison records myself. His name is Greg Johnson. He was a model prisoner by all accounts, didn't put a foot wrong. He was released a week early for logistical reasons to do with housing. Sarah Wallace had submitted a request for him to be re-homed elsewhere. The short paragraph that accompanies it describes a man who leaves me cold. But in a conversation with his prison therapist, Greg Johnson had claimed that he had broken Curfew because Sarah had pushed him out the door. Judging by what I've just read about him, I can't say I blame her. Something about his name nags at me. I flick back through the notes I made earlier. Johnson. Johnson. There it is.

"What are you looking at?" Rachel asks, sitting down at her desk.

"Do you remember the woman we spoke to earlier? The one who went out to see a man in the middle of the night? It looks like that man was Sarah Wallace's ex-husband."

"Oh my god," Rachel says. She turns to her slate and starts tapping at the keyboard, fingers moving at a million miles an hour.

The media liaison officer comes bustling over. I close my screen. "We need you to make another statement," she says. She thrusts a slate at me, and I have no choice but to take it.

"Are you sure that I'm the right person for this?" I didn't try that on Sue, because I know it wouldn't have worked, but it seems worth a try now.

"You did the earlier one," she says. "We need to show consistency."

I'm surrounded and ushered toward the door, and I find myself standing outside and facing what can only be described as a mob. It takes several minutes for the volume to decrease enough for anyone to hear me, and even then, I'm interrupted by random shouts.

I read the first few lines from the statement. Still working, new information coming in all the time, a difficult day for everyone, blah blah blah. But I stop when I get to the last line.

Maybe the dental records will come back and confirm that it is Sarah Wallace, and maybe Sue will be able to somehow pin it on Kate Townsend and her grief, despite the fact that there is no trace of Kate's DNA anywhere on the body. If that fails, maybe she'll be able to pin it on Scarlett Caldwell, because it's obvious now that we need to take a much closer look at her. Maybe it will all fall out the way Sue Ferguson wants it to, and in another hour or so, I'll be back on these steps to announce it.

But I can't do it. I can't read that last line. I won't lie. I won't pretend that we're close to solving this when we're not. Someone knows who our victim is. Someone is missing her, and they might not even have realized it yet. Perhaps it's time they did. I turn off the slate and look at the crowd. "We still haven't been able to identify the body," I tell them. "And until we do, it's going to make finding who did this very difficult. What I can tell you is that our victim is an adult female and that she was strangled and beaten. We believe that she's aged between eighteen and forty-five, she's white with dark hair, and she has no tattoos or scars or other distinguishing features."

I take out my own slate, quickly turn it on, pull up the photos I took of our victim's clothes. I hold it up. "These are her clothes," I say. "If you recognize them, please get in touch with us." I move it slowly from side to side, trying to give as many of them as possible a good look at it. I know the images will be widely shared in a matter of minutes.

There's one more thing I want to say. I can feel it on the tip of my tongue. I debate whether it's a good idea, but not for long. If I don't say something, if I don't at least try, Sue Ferguson and her team will continue to try to find a woman to blame, and younger officers like Rachel will help them. "I've been a police officer for thirty years," I say. "I've seen awful, terrible things. If this murder had happened before Curfew, there would be no doubt in my mind that it had been committed by a man. No doubt at all. I don't think we should be afraid to consider that possibility now."

What matters to me is what has always mattered: the truth. I don't care if it's unpalatable or unpleasant. Unless we know what really happened, we can't make sure it doesn't happen again.

I turn to go back inside. I see Rachel and Sue Ferguson. I didn't realize that they were there. I see the fury on Sue's face, and the shock on Rachel's.

I guess I'm in trouble.

CHAPTER THIRTY-THREE

Sarah

Sarah went to work on Friday with a heavy feeling in her stomach. It was hard to fathom that only a few weeks before, she'd loved this job so much that she'd thought she would never want to stop doing it. Her ambitions had been long-term and marked on a calendar she kept on her slate. Another six months, senior tagger. A year after that, center manager. She wasn't sure any of that was achievable now, given what had happened recently, with the death of Paul Townsend, and the missing tag key. It seemed like everything was going wrong. She felt anxious at work in case she made another mistake there, anxious in public places in case she ran into Greg again, and anxious at the Motherhouse now that she knew how easily she could lose her temper with Cass.

She told herself it wasn't forever. Once Cass went to university she'd be able to move to another town if she wanted, start again somewhere else. There were other Motherhouses and other tagging centers. She could even buy her own place if she had to, although she liked living with other women. It made her feel less alone.

She double-checked her bag and then got out of the car. The day went as well as could be expected. Her colleagues were in a sober mood. The men were unusually well-behaved. Sarah was glad. She was confident that she would be able to use a Taser again if the situation called for it, but she really didn't want to.

At least Mabel seemed cheerier. She brought Sarah a cup of tea. "I'm sorry I've been in such an awful mood this week," she said. "I know I've been horrible."

"It's not your fault," Sarah told her. "It's been a rough few weeks."

"It's not just this place," Mabel said. "I had a row with Helen."

"What happened?"

"I guess it doesn't matter if I tell you," Mabel said. "She got pregnant and it was a boy, so she decided not to keep it. Tom doesn't know. I told her she shouldn't be with someone she has to keep things like that secret from. She said I was jealous of the two of them."

"Sometimes you've got to let people figure things out for themselves," Sarah said. She realized, as she said it, that she would do well to take her own advice. Maybe she should just let Cass see Greg as and when she wanted to.

Mabel shrugged. "I don't care if she does or she doesn't."

Sarah suspected that Mabel was mostly trying to convince herself, but she let it slide. It wasn't her problem. She didn't want to get involved in petty squabbles about things that, at the end of the day, didn't really matter.

Halfway through the afternoon, Hadiya came into her room to tell her that the final report had come through from the tagging safety committee. They'd examined all evidence relating to the death of the man she had tased, including the coroner's report, and had concluded that Sarah had acted appropriately and wasn't at fault.

It felt as if a huge weight had been lifted. Sarah sat back in her seat and read it through another three times, just to be sure. Tears came to her eyes, but the emotion worked its way through her body quickly and she was calm almost immediately, ready to move on to the next man on her list, and the one after that, and she felt like her life had started to move forward again.

There was just one thing left to do, and that was to report the missing tag key, and she did it that afternoon.

"When did you last have it?" Hadiya asked.

"I'm not sure," Sarah admitted. "Everything has just been such a mess. I didn't report it straightaway because I thought that I might have put it somewhere silly and that it would show up, but it hasn't."

Hadiya exhaled. "You should have told me as soon as it went missing."

"I know." Sarah stared at the floor. "I've tried using the tracker, but the system can't locate it."

"The battery has probably died," Hadiya said. She picked up her coat, shoved her arms into the sleeves. "I really need to get going. We'll sort it out next week. It's not like anyone else can use it anyway."

It was a result that deserved a celebration. Sarah tidied her office and waited for Curfew, planning to buy a bottle of wine on the way home to share with Mrs. O'Brien, who had told her that it was important to savor the victories. And this was a victory. She had been faced with a man who was about to cause trouble, who wanted to cause trouble, and she had trusted her instincts and reacted. She hadn't waited for the trouble to happen first. That was where she had gone wrong with Greg. She hadn't listened to her gut, had chosen not to see what was right in front of her eyes because seeing it would mean having to do something about it and she hadn't known if she could. Never again. She would never doubt herself again. She was halfway across the car park when she saw something tucked under the windscreen wiper of her car. It was a note, written in block capitals on cheap white paper.

I KNOW WHAT YOU DID, YOU BITCH, AND YOU'RE GOING TO BE SORRY

It looked like the Townsends were escalating.

CHAPTER THIRTY-FOUR

Cass

I t was two days since Cass had seen Bertie. It felt like much, much longer. She'd thought about nothing else. She'd replayed their conversation and the kiss in the street over and over in her head until they took on a magical, cinematic quality. She remembered them as if she were an outsider watching her own performance. She'd messaged him relentlessly on Tuesday night, unable to stop herself, even though he'd told her he couldn't reply because his girlfriend was home and he didn't have any privacy.

By Wednesday afternoon, she felt like she was going mad. She desperately wanted to know what he was doing, what he was thinking, if he was thinking about her. She wanted him to break up with his girlfriend and was finding it increasingly difficult to understand why he hadn't. He made her wait so long between responses that she spent break time crying in the toilet, stifling her sobs with her sleeve in the hope that the other girls wouldn't hear her. She swung from fierce joy to deep depression and back again in a heartbeat, and to make things worse, she had no girlfriends she could talk it over with. There was no one to help her clinically dissect his messages. She knew his iDate profile word for word and yet couldn't stop checking it to see if anything had changed.

The only person she could talk to was Billy, and she was avoiding him because he desperately wanted her to put his tag back on. "Please," he'd begged her at school that day. "Come over after school. Or we could do it now, if you want. We can go down on the field, where no one can see. I've got the tag, look." He had pulled up the leg of his trousers and shown her. He'd put it on his ankle and bound it with tape.

"No," Cass said. "Let's wait a couple more days."

"What for?" Billy asked.

"Because I want to," Cass told him, and headed back into the girls' toilet, where she knew he couldn't follow. The power she had over him went a long way toward compensating for the fact that she was unable to make Bertie or her father pay her any attention.

She was too afraid to push Greg. That left Bertie. Cass got through the last lesson in a daze, and when the bell went, she left without waiting for Billy. She caught the bus into town. It was after four by the time she got there.

She hurried to Coffee Stop. She could see through the window that Bertie was inside. Her heart lifted. She took a moment to check her hair in the window, chewed on her lips to make them pinker, then pushed the door open and went in. She hurried up to the counter. "Hello, Bertie," she said brightly.

He wasn't alone. There was a woman behind the counter, small and blond, wearing the standard uniform of black trousers and polo shirt. Her gaze slid lightly over Cass and then went back to the coffee machine, which she was cleaning.

"Hi," Bertie said, and he flicked a quick glance at his colleague. "What can I get for you?"

It wasn't the response that Cass had been hoping for. He didn't even look pleased to see her. She didn't understand. "Vanilla latte," she said.

She had to fumble in her bag to find her slate so that she could pay, and her drink was made by the blond woman and she didn't do a very good job. Cass found a seat at an empty table and sat facing the counter and playing with her slate. She felt utterly crushed.

Then her slate pinged to say she had a message. It was Bertie. She shot a swift glance at the counter, but he didn't look her way.

What are you doing here?

> I wanted to see you

It's not a good time

The woman behind the counter said something to him, and whatever it was must have been funny, because he laughed.

Cass took another sip of the latte. It was suddenly too sweet, too much, and she found that she didn't want it. She left it half-finished, got up from the table, and walked out. She felt wobbly and disappointed and had to work extremely hard not to burst into tears. In the end, she failed before she'd even made it round the corner, and she stood there, wiping her face with her sleeve and sniffing.

That was where she was when Bertie came out and found her. He approached her slowly, with his hands hidden in his trouser pockets. "Cass?"

"What?"

"Why are you crying?"

"I'm not crying."

"Yes, you are."

She gave her face a determined wipe and swallowed hard. "Why do you care?"

His expression darkened. "What did I do to deserve that?"

Cass scraped at the ground with her shoe. "Nothing," she muttered.

"Look," he said. "You caught me by surprise, that's all. You know my home situation is difficult, but the people I work with don't."

She peeped up at him. "I didn't mean to cause trouble."

"Yeah, well." He tucked his hands in his pockets. "I'll message you later, all right?"

"All right."

"But you can't just turn up out of the blue when I'm at work. If you come in, and there's another member of staff working with me, we don't know each other. Okay?"

"Right," Cass said. She managed to give him a smile. She lingered, hoping for more, hoping he might sneak a quick kiss, but he didn't.

"You're too good for me," he said. "I don't deserve you." He tipped his head back and rubbed his hands over his face. "I've got to go. Later, yeah?"

"Yeah," Cass said. She fidgeted with her jacket as he went back inside. Her eyes were sore and the skin on her face felt uncomfortably tight. She'd made a fool of herself. She headed to the bus station with a sick feeling in her stomach. All she wanted was to hide away from the world. But the outside world had a way of making itself felt, and on the way home, she had a message from her dad.

Need to talk to you about something. Message me ASAP.

When she did, he asked her to come to Riverside to see him. She didn't want to go, not really; she didn't want to face the smell of urine in the entrance hall, or the dingy stairs, or the man who lived in the flat next door to Greg's. But she went anyway.

It took a certain degree of courage to climb the stairs and knock on his door. On top of the general grossness of the place, she was afraid that he would still be angry with her. His reaction when she'd told him about the tag key had made her feel like a burst balloon. Shriveled and useless. Over the past couple of days, more memories had come back to her, and she could no longer pretend that she'd never seen her father's temper before. The red face and the unblinking stare had both been familiar. The difference was that she'd never been on the receiving end of it. She'd never expected to be. Greg only got mad with Sarah, and it was always Sarah's fault.

With Cass, he'd always been cheerful and kind. He was the man who would sneak her sweets in bed, who would buy her the toy she wanted when Sarah said no, who had taken her to have her ears pierced after her mother had forbidden it, saying she would end up with an infection.

Sarah had been right about that much, at least. Cass could still remember waking in the middle of the night with her ear hot and throbbing, how she'd crept into the bathroom and taken painkillers from the cabinet. Sarah had taken her to the doctor's for antibiotics even though Greg had said she was overreacting and it would clear up in a couple of days. She'd forgotten about that. She touched her ear now, felt the little silver stud.

Greg opened his door as she got to the top of the stairs. He opened his arms as she walked up to him and greeted her with a massive hug, rocking her from foot to foot. "It's great to see you," he said. "How's your week been?"

He said nothing about the last time they had met. But if he wanted to act like it hadn't happened, Cass was happy to go along with it. Her entire body seemed to relax. "All right," she said. "How about you?"

"Nothing exciting to report here," he said. He exhaled loudly. "Where are my manners? Come in." He stood back to let her into the flat. "Had my tag checked again this morning, which is about as good as it gets for excitement these days."

"You went to the tagging center?" Cass asked, thinking of her mother, a slight sense of panic constricting her insides.

"No, they come here. We're not allowed to go to the center."

"Oh my god, they really do treat you like criminals, don't they?"

"They certainly do." He sat down on the sofa, resting his tagged ankle on his knee and rubbing it. "I think my tag has been put on too tightly. Bloody thing is cutting into the skin. But they wouldn't loosen it for me. Said it was fine."

"How can it be fine if it's doing that?"

"Exactly what I said. They told me to get some antiseptic cream to see if that helped, but it's a bit beyond my budget."

"I'll get you some," Cass said eagerly. "What kind do you want?"

"I'm not sure," he said. "We could go to the shop round the corner, see what they have?"

"Sure," Cass said.

When they got there, she found herself buying him not just antiseptic cream, but moisturizing lotion and baby oil. "Thanks, Cassie," he said as they were leaving, the bag in his hand. "This'll make a huge difference."

"You're welcome," Cass said promptly, squashing her irritation as she thought about what she'd have to do without because of his shopping spree. But this was her dad. He didn't have anything. It was only a few toiletries, and she didn't want to do anything that might make him angry with her again.

Afterward, they walked slowly back to Riverside, with Greg stopping every few meters to rub his ankle. He asked Cass if she wanted to come in for a cup of tea and a biscuit, and although she couldn't imagine anything worse, she didn't say no. The tea was weak and the biscuits were cheap digestives. The man living in the flat underneath had his music on full blast. Cass could feel it coming up through the floor.

Greg rubbed at his ankle again, and then tugged up his trouser leg and showed her the tag. The skin around it was red and sore, and it was clear even to Cass that the tag was too tight. "I can't believe that they think that's acceptable," she said.

"I don't think our well-being is their top priority."

"Well, it should be. They've got a duty of care."

"I wouldn't fancy telling them that." He drummed his fingers on his thigh, then he sighed. "Look, I know I lost my temper with you the last time we met. I was just so shocked when you told me that you had a . . . that you've got that thing. You have still got it, haven't you?"

"Yes," Cass said.

"Do you think that you could . . . no."

"What?"

"Could you loosen it for me? Just a bit?"

Cass knew that she shouldn't. She didn't want to mess with another tag. But on the other hand, this was her dad, and he was only asking her to loosen it. She remembered what she had seen at the tagging center, what her mother had done to that man who had complained that his tag was too tight. That was the last thing she wanted for her dad.

"I can try," she said. She opened her bag and found the key. She turned to the side a little so that he couldn't see her activate it, worried that it might not work, but it turned on just as it had before. Then she unlocked his tag. She did her best not to touch his sore skin. He winced anyway. She adjusted the strap and was about to lock it again when Greg leaned in, looking at it. He tested the ease with his thumb.

"Can you make it just a little bit looser?" he asked. "Part of the problem is that sometimes my ankles swell and that makes it worse."

"Of course," she said, making it a bit bigger, then at a silent signal from him, a bit bigger still. Eventually he seemed satisfied, and she locked it.

"Much better," he said, rewarding her with a smile and an offer of another biscuit. Cass declined. She checked her slate and said she had to leave. Greg asked her to message him so that he would know that she'd got home safely. He said it had been great to see her, and that he'd missed her so much.

Maybe taking the tag key hadn't been such a mistake after all.

CHAPTER THIRTY-FIVE

Pamela

Present Day
2:25 p.m.

After I give that second statement to the media, I find myself once again shut in an office with Sue Ferguson. I'm seated in a chair. She's on her feet. The power play is not lost on me. I let her fury rain down on me. It peppers my skin. It burns.

"How could you be so stupid? So careless?" With her hands on her hips, she strides from one side of the room to the other. "What about this situation is so difficult for you to understand?"

"I wasn't careless," I say. "I was truthful."

"The public doesn't need the truth." All the rage seems to leave her then, and she sinks down into a chair at the other side of the desk and puts her face in her hands. She groans. "You're an experienced officer, Pamela. You know that this is about more than just finding a killer."

Actually, I don't. To me, that's the only thing that matters here. "How can it possibly be about more than that?"

She stares at me as if she can't believe how dense I am. "Because of Curfew," she says.

"What? That it can't have been a man because he couldn't have gone outside without being caught? Because I've got to tell you, Sue, I think that there's a pretty good chance—"

"Stop right there," she says, interrupting me. She pinches the bridge of her nose. "Don't even go down that path. Do you understand me? I won't allow it. I already warned you about what would happen if you did this, Pamela."

That's when I finally understand. She hasn't been sent here to solve this. She's been sent here to solve it in the right way. That's what happened in those other cases, the hit-and-run and the stabbing. That's why no one who worked on either of them will talk to me. Because they know. I wonder what was said in order to keep them quiet.

"Curfew works," she tells me. "That's the only reason we've been able to keep it for as long as we have. You and I both know what a difference it makes. How many women it has saved. But it's fragile. We could lose it, Pamela. It wouldn't take much. Laws can be unmade."

And all it would take would be the arrest of one man.

"The evidence we need is there," she says. "And we are going to find it. We know that Sarah Wallace is definitely missing. She didn't turn up for work this morning; the women at the Motherhouse don't know where she is; she isn't answering her slate. Rachel came to me a short while ago with the name of another person of interest. Scarlett Caldwell. It appears that she has a connection to Sarah Wallace, and her slate data indicates that she was out last night. I've already sent officers to pick her up, and we're working on potential motives."

"What about the male DNA on the body?"

"There could be any number of explanations for that."

"Such as?"

Sue ignores me. "The most important thing is that we tell this story in a way that the public will understand. In a way that makes sense."

But this isn't a story, I think to myself. *This is a woman, battered to death and dumped in the park. It's not a work of fiction. Her life was taken from her and we owe it to her to find out the truth, even if it reveals some truths about Curfew that we don't want to hear.*

"Are we on the same page here, Pamela?" Sue asks me.

I run my tongue over my teeth. My mouth is parched. I can't remember the last time I had something to drink. I've run a night shift into a day shift without sleep and I can feel it in every part of my body. I'm too tired for this. "Actually, I don't think we are," I say.

My slate buzzes, sparing me from whatever Sue Ferguson is about to say in response. I take it out of my pocket, check the message. It's from Michelle. "Dental records are back," I say. Sue Ferguson's slate buzzes, too, presumably with the same information.

"Shit," Sue mutters as she looks at her own slate.

It's not Sarah Wallace.

Before either of us can say anything, Rachel rushes in. She doesn't even bother to knock. "We've got something," she says. Her face is flushed, as if she's run a hundred meters and not just across an open-plan office. "A missing woman. Just reported. I think . . . something about this one is different. This is the second person to say they don't know where she is."

"Who is it?" I ask Rachel. "Can you ping me the details?"

She does, and I look at them. I look at the name, the photo, and in my mind, the battered face merges with this one. A terrible sadness settles inside me, like a layer of falling snow. "It's her," I say. "She's our victim."

When I glance across at Sue Ferguson, her expression is grim. This is the woman who just told me that she's willing to lie about what happened if telling the truth will damage Curfew.

I wonder how she's going to spin this.

CHAPTER THIRTY-SIX

Cass

On Monday, Cass got up early and left the Motherhouse while Sarah was still in bed. She had things to do. She knew that she was taking a risk, missing another day of school, but she had a plan for that. She was allowed three days a month of period leave if she needed it, and she'd decided that today, she did.

At the center of her plans was Bertie. He'd been so understanding, so kind when she'd messaged him the previous night. He'd forgiven her for turning up at his work. He knew exactly what she was going through with the women in the Motherhouse because he was going through it, too, with his girlfriend. He said that her friends were making life difficult for him, too.

She'd wanted him to meet with her. He'd been reluctant, but Cass didn't take no for an answer, and in the end he agreed. Same time, same place. He was late again and she was beginning to think that he wasn't going to show up, but he did.

He didn't want to go for coffee, or for a walk by the canal or around the park.

"Where do you want to go, then?" Cass asked him. She couldn't believe that he was here and already wanted to leave.

"I don't know," he said, his voice low. His eyes were very dark. "It's just . . . I don't like being somewhere we might be seen. She's got a lot of friends."

Cass didn't understand. He'd been fine with this before. "Well, we can't go to mine," she said. That was out of the question. No men allowed at the Motherhouse, not that she'd take him there even if they were. "How about your flat?"

"I don't think that's a good idea."

"I really want to spend some time with you," she told him. "I thought you wanted to spend time with me, too."

He looked away from her.

"Please," she said. She felt utterly embarrassed and pathetic as she said it, but she didn't know what else to do.

He sighed. He took her hand and led her along the cobbled street and round the corner until they were out of sight of everyone. Then he stopped. "I really don't know if this is a good idea."

Cass felt frustrated tears prick at the back of her eyes. "Why not?"

"You wouldn't understand."

"Try me." She wondered what he was thinking. She wondered if she should try to kiss him again. She took a step closer, then another, then she lifted a hand and touched the front of his jacket. He didn't try to stop her. "You can trust me," she told him. "Remember?"

He smiled and shook his head a little. "You're way too smart to get involved with a fuckup like me."

No one had ever needed Cass the way that he did. No one had ever made her feel wanted like this before. "You're not a fuckup," she said. "What is it you want, Bertie? Tell me. It's all right. You don't have to be afraid with me." She felt so grown-up, so certain, so in control. It was intoxicating. "I just want to be alone with you."

She laced her fingers through his and silently willed him to say yes.

They took the short journey to his flat in near silence. They sat with their bodies pressed up tight against each other. Concern that someone might see them seemed to have completely fled. He tucked her into the porch as he unlocked the front door, and Cass stepped into the flat, a stranger's flat, the one she knew he still shared with his ex-girlfriend, though she barely saw it. She could see only him. Her heart was pounding hard enough to burst out of her chest, and when he finally slid his arms around her waist, then bent his head and kissed her, she thought she would burst with happiness.

He backed her into the bedroom and began pulling at her clothes, and she let him. His mouth was everywhere. She gave as good as she got, not wanting him to pick up on her lack of experience. And then he was unbuttoning his jeans and he was in her. In a couple of minutes, it was done. He grunted and his entire body went rigid, and then he rolled off her and lay sprawled on the bed.

Cass ventured a hand across his chest. "Are you okay?"

"Fine," he said. He yawned.

"Did you like it?"

"What? Oh. Yeah."

She lay back, stunned and unsure about what had just happened. She opened her mouth to ask and then thought better of it. A cold sense of unease began to creep across her skin. She tugged at the duvet, wanting to climb under it, but he was too heavy and she couldn't get enough of it free to cover herself. She lay there instead, her skin rapidly cooling, wondering if she should put her clothes back on, not wanting him to think she was a prude, feeling the warm, sticky mess between her legs start to slide along her thighs.

The sound of the front door opening disturbed her thoughts. A female voice called out. "Hello? Anyone home?"

Cass sat bolt upright. Was it his girlfriend?

"Shit," Bertie said. "What the fuck is she doing here?"

Before either of them had the wherewithal to move, a woman

pushed open the bedroom door. She carried a shopping bag in one hand, and she was wearing big gold earrings and a black puffer jacket, a combination that would make Cass break out in a cold sweat whenever she saw it again in the future.

"Cass?" she said. "What are you doing here?"

Cass didn't respond. She seemed to have forgotten how to talk.

Mabel's gaze went to Bertie, then Cass, and back to Bertie again. "You fucking bastard," she spat. "I fucking caught you, you fucking bastard."

Bertie scrambled for his jeans. "Get the hell out of my flat, Mabel."

"Your flat? I don't think so. You wait until Helen hears about this. You'll be out of here and back in your shithole bedsit, where you belong, before the end of the day."

"You stay away from Helen, you fucking dyke."

"What did you just call me?"

Cass slid silently to the edge of the bed. She scooped up her clothes with shaking hands. She pulled on her T-shirt and got her skirt to her waist, not bothering with her underwear, and headed for the door. Neither of them seemed to notice her.

She paused inside the front door just long enough to drop her shoes to the floor and work her feet into them, though it took longer than it should have, she was shaking so badly. It was as she stood there that the second bombshell was dropped on Cass. A trio of photographs in frilly little frames hung on the wall just inside the door. Bertie and his girlfriend.

His girlfriend.

Miss Taylor.

Cass fled.

CHAPTER THIRTY-SEVEN

Helen

Helen got ready for work on Tuesday morning feeling better than she had in days. Her energy levels were up and the sallow tint had finally gone from her skin. Things had got much better between herself and Tom since she'd promised to stop talking to Mabel. Maybe he was right. Maybe their friendship had been part of the problem. Mabel had tried to ring her a couple of times on Monday night, and in the end Tom had taken her slate and blocked the number. He'd been lovely to her afterward. He'd finally cooked her the long-awaited meal, and he'd run her a bath.

Helen got her makeup bag out and did her makeup at the mirror just inside the front door, where the light was best. She'd hidden the white box containing the remaining abortion tablet inside the bag. At some point she would throw it away, but at the moment she wanted that reminder of what had happened, and how difficult it had been. She wouldn't let herself slip into thinking otherwise and making another foolish mistake.

Even her hair behaved when she tied it up. Her first lesson went so well that she stopped feeling like the worst teacher in the world. She used the free period after that to catch up on her marking.

She'd been given the pleasure of being on duty at lunchtime, so she took her bottle of water and wandered the grounds, pausing to check that everyone was where they should be. The sky was clear. Life was good again. She'd turned a corner. She and Tom were going to get through this. Yes, he had quirks and irritating habits that she hadn't known about, but she would learn to put up with them, and in a year or so she'd get pregnant again, and this time it would be a girl. She could feel it.

She rounded the corner of the main building, intending to go back inside and refill her bottle. She didn't get that far. A huddle of year thirteen girls stood in front of the doorway. They were speaking quickly, so engrossed in conversation that they didn't hear Helen approaching. She stood at the edge of the huddle, quietly listening in.

"You're such a fucking liar, Cass."

"I am not!"

"There's no way. I don't believe you. I just don't believe you."

"You can believe what you like. Makes no difference to me."

A titter ran through the group. "'Course not."

Billy was there, too. Helen hadn't noticed him, standing as he was at the edge of the group. His rucksack hung from one shoulder, and he wasn't wearing a coat. "Stop it," he pleaded, but no one was listening to him.

Helen pushed her way through the group, not surprised to find Cass standing in the center, thin arms folded across her body. She spun around as Helen moved in.

"What's going on here?" Helen asked. She kept her voice calm as she looked at them, making a mental note of who was there.

"Why don't you ask her?" said one of the other girls, gesturing at Cass.

"I'm asking you," Helen said.

There was some more giggling, and shoving. "What's wrong with you?" Helen said to them. "You're year thirteens!"

It was Amy Hill who spoke up. "Miss, your boyfriend works at Coffee Stop in town, doesn't he?"

"That's none of your business."

"We know he does, Miss. Kimberly Smith saw you with him the other week."

"I don't see what that has to do with anything," Helen said. All of a sudden, she found herself the focus of attention. Cass had been forgotten about. The girls were only interested in her now. And Tom.

Amy smiled. She reminded Helen of a snake. "Cass reckons she shagged him."

The world seemed to stop. All around them, silence fell. Even the birds seemed to stop tweeting. Helen felt dizzy, as if the ground were moving under her feet. "Clear off, all of you," she said.

She caught Cass by the arm before she could leave. Billy loitered a couple of meters away. Helen was too furious to tell him to leave. "Care to tell me what that was about?"

"Nothing, Miss," Cass said defiantly. Her face was bright red, her arms wrapped tightly around herself.

Helen had been a teacher for a long time, and she knew how to spot a liar, and she saw one in Cass's bony, pale face, the defiant angle of her shoulders, the eyes rimmed with far too much black eyeliner. A child in adult's clothing.

Tom wouldn't be interested in that.

Would he?

"Why do the other girls think that you know my boyfriend?"

"None of your business."

"I think it is my business, actually."

Cass made a sound that should have been a warning. "Why? You've got no idea how he feels. You don't know him, not like I do."

"Excuse me?"

"He told me," Cass said boldly. "Don't bother trying to deny it. Your relationship has been over for ages anyway. He wanted to tell you, but he didn't know how you'd take it. You've totally crushed him. He was depressed before he met me. Actually depressed."

"He's not depressed," Helen said. It was the only bit of what Cass had just said that her brain seemed able to respond to.

"You think you're so clever. You stand there in front of us and you spout all that crap about Curfew and how great it is, how much better things are now that women get to push men around and stop them from living a normal life. I guess it makes sense that you'd be a complete bitch at home, too."

Helen inhaled, air rushing into her lungs. The world seemed to start turning again. "That's enough," she said.

"Running him down all the time, controlling the money, never letting him buy anything. He's tried so hard to make things good for you and you don't even notice. All you do is criticize."

"I said, that's enough!" Helen shouted. Shocked, she pressed the back of her hand to her mouth, her teeth grazing the sensitive skin there. She'd shouted at her pupils before, but she'd always been fully in control. She'd never truly lost her temper. Not like that.

She slowly lowered her hand. "I don't know where you're getting this from, Cass, but none of it is true. You must know that." Something occurred to her, and she latched on to it. "Where did you meet him? Was it at Coffee Stop?"

Cass's bottom lip wobbled.

"It was, wasn't it? I bet he was nice to you." That had to be it. A lot of young women went to Coffee Stop. It wouldn't be the first time that one of them had tried to flirt with Tom, mistaking his professional manner for something more. "You have to understand, Cass, he's nice to everyone. It doesn't mean anything."

And Cass, poor, lonely Cass, with her father who had just been released from prison, had taken a few words of kindness from a good-looking older man and built an entire fantasy relationship from them.

Helen felt sorry for her.

"He's on iDate!" Cass screamed at her. "That's how I met him. I'm not some random girl that he was just flirting with—we've been seeing each other for weeks. We had sex in your flat."

Before Helen could say anything else, Cass turned on her heel and ran, cutting across the grass to get into the building. Helen watched her push open the door and sprint through. It swung shut behind her. Helen debated going after her but decided against it. Her entire body was shaking. She was incredibly aware of her skin and the roots of her hair and the rustle of the leaves as they danced in the wind.

It couldn't be true. Tom wouldn't. He wouldn't. He wasn't that sort of man. But as she took out her slate and signed into iDate, Helen was forced to admit that she didn't really know what sort of man he was.

And she couldn't say that she hadn't been warned.

CHAPTER THIRTY-EIGHT

Cass

Cass didn't really know why she had told the other girls at school about Bertie. Maybe because they'd caught her at a bad time. They had said something about her dad and about her clothes and then they'd asked her if she'd let Billy take her virginity yet and she'd snapped. She'd just wanted them to go away. To leave her alone. She'd wanted to show them that she was better than them, that she'd experienced something none of them had.

She certainly hadn't intended to say any of it to Miss Taylor, but then she'd stood there in her pretty pink cardigan and silk blouse and Cass had felt hate well up inside her and the words had just tumbled out. What made it worse was that it had been clear that Miss Taylor didn't believe her.

Before she'd slept with Bertie, Cass had imagined how it would play out when he finally told his girlfriend that he was leaving her. She'd known that she'd probably have to face the woman down, but she'd imagined herself being cool and controlled in the face of the other woman's hysteria, knowing that what she and Bertie had was beyond anything he'd ever had with her. But it hadn't been like that at all.

She'd screamed at Miss Taylor. Her face burned as she thought about it. As she rushed through the corridor and down toward the basement exit, Cass knew she would never come back to this school again. She was done.

More than anything, in that moment, Cass wanted her mum. She'd never felt so alone, so hurt, so ashamed. She'd been walking for almost half an hour before she realized that she'd walked to the town center. She found herself outside Coffee Stop. She didn't go in. She stood on the other side of the road, watching through the window as people milled around inside. He was in there. She could feel it. She didn't need to see him to know.

Cass didn't know what she was going to do until he walked out of the building at half past two. She followed him. Not too close, just close enough to keep him in sight. She willed him to turn around and see her. Her heart burned with a painful, deep-seated longing. She imagined a moment when their eyes would meet. He would stop. She would see his surprise. And then she would see the moment of relief when he realized it was really her. Perhaps he would walk toward her, and it would be obvious that he was trying not to run. He would wrap his arms around her and tell her that he'd desperately wanted to message her, but he couldn't. There would be a reason. Perhaps he had broken his slate or lost it. He'd explain everything—Miss Taylor, the way he'd behaved yesterday, the things he'd said to Mabel—and she wouldn't feel so grubby and used.

Right at that moment, he reached into his back pocket, took out his slate, and looked at it. Cass heard herself make a funny little noise. She followed him for another fifteen minutes. She knew, with every step she took, that she was making a mistake. But she couldn't seem to stop. He was like a magnet, pulling her with him.

He turned onto his street. Cass recognized it immediately. He slowed his pace a little, as he reached into his pocket again, fishing for keys, his head bowed, his attention still fixed on his slate. The keys jangled as he pulled them out. He started to whistle, a happy, jaunty tune. It wasn't the tune of a man who was heartbroken. It was an arrogant, snappy, attention-seeking noise.

"Bertie," Cass called. She didn't know why she'd said it, why here, why now.

He stopped whistling and turned. He saw her. "What the fuck are you doing here?"

"You didn't reply to any of my messages. I was worried about you." Not exactly the truth, but close enough to it that she convinced herself it was.

"Go home, Cass."

Cass cut the distance between them. "No," she said. "Not until you tell me what's going on. Why have you been ignoring me? Why didn't you message me . . . after?"

There was the sound of a car approaching. "Shit," he muttered. He grabbed her arm and steered her toward the door, jamming the key into the lock and pushing her inside. He slammed it shut behind him. Cass stood still. She didn't know what to do with herself. She fidgeted with the strap of her bag, refusing to look at the framed photo of Miss Taylor hung up on the wall. Her heart was beating uncomfortably fast. "Bertie," she said again, but he was in no mood to hear it.

"What the hell were you thinking, coming here?" he raged at her. "Someone could have seen you. Seriously, do you not think about anything? Are you really that stupid?"

That wasn't an explanation. That didn't make her feel any less grubby or used.

"Why would it matter if someone saw me?"

"Why would it . . . Jesus H. Christ." He pinched the bridge of his nose. The face that she'd thought so wonderfully handsome was suddenly anything but. Anger made him very, very ugly indeed. "Do you think that I want the whole street to know about you?"

"I don't know," Cass said. Her voice came out raw and high-pitched. "If I did, I wouldn't be asking."

She could feel a strange, sinking sensation in the pit of her stomach, as if it had hardened into lead and was moving lower and lower. She felt as if her feet were glued to the floor. All the magazines had warned about this, too. But she'd never thought it would happen to her. This was something that happened to other women, the boring ones who didn't know how to keep a man interested, who said the wrong things, who couldn't spot a jerk.

"Look," he said. "You and me, it was a casual thing. It wasn't anything serious."

"But you told me how miserable you are with her. You said that it was different with me, that I was different, that you thought that we could be something serious, that this was it."

"That was just talk. Everyone says shit like that in the heat of the moment. It doesn't mean anything."

"But I slept with you!"

"So?"

"So didn't you like it?" Maybe that was it. Maybe that was the reason. She could do better, she knew it, if he'd let her try again.

He stared down at her in disbelief. "It was just a shag."

Cass felt her jaw go slack and her mouth slowly fall open. The man that stood in front of her now was a completely different person to the one she'd climbed into bed with. The sense of betrayal that she felt was immense. It poured through her, as chilling as a bucket of cold water, and just like that, her feelings changed. She knew what he had done. And worse than that, she knew exactly what she was and what she'd done. "You lying scumbag," she said quietly. She felt a little hysterical. "You're just one of those cheap liars."

"And you're just a stupid little tart. Did you really think I'd dump my girlfriend and give up this"—he gestured around them—"for someone who is still at school?"

"You said this was your flat!"

"Of course it's not my flat. I work in a coffee shop three days a week! Do you really think I could afford this on what I make?"

"I don't know," Cass said coldly. "I don't know what you make."

She didn't know anything about him, she realized. Not really. She'd thought that she did. But those had been just words. Empty promises, filled with nothing but crap. He had fed her the lines and she'd sucked them all in because they had made her feel special and pretty and wanted. They'd made her feel like she was better than the other girls at school. She'd loved the sense that she knew something that they didn't. It had filled her body and powered her like a sugar high that lasted for hours and hours and hours.

Now it was gone, and what it left behind was terrible. It was as if her insides had been scraped raw. She felt small and thin and hollow. *He was supposed to fall in love with me*, she thought to herself desperately. *But he didn't and I don't know why not.*

She latched on to that thought. All that mattered to her now was staying here long enough to find the answer. There had to be something. Perhaps if she could find out what it was, she could change his mind. Make those things that he had said to her still be true. She pushed back against her anger and acceptance, both of which were still too terrifying, and clung to the idea that she could turn this around.

She took a couple of steps back, then found her courage and turned and walked into the flat. They would talk this out like adults. Sure, they'd both just said some horrible things, but that was a sign of passion. It meant that there were feelings there, deep, scary feelings that they were both too damaged to face up to. Well, maybe they could face them together. She hadn't been into the living room before. It was a neat, white room with a pale sofa and a pale rug. Cass perched on the edge of the sofa.

"What the fuck do you think you're doing?" he yelled at her.

"Sitting down so that we can talk this through like grown-ups rather than screaming at each other."

"There's nothing to talk about!"

"I think there is."

"That's where you're wrong."

Cass patted the seat next to her with a shaky hand. "Sit down."

He filled the doorway with his body and his anger. His face was bright red and a vein stood out on the side of his neck. He was perfectly still, but the air around him seemed to be vibrating.

Cass shifted nervously in her seat.

"Don't patronize me," he said.

"I'm not! But I really think we should talk about this."

"About what?"

"About you and me!"

"There is no you and me. There never was."

"But you said—"

"Yeah, yeah." He cut her off with a slash of his hand through the air. "And you were dumb enough to believe it."

Cass shot to her feet. "I thought you were different," she told him, though different to what, she didn't know. She said it because it was what women said in the books she'd read and the old TV series that she watched when her mum was out. "I thought I meant something to you."

He tipped his head back and stared at the ceiling. "I don't fucking believe this," he muttered. "Fucking bunny boiler."

Cass didn't know what that meant, but it obviously wasn't a compliment. "No, I'm not!"

"Look, just take the hint, will you? I'm sorry that you thought this was serious, but it was never more than a casual thing."

"You lied. You're a liar." Her throat felt strange and her bottom lip wouldn't stop trembling.

"You didn't tell me you were still at school."

"You didn't tell me that your girlfriend is Miss Taylor," Cass replied.

He just stared at her like she was something he'd found on the bottom of his shoe, and Cass found herself wondering how she could ever have thought him attractive. There was nothing appealing about him now. In the blink of an eye he had changed completely. It was as if she'd imagined him, created a person who didn't exist and slotted him into the body that stood before her. The hairs on the back of her neck rose as she realized that she was shut in another woman's flat with a stranger.

The thought that this was Miss Taylor's flat somehow made it worse. But still, she couldn't bring herself to leave, not yet, and if he tried to make her, she would resist. She wanted to hurt him first. She wanted to make him feel what she felt. She experienced the oddest sensation, as if the ground were moving under her feet, and had to fight to catch her breath before it settled.

"You're an utter bastard."

He shrugged. "If you say so."

He didn't care. He saw her pain and it meant nothing to him. She meant nothing to him. "Fine," she said, though she was anything but. She kicked her way past the coffee table, bruising her shin as she did so, though she barely felt it. She shoved her way past him, a final hard contact that she would remember for days afterward.

She stomped down the short hallway toward the front door and that photo of Miss Taylor, beaming as if she were the happiest woman on earth. When she saw that picture, Cass stalled. She stared at it for a heartbeat, then she turned and looked at him. "Do you love her?" she asked him.

He laughed. "Oh my god," he said. "You're unbelievable."

"It's a simple question. Yes or no. You can't even answer it, and you think I'm pathetic?"

He laughed again.

Cass grabbed the picture and threw it at him. His hands came up and he batted it down. It hit the floor hard and the frame came apart on impact. "Fucking bitch!" he shouted at her. "Get out! Just get out!"

"Don't worry, I'm going," Cass spat at him. But before she did, she grabbed the coats and jackets from the hooks by the door and threw those at him, too. The vase from the little table went with them, as did the bowl of keys and change and a saggy little makeup bag. It wasn't fastened properly and it split when it hit the wall, showering him in eyeliner pencils and old hair bands and a white box, the type that medicines came in. It looked oddly pristine and new among the cheap cosmetics.

"I hate you," she told him, and then she seized the door handle and flung the door open and ran out.

Eventually, she found herself down by the canal and decided to follow the path. It would take her home, and it was quiet, which meant that she could cry in peace. Everything in her life was a disaster. Everything was going wrong. She had no friends, and now no boyfriend. She had nowhere to go apart from the Motherhouse. She had nothing.

She pulled out her slate and messaged Billy. He'd be on her side.

He didn't even bother to reply.

CHAPTER THIRTY-NINE

Sarah

Sarah had been having a surprisingly good morning, all things considered, until Mabel knocked on her door. She'd told Hadiya and the women at the Motherhouse about the note on her car, and admitted that she thought the Townsends were harassing her. Everyone wanted her to go to the police. Sarah had promised that she would, although she was still thinking about it. Kate Townsend was grieving. She wasn't thinking straight. Sarah didn't want to make things worse for her. It wasn't Kate's fault that her father had been what he was.

Mabel closed the door quietly behind her and stood there with her back pressed against it and a look in her eye that said a conversation was coming that Sarah was not going to enjoy.

There was a shifty, embarrassed expression on Mabel's face, and her eyes darted all over the room, looking at everything but Sarah. "I've got to tell you something."

"Go on," Sarah said. She leaned back in her seat, trying to look casual as she braced herself for what she was pretty sure was going to be bad news.

"It's about Cass."

Sarah braced harder. "What about her?" she said. Was it the tag key? Did Mabel somehow know that Cass had taken it?

Mabel flushed and blinked several times in quick succession. "I . . . I sort of caught her somewhere she shouldn't be."

Not the tag key. Sarah exhaled. "What sort of somewhere?"

"This is so hard to say."

"Then just say it. Don't faff around. Just spit it out."

Mabel rubbed a hand over her face. "I caught her in bed with Helen's boyfriend."

There was so much in that that it was impossible for Sarah to unpack it all at once. She started with the first question that came into her head. "What? When?"

"Yesterday morning. I nipped over to Helen's flat during my break to drop off a couple of things that she left at my house, and the two of them were there."

"But Cass was at school!"

When Mabel didn't say anything, simply folded her bottom lip inward and bit down on it, Sarah was forced to rethink that statement. She sank slowly down onto her desk and sat there, barely noticing the keyboard digging into her right buttock. She had no proof that Cass had been at school. And Cass had certainly proved her willingness to skip school when it suited her. She couldn't even begin to process the thought of Cass in bed with Tom Roberts. She reached for her bag and groped inside it for her slate. "Are you sure it was her?"

Mabel nodded. "I'm so sorry. I know I should have said something yesterday, I just . . . I didn't know what to say. I told myself it was none of my business, but then I thought, if she were my daughter, I'd want to know."

"Where the hell did she meet him?"

"She just turned eighteen," Mabel said. "Maybe she joined iDate. That's how Helen met him. It wouldn't surprise me at all to find he's still on there. And he works at the Coffee Stop in town. Didn't you tell me Cass likes to go there?"

"Does Helen know?"

"I doubt it."

"Are you going to tell her?"

"I tried to call her last night," Mabel said. "She didn't answer."

"Go and see her," Sarah said. "She has to know about this."

"She wouldn't believe me."

"Maybe not," Sarah said. "But he just handed you his arse on a plate. Don't waste the opportunity."

It was only after Mabel had left the room, closing the door behind her, that Sarah allowed herself to put her head in her hands and silently scream. She should have seen this coming. She'd been fully aware of Cass's rapidly growing interest in the opposite sex over the past six months. But she'd always thought it would be Billy, and she'd imagined a month or so of an overblown, dramatic relationship that would end, predictably, in tears, but be of no real consequence a year down the road.

An adult man with a serious girlfriend was something else entirely. How could Cass be so easily taken in? *Very easily*, Sarah realized. She'd been given a bit of attention by an attractive man and she was too young and too naive to see him for what he really was. Sarah phoned the school, which quickly confirmed that Cass hadn't been there the previous day.

Sarah considered telling Hadiya that she needed to leave early again but decided against it. She worked through each appointment briskly and methodically. She made sure that everything was done correctly. By the end of the day she was exhausted, and headed out to her car with her head full of thoughts of what lay ahead of her that evening.

The sense of unease that she'd felt when she crossed the car park before didn't bother her this time, primarily because she was too busy thinking about Cass to spare any attention for her surroundings.

It was a mistake.

But this time it wasn't Kate Townsend. It was Greg.

He was standing next to her car. He was wearing an ugly pair of shorts and black trainers with white socks. His hands were buried in the pocket of a zipped-up hoodie.

"What do you want?" she asked him, coming to a halt a few meters away. "Why are you here?"

"I wanted to talk to you," he said. "I can't come to the Mother-house. You made that very clear. I can't call you. What else am I supposed to do?"

"You're supposed to leave me alone."

"I would love to," he said. "Trust me. I'd like nothing more than to never see you again, but unfortunately, you're making that impossible. We need to talk about the divorce. More specifically, about spousal maintenance."

Sarah thought of her Taser, locked in her desk drawer, and wished she had it with her. She'd like nothing more than to watch him collapse and wet himself. "Go away before I call the police."

"Feel free to call them," he said. "I'm not breaking any laws. It's daytime and this is a public place."

Sarah reached into her bag for her slate anyway. Perhaps if he thought she really would call them, he would leave. She tapped at the screen.

"Maybe I'll tell them that you assaulted Cass," he said.

Sarah froze. Her stomach heaved.

"You didn't know I knew about that, did you?" he continued, smirking at her. "Maybe I'll also tell them that you rushed up to me in the center of town and started screaming at me. I'm sure they'd be interested in that. Men do still have some rights. Not many, but some. We're allowed to go about our business in peace as long as we stick to Curfew."

"Piss off, Greg."

"I always knew you had a temper," he said. "I didn't know there was actually something wrong with you. But there is, isn't there? How could you attack your own daughter?"

"I didn't attack her."

"That's not what it sounded like to me."

"I am not having this conversation with you."

"You should be careful," he said as she finally managed to get her legs to move and rushed past him. "You've already ruined my life. I won't let you ruin Cassie's as well."

Sarah wrenched open the car door and moved behind it, needing the protective barrier of steel. "Is that a threat?"

"That's up to you, isn't it? But let me make one thing clear, Sarah: If you lay another finger on my daughter, I will ruin your life."

She dropped into her seat, slammed the door, and gunned the engine. She shot out of the car park so fast that she almost hit a car coming the other way, her heart beating up into her mouth as she slammed on the brakes and just missed hitting it. At the end of the road, she had to face the fact that she was far too shaken up to drive, so she swung into a side street, parked up, and sat for a good ten minutes with the engine still running.

She didn't know what to do. But she couldn't go on like this, and she was not giving Greg a penny. She thought about going home, packing a bag, and leaving. Let Greg take care of Cass. He seemed so concerned about her welfare. Let him deal with a potential accidental pregnancy or an STD. Let him deal with the fallout from the school every time Cass played hooky. Maybe Cass would behave for Greg. The two of them were welcome to each other. This was the problem with motherhood. You could never really escape the man you'd had the baby with. He was in your life forever, no matter how hard you tried to keep him out.

But try as she might, Sarah couldn't talk herself into it. In her mind, Cass was still the beaming toddler with the thin, soft hair, the five-year-old who had loved chocolate buttons, the ten-year-old trying to do cartwheels in the garden. The eighteen-year-old who had completely fucked up and was going to need her mum once she realized what a horrible mistake she'd made.

The treacherous child who ran to her father every time Sarah did something she didn't like.

She went back to the Motherhouse and waited for Cass to come home.

When she did, she was going to kill her.

CHAPTER FORTY

Helen

Helen hurried straight home after work that afternoon. There was no avoiding the conversation that lay on the other side of her front door. But as she reached the end of her road, she saw a familiar figure waiting on the corner. It was Mabel. Helen didn't want to speak to her, but it meant delaying the inevitable conversation with Tom. So she pulled over and let Mabel approach.

She wound down the window, but she didn't get out of the car.

"I've got to tell you something," Mabel said. She launched straight in. No niceties, no small talk. "It's about Tom."

Helen felt her heart sink. Not this again. "Whatever it is, I don't want to hear it."

"Well, you need to." Mabel paused for breath, but not for long enough for Helen to get a word in. "I don't know how to say this, so I'll just say it, and I know you're going to be angry, but you've got to understand that I wouldn't make something like this up. I called in at your flat yesterday to drop off your stuff. Tom was there and he was in bed with this girl. I honestly didn't know what to do. I work with her mother, Helen; she's barely eighteen. She's still at school. I tried to call you last night, but you weren't answering your slate."

Each word was like a bullet. Helen was too numb to feel them.

Yesterday. This had happened yesterday. They'd had dinner to-gether the night before, cottage pie, and they had slept in the same bed, her bed, and all the time he'd been keeping it a secret and she'd had no idea, and everyone at school knew about it. He'd blocked Mabel's calls. Now she knew why.

"I have to go," she said. She put the car in gear and drove off, glancing in the rearview mirror to see Mabel standing at the side of the road, watching her. It made Helen feel ill. She hadn't wanted to believe Cass Johnson. She'd been very close to talking herself out of it.

But there was no talking her way out of it now. She parked out-side her flat, grabbed her bag, and walked up to the front door. Tom opened it just as she was about to slide her key in the lock.

He stood there, looking down at her, and there was something very dark and dangerous in his eyes, and his height and his size, the things she'd found so attractive about him, were terrifying.

Instinctively, Helen knew that she should leave, she should run, but the order didn't make its way to her legs fast enough. Tom grabbed the front of her blouse and pulled her inside the flat. He shoved her in front of him and kicked the door shut, bang, and his grip on her blouse tight-ened until the fabric pulled against her back. "You bitch," he said.

"Let go of me!" She grabbed his hand and tried to make him let go, but he was too strong and it didn't work. He shook her so hard that her head jerked back and forth and her teeth snapped together. Why was he doing this? Had he seen her talking to Mabel?

"When were you going to tell me?" he shouted.

"Tell you what?"

"Don't get smart with me, Helen. You know exactly what."

He pushed her back, holding her up when she stumbled, and through the door into the living room, where he shoved her down onto the sofa. She sprawled there, trying to get her breath back, her heart racing at a million miles an hour.

"That," he said, pointing a shaking hand at the table.

There, in the middle of the empty space, was the box containing the remaining abortion pill, the one she'd hidden inside her makeup bag. He'd gone through her things, her private things. "That's not mine," she said, because denial was the first and easiest thing that came to mind.

"Then whose is it?"

"Mabel's."

"Mabel? Sorry, darling, but you'll have to do better than that."

Helen reached for it, but he was too quick for her, and he got there first. He snatched it up and threw it in her face. "Abortion pills, Helen? Why do you need abortion pills?"

"It's an old box. From a long time ago."

"The label says they were prescribed last week."

He loomed over her, and Helen found herself pinned in place, unable to move. "How did you get pregnant? I thought you were on the pill."

"I . . ."

"Was it mine?"

"Yes, of course it was! I'm not the one sleeping with other people," she said, but he didn't seem to hear.

"Did you get rid of my baby, Helen?" he asked, his voice low and very, very dangerous.

She wanted to lie, but she was terrified that it would only make it worse, and she certainly wasn't going to tell him the truth, so she took the only option left, which was to say nothing at all. She could hear blood pounding loudly in her ears. Her mouth was dry. Her gaze kept slipping to the box on the table and when it slid back to him, she couldn't look past the logo on his shirt. She couldn't look him in the face. She tried, wanting to find some degree of kindness there, some sign that he was going to be reasonable about this, but she was afraid to look and find that it didn't exist.

"Answer the bloody question!" he yelled at her, and his voice was so loud that it shocked a response out of her.

"Yes," she whispered.

CHAPTER FORTY-ONE

Cass

Cass had spent the evening stewing in her thoughts and her anger, hiding from her mother in the laundry room of the Motherhouse. They'd had the most horrendous falling-out. Sarah knew that she'd been seeing Bertie. Mabel had told her. It felt to Cass that the whole world was against her. Not just her mother, or the women in the Motherhouse, but everyone. Just after nine, Mrs O'Brien had walked into the laundry room with an armful of sheets, and so Cass had fled back upstairs and shut herself in her bedroom.

She circled around and around, analyzing everything that had happened between her and Bertie, or Tom Roberts, as she now knew him to be. She replayed everything that he had said and the way that he had said it. She read and reread their iDate conversations until she felt like she was going mad. Was it her? Had she imagined everything? Was the way he had behaved normal? Was she at fault for reading too much into it, for wanting it to be something it wasn't? Was she as naive as Sarah had said? Eventually, cried out and completely exhausted, she was finally able to answer that question.

He had lied.

And yes, she was naive, because she had believed him. Well, she wouldn't do that again. Her eyes had been opened. She'd heard stories about that sort of male behavior, but she'd dismissed them, certain that no one could be that selfish or that awful, and that there were always two sides to every story. What about the women? What about their role in all of it? No one ever talked about that.

Now she understood why.

Men were shit.

They were exactly what she'd refused to believe them to be. They were cruel and manipulative, and they didn't care and they lied and they would do and say things they didn't mean in order to get what they wanted or get out of doing things they didn't want to.

She wished that the past couple of weeks had never happened. She wished that she could take it back, all of it, but she couldn't. It felt like she'd been in a fight. Physically exhausted, emotionally battered. Everything hurt. She'd been a fool and she knew it. Her only hope now was that she could somehow manage to undo some of it and deny the rest. She couldn't cope if her mother ever learned the truth.

Because if she accepted that the women of the Motherhouse had been right about men, that meant that they were right about Curfew, and that Cass had been wrong about everything. As her thoughts circled around and around again, there was one that was louder than all of them.

She had to put Billy's tag back on.

She slipped out of bed and got dressed, pausing only once to check the time on her little alarm clock. Two in the morning. She retrieved the tag key from its hiding place and put it safely inside her trouser pocket, then opened her bedroom door a crack and listened. No sound.

She snuck down the hallway to the door, holding her breath as she opened it with her heart pounding, then made her way outside. The street was deserted except for a prowling cat that gave her a wide berth, and no one disturbed her as she ran over to Billy's street. She decided against knocking on the door and instead went round to the back of the house. "Billy!" she hissed. It was a futile effort. He would never hear her. She knew that even before she did it, but she tried anyway.

She looked around. The path that ran along the back of his house consisted mostly of dirt and gravel. She picked up a couple of stones and weighed them in her hand. The first one didn't even make it up past the kitchen window. The second was almost on target, though. She rooted around for a couple more and was just about to have another try when the window opened and Billy climbed out. Cass watched as he lowered himself down onto the flat roof of the kitchen extension, and from there, down to the ground. He jerked to a halt when he saw her, looking like a deer caught in the headlights. "Cass? What are you doing here?"

"I could ask you the same question! What are you doing outside?"

Billy glanced at the house, then back at Cass. He ran over to her and pulled her into the shadows at the side of the garden, where the two of them crouched down, out of sight. "They're arguing again."

"So?"

"You're the one who said I should sneak outside for a bit of peace when they started going at it!"

"I didn't mean it! What the hell is wrong with you?"

When he'd begged her to put his tag back on, she'd refused because she'd liked how powerful it made her feel, had liked his dependence on her, the degree of control that she felt. He had seemed so desperate for it that it had never occurred to her that he would actually break Curfew, even though she had been the one to suggest it. Seeing him outside now, in the dark, made her feel sick.

"If you didn't want me to break it, you should have put my tag back on when I asked you to."

"This is not my fault." She wouldn't let Billy blame this on her.

This was his choice, and his alone. "Anyway, I came over to put your tag back on."

"Now?"

"Yes, now!"

"Well, you can't do it here! If you put it on now, the police will know I'm outside," he said. "You'll have to do it tomorrow."

Perhaps only a day before, Cass would have agreed to that. But not now. "It can't wait," she told him. "My mother knows I've got the key." She didn't know if that was true or not, but Sarah had certainly suspected that Cass had taken it. She paused, thought it through, made her decision. "I told her that I took your tag off," she lied. "She knows you're untagged, Billy. She said I had until tomorrow to put it back on and then she'd have you called to the center for a random tag check."

Billy's breathing sounded rough. "Why did you do that?"

"I had to. Do you think I would have done it otherwise?" She couldn't see him well in the dark, which made it difficult to know what he was thinking. Up until now, Billy had always been reliable, and she'd always been able to predict what he would do. She couldn't do that anymore. She got slowly to her feet.

Billy muttered something that she didn't quite catch, and then he stood up, too. "We'll have to climb back in," he said.

Cass looked at the extension roof. "I can't do that!"

"Then what else do you suggest we do?"

"You'll have to open the door and let me in."

"My parents are downstairs!"

"That's not my problem," Cass said. She pushed him, and he stumbled forward, then moved silently over to the fence. She watched as he climbed up onto it, then pulled himself up onto the extension roof, and from there to his bedroom and back in through the window. Billy wasn't athletic or particularly fit, and yet he got himself back inside easily. Cass crept over to the back door, trying to keep to the shadows as much as she could. She felt sick. She wished, now, that she had never taken the key, had never used it, her prior ignorance a millstone around her neck.

She waited what felt like forever before she heard the sound of the door being unlocked, and Billy's face appeared in the gap. "You'll have to do it here," he whispered.

"It's too dark. I can't see well enough."

He swore and opened the door a bit wider. "Quiet," he hissed at her as she pushed past him. She could hear yelling coming from the living room. There were a couple of empty wine bottles on the worktop. Billy grabbed hold of her sleeve and pulled her toward the stairs. She followed him upstairs and into his bedroom. He carefully closed the door.

Cass was suddenly very aware that she was locked in his room in the middle of the night, that no one knew where she was, and that he was untagged. She had never felt more vulnerable.

He sat on the bed, pulled up the leg of his jeans. "Did you really do it?" he asked.

"Did I really do what?"

"Did you really sleep with Miss Taylor's boyfriend?"

His tag was on his ankle, still held on with tape. He pulled it off.

"That's none of your business." She tried to turn on the key. Nothing happened. "It isn't working!" she said, panicking.

"What do you mean, it isn't working?"

"The key. It's dead. It isn't working."

He snatched it from her hand. He examined it. And then Billy, thin, spotty, harmless Billy, lost his temper.

CHAPTER FORTY-TWO

Pamela

Present Day
3:20 p.m.

He answers the door promptly. His hair is a mess and his face has the puffy, gray look of someone who has been up all night, but his clothes look clean and I would bet money that he's just got changed. "Hello?" he says, phrasing the word as if it's a question.

"Tom Roberts?"

"That's me."

"Can we come in?"

"Is this about Helen?" he asks, and all the color seems to drain from his face. "Oh my god, it is, isn't it?"

"It's probably best if we talk inside," I say gently.

The words seem to register this time. He moves aside to let me in.

Sue Ferguson wasn't best pleased when the dental records came back and positively identified the body as one Helen Taylor, aged thirty, a teacher at a local school. The boyfriend reported her missing after the photos of her clothes were circulated online. Sue's team are currently trying to connect her to Kate Townsend or Scarlett Caldwell or any of the other women who were outside last night. I doubt they'll succeed.

Rachel volunteered to talk to the boyfriend. Sue Ferguson agreed. I doubt she will be too happy when she finds out that I'm here, too, but there's nothing she can do about it.

The flat has a small, bright entranceway. The walls are white and there are framed photographs everywhere. I feel a pang of grief when I recognize Helen Taylor in some of them. In life, she'd been bright-eyed and cheerful. Every single picture has someone else in it. The boyfriend appears in only a few of them, all very recent additions if I'm any judge. Some are of school classes, huge teenagers crowded around Helen, awkward smiles everywhere. A tall, curly-haired woman is in many of the others. She needs to be identified and interviewed. I make a note of it on my slate.

To the left is a bedroom, to the right a small kitchen, at the end a living room, and I follow Tom through to there. I left Rachel outside and told her to talk to the neighbors. Our car will bring them out. She wanted to argue, I could tell, but I quickly shut that down.

Tom runs a hand through his hair. It flops back down over his forehead. His knuckles are raw.

I've seen injuries like those before.

"You should probably take a seat," I say. I allow myself a quick glance at his leg. He likes his jeans snug and I can see the telltale bulge at his ankle, though after my earlier conversation with the manager of the tagging center, I don't see it as a barrier but as an obstacle, and obstacles can be overcome. The fact remains that in order to kill someone, what you need above all else, perhaps even more than motive or physical ability, is opportunity. Access to them in a place where they are alone and vulnerable.

A woman is never more alone or more vulnerable than when she's at home.

He looks behind him, as if checking the position of the sofa, and then does as I've asked. He picks up a cushion and hugs it to himself, one bare forearm trapping it against his body. As well as the raw knuckles, there's a bruise on his wrist, and when he sees me looking at it, he glances down at it, too. "Fell off my bike," he says.

I ignore that. "I understand that you reported Helen missing."

"Yes," he says. "I'm really worried. No one seems to know where she is. We'd had a bit of an argument, and she went to stay with a friend last night, and I thought she was still there, but then I realized that she'd left her slate here, and I can't get hold of her, and I saw the thing on the news, and I thought, well. I thought . . ."

I don't let him continue. "I'm afraid that I've got some bad news. We found Helen's body this morning."

"Oh, god," he says. "Oh my god."

He leaps to his feet and starts to move around the room, seemingly disoriented, his hands digging into his hair. "What happened to her?"

"We're not sure yet."

"But it's definitely her?"

"Yes. We have confirmed identification. There's no mistake. I'm sorry. Is there someone I can call for you?"

"I'll do it," he says, and he goes through into the kitchen, and a few seconds later I can hear him talking. The words are frantic, urgent, high volume. When I peek through the doorway, he's on his slate. I decide to let him continue, one ear on the conversation as I take a good look around the living room. It's neat and tidy, a very feminine room, with pale walls and pale furniture and knick-knacks everywhere. The only thing that looks out of place is the big TV and the sleek gaming system wired up on the floor below it. Their Cohab record says that they hadn't been living together long, and I guess that this was Helen's flat and that he and his gaming system moved into it. I can imagine a young single woman spending many happy hours relaxed on that sofa, reading one of the books from the shelf, drinking tea from a pretty mug.

He comes back in. "My friend is coming over," he says. He scrubs a frantic hand through his hair. "I don't know what to do. What am I supposed to do? Her parents. I have to tell her parents." He starts poking at his slate again. He hasn't asked if he can see her, which strikes me as unusual, nor has he tried to tell me that I've made a mistake and it can't be her. I've seen people respond to news like this in all sorts of ways, and I've learned never to judge. But I can't help but think of Helen alone at the morgue.

"We'll take care of that," I say. "Tell me about Helen. How long had you been together?"

"We just got our Cohab certificate a couple of weeks ago," he says. "It all happened very quickly. Helen was the love of my life, you know."

It's at this point that he crumples, and I'm very relieved to hear a knock at the door. I open it to find Rachel standing there with a worried-looking young man. "One of his mates," Rachel mouths at me. He's got keys in his hand, as if he was about to let himself in. I stand out of the way to let him past, and he discreetly puts the keys down in a bowl on a table by the door. They're on a key ring shaped like a sunflower. I notice a couple of empty picture hooks on the wall above the table. They look lonely and out of place. I wonder what happened to the pictures.

"What do you think?" Rachel asks me.

"Helen Taylor was a nice woman," I say.

"Awful for the boyfriend," Rachel says.

"Hmm," I reply. "Unless he did it."

"You're obsessed," Rachel says. "Do you know that? Completely and utterly obsessed with pinning this on a man."

"And what if I'm right?" I ask, keeping my voice low. "He fits the image on the CCTV, and he's certainly physically strong enough to have carried the body. There are the cuts and bruises on his hand entirely consistent with the injuries inflicted on Helen's face and body."

"And he's wearing his tag," Rachel points out angrily.

"Yes, he is," I say. "We should have it looked at, make sure it's working properly."

I get Rachel to call Sue Ferguson and ask to have some of her officers and a counselor sent to the flat. As soon as our replacements arrive, Rachel and I return to the station.

Sue's team have already identified the friend, a woman called Mabel Bright, and officers have been sent to speak to her. Kate Townsend and Scarlett Caldwell have been abandoned as suspects. I debate asking if we can have Tom Roberts's tag examined and decide against it. Sue will never agree. I go down to the cafeteria. The food tastes like nothing. I drink two double-shot coffees, which have the sole effect of making me need to pee.

My gut tells me that the answer to what happened to Helen Taylor, and why, is in that flat. It's in the missing pictures on the walls and the expensive gaming console. Perhaps the boyfriend is innocent, but then again, perhaps not. Perhaps I am obsessed with pinning this on a man, and Tom Roberts just happens to be available. Perhaps, even if he did it, it is better for all of us if that never comes to light.

And perhaps not.

I am a month away from retirement. What's the worst thing they can do to me? I've got no career to protect. I pick up my slate and ring Hadiya at the tagging center. I tell her that the body isn't Sarah Wallace. She bursts into tears. When she's recovered, I ask her to pull Tom Roberts's tagging record. Yes, he had had his tag checked recently. It malfunctioned and he came in to have it replaced. Sarah Wallace had done it. More interestingly, it turns out that Mabel Bright is also a tagger.

A man could break Curfew if a tagger removed his tag.

I thank Hadiya for her time.

"I hope you catch whoever did this," she says.

"Yes," I say. "So do I."

I go outside. I use my slate to do a little digging into Mabel Bright. I find a young, cheerful woman with an active online life, but she's careful. She doesn't give much away. I decide to let Sue investigate Mabel, for now.

I look at Helen Taylor's online life instead. It doesn't take me long to find something. It wasn't posted by Helen herself but by pupils at Burnside, the school where she works, and it has something to do with Cass Johnson.

The daughter of Sarah Wallace. Everywhere I turn, I run into Sarah Wallace.

I dig into Cass a little more. She recently turned eighteen, and on her birthday, she joined iDate. My job gives me access to private messages and photos, and I look to see who she was in touch with, and when I see, it gives me chills. Her slate was also on the list of those that were outside.

I decide it's time to visit the Motherhouse.

CHAPTER FORTY-THREE

Sarah

Sarah hadn't heard Cass leave the flat, but she heard her come back in. She was sitting on the sofa in the living room, holding a cup of tea in both hands and watching the news on the TV, hyperaware of the empty bed in her daughter's bedroom. A body had been found in the park. For several terrifying minutes, Sarah had thought that it might be Cass. She had lived the possibility that her daughter could be dead. It had taken her back to the silent seconds after Cass had been born, when she'd waited to hear her cry. Hearing the door open and Cass walk in had been like that first newborn mewl.

"Cass," Sarah called. "Come in here."

She heard the hesitation in her daughter's footsteps.

"Now!" she bellowed.

Cass did as she was told.

"Where have you been?" Sarah asked her.

"Out," Cass said. Her eyes darted to the television. "That's the park," she said. "They found a body?"

"Apparently so," Sarah said.

"That's weird," Cass said. "I wonder who it is."

"They don't know yet. I thought it might be you," Sarah said quietly. She felt tears burn at the back of her throat. "I can't tell you how glad I am that it isn't."

She wrapped her arms around Cass's waist and steered her toward the sofa. "Sit down," she said, kneeling in front of her only daughter, and looking up into the face that only a few days before had reminded her so strongly of Greg that she'd felt an overwhelming surge of hatred. Now she saw only a child she loved. She tried to sound calm. She felt anything but. She put her hands on Cass's knees and gripped them firmly. "Don't do that again, Cass," she said. "Don't sneak out in the middle of the night without letting me know. I know it won't really be sneaking out if you do that, but we could pretend, right?"

Cass pressed her lips together tightly, and she blinked several times in quick succession. "Mum," she said. "Can I tell you something?"

"Of course."

"I did something really bad." She couldn't meet Sarah's gaze, looking at the floor instead.

Here goes, Sarah thought to herself. "Has this got anything to do with Tom Roberts?" She felt a knot in her belly. She remembered him only too well. The charm, the smile, the casual vanity. She looked at Cass and knew how vulnerable she would have been to all of that. "Tell me you used contraception."

"Mum!" Cass went bright red. "It's not that."

There was something worse? "Tell me."

Cass tried to speak. She couldn't get the words out. She cleared her throat. "You're going to be so mad at me. Promise you won't be mad."

"I'll do my best," Sarah said.

Cass took a deep breath, then spewed out the words that would give Sarah nightmares afterward. "I lied when I said I didn't take the tag key. I did take it. I figured out how to make it work and I took Billy's tag off and now it's stopped working and I can't put it back on, and you've got to help us, Mum. He's untagged. He's bloody well untagged, and it's my fault, and he's been going outside, I caught him, and . . ." She ran out of steam. Tears started to fall, big fat ones that rolled down her cheeks and dripped off her chin.

Any feelings Sarah might have had about her daughter embarking on an entirely inappropriate relationship with Tom Roberts disappeared. It was nothing compared to this. "Have you got the key?"

"Yes," Cass said. She fumbled in her pocket, produced it. She held it out.

Sarah took it, and as her fingers closed round it, several things happened at once. There was an overwhelming sense of relief. There was also, she was surprised to find, a sense of calm. She had been so convinced that Cass had taken the key, and then so full of self-disgust and doubt when Cass had denied it and she had been unable to find it. She had hated herself for searching her daughter's room. Now all that faded away.

She touched the screen, tried to turn the key on, but as Cass had said, it wasn't working. "It's been deactivated," she said. "It's what we do with keys that go missing."

"I didn't know that," Cass said in a small voice.

"I'll have to book him an appointment at the tagging center," Sarah replied. Her mind worked quickly. "If I see him, I can put his tag back on without anyone finding out."

"Can we do it today?" Cass asked hopefully.

"No," Sarah said. "Probably tomorrow at the earliest."

The news was still playing in the background, and she picked up the remote and turned it off. She didn't want to listen to it. She got to her feet, started to pace. She'd have to make the appointment without raising suspicion, and make sure that she was the one Billy saw. It wouldn't be easy.

"It can't wait that long!" Cass said. "He broke Curfew! He can't have it off for another night. What if he does it again and this time he gets caught?"

If he did get caught, there would be difficult questions, and Sarah had no doubt that Billy would answer them, and that would lead to Cass, and Sarah didn't want to think about how much trouble her daughter would be in if anyone found out what she'd done. Her priority now was to protect Cass. She had to fix this situation. And more importantly, she could fix it.

"I'll have to go to the tagging center, see if I can get hold of another key," Sarah said. She got dressed quickly, throwing on her work trousers and shirt. She came out of her room to find Cass anxiously tapping at her slate. "What are you doing?"

"Messaging Billy to let him know what we're doing."

"Don't," Sarah said. "In fact, turn it off."

"Why?"

"They're trackable," Sarah said. "And your messages can be read. We don't want any chance of that."

Cass did as she'd been told. The two of them crept downstairs and went out to the car only to find that both front tires were completely flat.

"Not this again," Sarah said. She kicked one of them. She could see where it had been slashed.

"I don't understand," Cass said, looking at them. "How can they both be flat?"

"I've been having some trouble with the family of that man I tased. There have been a couple of other . . . incidents." Though she hadn't thought that Kate Townsend would go quite this far.

"But you never said anything! And this isn't just a bit of trouble, they've damaged your car. You should tell the police."

"I don't think this is a good time to have anything to do with the police, do you?" Sarah asked gently.

Cass flushed. "No."

"Come on," Sarah said. "We'll take the bus."

But after twenty minutes with no sign of a bus, Sarah decided that they should walk instead. It took them almost an hour to get to the tagging center. Three police cars drove past them as they walked, and with each one, Sarah grew increasingly nervous.

It was still early when they got to the center, and it was still closed. They waited in the car park. There was a distinct smell of urine, and Cass held her nose and complained about it.

The longer they waited, the more Sarah began to think that this was a bad idea. Hadiya would want to know why she wasn't doing a full day's work, and the last thing she wanted was to get caught trying to sneak a key out of the building. She wasn't even sure how Cass had got away with it.

"This isn't going to work," she muttered, dragging Cass into the bushes as Hadiya's car pulled into the car park. "We'll have to find another way."

CHAPTER FORTY-FOUR

Cass

S arah had wanted to go back to the Motherhouse, but Cass persuaded her to wait. "Please, Mum," she said. "We've got to do this today. He broke Curfew."

They waited on a bench at the other side of the road, watching the tagging center, but neither of them made any attempt to get nearer. But what they did do was talk. It was easier somehow, sitting here, not looking at each other. More than an hour passed before either of them made an effort to move. They saw another two police cars, and a van.

"Do you think it has something to do with that body in the park?" Cass asked.

"I don't know," Sarah said. "But I don't like it." She took Cass's hand. "Come on."

"Where are we going?"

"To the train station."

"But the tag key . . ."

"I know," Sarah said. "But it's not going to happen."

They walked into town, past the bus station, which made Cass think of the horrible conversation she'd had with her dad, when she had told him she had a tag key and he'd lost his temper. She wanted to tell Sarah about it. She wanted to tell her everything. Her body felt like it was overflowing. She hadn't expected her mother to be so decisive, so fierce, or so firmly on her side. She had only told Sarah about Billy because she had run out of other options.

At the train station, Sarah bought tickets using an assortment of notes and coins from her purse and the bottom of her bag. They got on the first train into London. "I want to be somewhere that we won't run into anyone, just for a few hours," Sarah said. Cass couldn't argue with that. She didn't want to be in the town center, where there was a chance that she might run into Tom. They went to the museums and ate sandwiches in a park, even though it was cold. But they couldn't stay away forever, and when they got back to the Motherhouse, bad news was waiting for them.

"There's a policewoman here," Mrs. O'Brien said. "She wants to talk to both of you."

"Any idea what it's about?" Sarah said, and it didn't escape Cass's notice that Mrs. O'Brien gave her mother's arm a squeeze as she went past. There was something in the contact, a kindness, that made Cass wish for the same. It took her very much by surprise when she got it.

"Whatever it is, it will be okay," Mrs. O'Brien told her.

The policewoman was waiting for them in the communal dining room. No one else was in there. Someone had given her a cup of tea and a plate of biscuits. Cass could feel her hands shaking. She was grateful for the steady presence of her mother.

"Hello," the policewoman said. She stood up as they approached. "Sarah Wallace?"

"Yes," Sarah said.

"And you must be Cass." She smiled, but Cass couldn't bring herself to return it.

"What is this about?" Sarah asked.

"Please, sit down. My name is Pamela, by the way."

Sarah pulled out a chair, and so Cass did the same, and they sat next to each other. She felt for her mother's hand under the table, and when she found it, Sarah gripped hers tightly and didn't let go.

"You've caused us some trouble today," Pamela said. "I can't tell you how relieved I am to see the two of you."

The door of the dining room was open, and Cass could see Mrs. O'Brien lingering outside. It helped, too. It didn't seem nosy anymore.

"I'm not sure I understand," Sarah said.

"No," Pamela said. "Probably not. But let's not worry about that for now. Cass, can you tell me what you know about a man called Tom Roberts? You might know him as Bertie?"

That was not at all what Cass had been expecting.

"Am I in trouble?" she asked.

"Not with me," Pamela said gently.

Cass swallowed. "He works at Coffee Stop in town, and he used to talk to me when I went in. I found him on iDate," she admitted. "We started messaging each other. I . . . we met up a couple of times. But that was it. I'm not seeing him anymore. I found out that he had a girlfriend and he lied about it."

There. She'd said it, and she'd put as much of the truth into it as she wanted to share.

"What was he like?" Pamela asked.

"He was nice, at first," Cass said. "He said that he liked me." She blushed. "But he didn't. He was just pretending. And then he became really horrible."

"In what way?"

"Just some of the stuff he said. He was really nasty."

"I see," Pamela said. "Did he become physically aggressive?"

Cass felt Sarah shift in her seat. "No," she said. "Nothing like that."

"What is this about?" Sarah demanded.

The policewoman studied her for a moment, then she got out of her seat and closed the door. When she sat back down, her demeanor had completely changed. "I assume you're aware that a body was found in the park this morning."

"We saw something on the news, yes," Sarah said. "But we've been out all day, and we've both had our slates turned off."

"The body is that of Mr. Roberts's girlfriend, Helen Taylor," Pamela said. "I understand that the two of you know Helen."

And with those words, the world changed, and Cass with it. She would never be the same after that. Just as Helen Taylor had been changed by the death of Susan Lang, so Cass Johnson would be by this.

Her entire body started to shake. She wanted to say something, but she couldn't speak. She could only look at Sarah, a silent plea for help, and she found it in Sarah's arms, which came around her and held her closely.

"Helen Taylor is one of Cass's teachers," Sarah said. "Cass didn't know that Miss Taylor was Tom's girlfriend when she started seeing him, and she ended the relationship as soon as she found out."

"Was Miss Taylor aware that you were seeing him, Cass?"

Cass could only nod. She wanted to be away from this, from all of it. She wanted to turn the clock back and erase everything she had done. She wished that she had never met him. She wished that she had told Miss Taylor that she liked her shoes. She wished that she had listened to her mother.

But what had been done could not be undone.

"Thank you," Pamela said, getting to her feet. Cass thought that she might say something else, but she didn't. Instead, she pushed the plate of biscuits gently toward Cass. "If I need to ask you anything else, I'll be in touch."

"You should speak to Mabel Bright," Sarah said. "She's a tagger, too. She's Helen's best friend."

"I will," Pamela said. She got as far as the door before she turned back around. "By the way, Cass, I meant to ask you about your slate."

"What about it?" Sarah asked.

"We tracked all slates outside last night, and Cass's was one of them."

"It can't have been," Cass said. She'd left it here when she went to see Billy, she was sure of it.

"Can I see it?" Pamela asked.

Cass took it out of her bag. She held it out to Pamela, who swiped through to settings and checked the location data.

"Well, that confirms it," Pamela said. "Do you have another slate, by any chance? This one looks very new."

"She lost her old one," Sarah said.

"When?"

"A week ago. This one is a replacement. They told me the old one would be deactivated. I guess it wasn't."

"Apparently not," Pamela said.

She thanked them both for their time, and then she left.

Sarah turned to Cass. "Right," she said. "What really happened to your old slate?"

CHAPTER FORTY-FIVE

Pamela

Present Day
4:35 p.m.

take Sarah Wallace's advice and I go to see Mabel Bright. She lives in a pretty little terrace in the old part of town. I message Rachel before I go in, requesting an update. Rachel tells me that Mabel has been ruled out. She was at her parents' house last night, and they have CCTV in the garden. Mabel went in and didn't come out until seven this morning.

I knock, and when she answers, she looks utterly broken. She's tall, but her body is folded over as if her spine is collapsing, and her face is puffy from crying. "I told the officers who came earlier everything I know," she says.

"I appreciate that," I say. "And I'm sorry to have to trouble you again. There are just a few more things we need to talk about. Can I come in?"

She lets me in. I get the impression that she's too exhausted to resist. She doesn't even close the door behind us, leaving me to do it. We go through into a cheery living room. There's a photo of Helen on the mantelpiece, and I think, yes, I can see the two of them being friends. "She wasn't here last night," she says. "I know Tom is saying she was, but she wasn't. I went to my parents'. I'd had a bad day and I didn't want to be on my own."

"When did you last see her?"

"I spoke to her yesterday afternoon. I wanted to tell her . . . I caught Tom in bed with someone else."

"Cass Johnson."

She looks down. "Yes."

"I've already spoken to Cass," I say. "She told me what happened. I know that she contacted him through iDate."

"Fucking bastard didn't even delete his account. Can you believe that?" She sits up straight, as if she's found a source of energy somewhere. I suspect that it's her hatred of Tom Roberts. "He was telling Helen how in love they were, and all along, he was hooking up with teenage girls he met online."

"How did Helen take the news?" I ask.

"Not as badly as I thought she would," Mabel tells me. "To be honest, from the way she reacted, I think she already knew, though I don't know how she found out. I tried calling her on Monday and she didn't answer. We hadn't been getting on very well."

"Can I ask why you weren't getting along? Had something happened?"

She rubs her eyes. "You could say that. She got pregnant, you see, and when she found out it was a boy, she had an abortion. She didn't tell Tom about any of it. I said that I didn't think she should be with someone who she had to keep secrets from. That's not a healthy relationship."

I believe I may just have found a motive. Men have killed for far less. And secrets have a habit of finding their way out into the open.

"She said I was jealous of the two of them," Mabel says. "I put it down to her being in a bit of a state, which was understandable, really. I thought if I gave her a few days to calm down, it would sort itself out. She'd left a couple of things here, so I dropped them off at her flat on Monday morning—I've got a key—and that's when I caught Tom with Cass Johnson."

Slowly, the pieces are beginning to slot into place. "How did you know it was Cass?" I ask.

"I work with her mother. Sarah brought Cass to the tagging center for a work experience day a couple of weeks ago. It was a really messed-up day. I had a problem with one of the men who came in. Sarah tased him. He died of a heart attack. Awful."

Which brought the Townsends into Sarah's life, but despite the time spent on them this morning, I now know that they're irrelevant. "Sarah did Tom's last tag check, didn't she?"

"Yes," Mabel tells me. "It was an emergency appointment. There was something wrong with his tag. But Sarah sorted it."

That's the thing I was looking for. I get goose bumps. "What was wrong with it?"

"I'm not sure," Mabel tells me. I see the penny drop. "Do you think he did it?" she asks me. "Do you think he found some way to take his tag off and he killed her?"

I look at her tearstained face. "Yes," I say.

"Good," she says. "Because I do, too."

The feeling in my gut is overwhelming. But it's not enough. Where next?

I go to the counseling center and speak to the counselor who gave Helen and Tom their Cohab certificate. She describes Helen as polite, well educated, lonely. She describes Tom Roberts as vain, clever, lazy, opportunistic. "I thought they were a bad fit," she tells me. "Helen wasn't ready to hear it. I thought the best course of action was to let them move in together and give her the opportunity to figure it out for herself. I wanted to leave the door open for her to come back to me. I didn't consider him dangerous." She takes off her glasses and looks at me. "Did I make a mistake?"

"That's the big question, isn't it?"

My slate pings as I'm leaving. It's the pathologist, Michelle.

"The male DNA on the body belongs to the boyfriend, Tom Roberts," Michelle tells me.

I thank her and end the call. It's not enough on its own. I'd expect to find traces of him. But combined with the absence of other DNA, it's something.

After that, I head back to the station. I brace myself as I head in through the door. Ideally, I'd like to go back to the tagging center and talk to Hadiya again, but I have to at least pretend that I'm still part of the team.

"Where have you been?" Sue asks me as I reach my desk, and there's a knife-sharp edge to her voice.

"Gathering information," I say.

"Without clearing it with me first?"

"Yes." I don't try to deny it or pretend that I didn't know what I was doing. Her fury makes me want to take a step back. I resist. Rachel is sitting at her desk, watching the two of us. I wonder what she's told Sue in my absence. "I know you couldn't get anything on Mabel Bright," I say. "And you've got nothing on Kate Townsend or Scarlett Caldwell. Face it, Sue, you're going to have to start looking in a different direction. We can't be closed-minded about this."

She turns and walks away from me.

"We have to look at the boyfriend," I call after her. "You must see that."

She pauses. In the following silence, you could hear a pin drop. She whirls around. "If you're so convinced he did it, prove it," she says.

And then she storms into her office and slams the door. Everyone is watching me, waiting to see what I'm going to do next. I decide to take what she said as an order.

I tap through my slate, send a message, and then I turn to Rachel. "You're coming with me," I say.

"Where are we going?" she asks.

"We're going to bring Tom Roberts in for questioning."

"What? No!"

"I am your senior officer," I say. I've had enough of her attitude, of her ignorance, of her refusal to follow my lead. "Do as you're bloody well told, Rachel."

Thirty minutes later, we walk him in through the front door. His friend has come along for the ride. I've allowed it, but I make him wait in reception. If Tom Roberts wants someone to hold his hand, he can request a solicitor. All that matters now is doing what needs to be done as easily and smoothly as possible. I take Tom into an interview room, where Hadiya is already waiting. She has a small black case with her.

"We need to check your tag," I say to Tom Roberts.

"Why?"

"Just routine," I say casually. "We've got to rule out all possibilities."

Twin stripes of red appear across his cheekbones. He moves slowly, deliberately so, hitching up his jeans to reveal the band of black around his ankle. I turn on my slate and start to record.

"As you can see, it's fine," he says.

"I understand you had an issue with the previous one."

"I did, but I went to the tagging center and had it sorted. This is a new one. Look, am I in trouble here? Do I need a solicitor?"

"If you would like a solicitor, that can be organized for you."

He narrows his eyes. "No," he says eventually. "It's fine."

Hadiya carefully removes the tag. She thanks Tom for his patience and then I take her into the room next door.

"It might take a while," she says to me.

"That's not a problem," I say. "There's no rush."

I watch as she examines the strap and the casing. There's no obvious sign of tampering. Next Hadiya hooks the tag up to her slate and downloads the data from it. "That's odd," she says.

"What is?"

"It stopped transmitting just after midnight, and then it started again around four a.m."

"How is that possible?"

"Usually, they stop transmitting when they're removed, but he would need a key to do that. Where would he have got a key?" She drops her head into her hands. "We had a key go missing," she says. "But it couldn't have been used last night. The battery would have run out by now, for one thing, and I deactivated it as soon as I knew it had gone."

"Well, he took it off somehow," I say.

I head upstairs and report my findings to Sue. She looks exhausted and gray. Her hair has loosened into a halo of frizz. Gone is the confident, sharp-talking woman who walked into the station this morning.

"Send a team to search the flat," she says.

We find the tool kit that Helen bought him, the one he used to remove his tag.

And we find traces of Helen's blood in the kitchen.

Later, back at the station, after Tom Roberts has been charged, Sue Ferguson calls me into her office.

"You did it, then," she says. "You got the result that you wanted."

"I got the right result," I say.

"Did you?" she asks me. "Because I'm not so sure. The goal here was to protect women, Pamela, and to do that, we have to protect Curfew."

"So we should have let him get away with it? What if he did it again, to someone else?"

"He's just one man. He could only do so much," Sue says.

"Every dead woman is one too many! All of them count, Sue. Every single one. And every single one deserves justice."

"And what about the women who will be harmed if Curfew falls apart?"

CHAPTER FORTY-SIX

Sarah

After Pamela left, Cass and Sarah sat alone in the dining room. They probably should have gone back upstairs, but it seemed too far and too much effort, and now that Cass had finally started to talk, Sarah didn't want to do anything that might make her stop.

Helen Taylor was dead. Sarah threw up a bit in the back of her mouth when she thought about it. And however hard she was finding it, she knew that it was even harder for Cass.

"How can she be dead?" Cass kept saying, over and over.

"I don't know, love," Sarah said. She hugged her daughter and breathed in the scent of her hair, no longer the smell of a baby, but of a young woman. Mrs. O'Brien and a couple of the other women came in.

"What happened?" Mrs. O'Brien asked.

"They identified the body in the park. It belongs to a woman called Helen Taylor. She was Cass's teacher."

Cass started to shiver. Mrs. O'Brien took off her fleece and draped it across her shoulders. Sarah was grateful for it. She would remember the kindness of these women long after this was over. The television was turned on, and they sat together and watched as the story slowly unfolded, until at seven p.m., a sharp-suited woman appeared on the steps of the police station and told the gathered crowd that a man had been charged in connection with Helen's murder. It was Tom Roberts. He'd found a way to remove his tag without being caught.

Mrs. O'Brien turned the television off at that point.

A couple of the women began to cry. Others disappeared back to their own flats, to manage their grief and shock in private. Sarah took Cass upstairs. "I can't believe he did it," Cass said. "But he did, didn't he?"

"It certainly looks that way if they've got enough evidence to charge him."

"He didn't seem like a bad person."

"They never do," Sarah said. She bit her lip and tasted blood. She couldn't help but wonder how close to danger Cass had been. Far closer than she could comfortably think about.

"I thought Curfew didn't make any difference, but it does, doesn't it? I thought Tom was nice." Cass paused. "No," she said slowly. "That's not true. I wanted him to be nice, and so I told myself he was, even when it was obvious that he wasn't."

"You weren't to know," Sarah said.

"You knew," Cass pointed out. "That's why you became a tagger, isn't it? Because you knew. We can't trust men. They say things they don't mean, and they do it because we're daft enough to listen to them, and we pretend they won't hurt us, and they do, and he hurt Miss Taylor, he hurt her, and she didn't deserve that."

Cass was breathing fast. Sarah could sense a full-blown panic attack approaching. It was hardly surprising. "Don't think about that now."

"I can't help it."

"You're not the first person to make that mistake, Cass," Sarah said. Her mouth was dry. "Maybe it's time I told you about the day your father broke Curfew."

She felt Cass stiffen beside her. "What about it?"

"Why I did it," Sarah said. She licked her lips, trying to find the right words. "I wish I had told you sooner, but I didn't want you to think badly of him. Whatever he'd done, he was still your father."

She took a deep breath and dug into the memories of that final day. It seemed a lifetime ago. "I worked a lot. I had to. Your father and I . . . when you were small, we'd decided that one of us should stay at home and look after you, and when Curfew came in, it obviously had to be him. It made sense. He took care of you and the house, I earned the money, and for a long time, it seemed to be working. I thought we were happy. I thought he was happy."

"Mum . . ." Cass began, but Sarah cut her off.

"Let me finish," she said. "Looking back, I think it started when you were fifteen. That's when I first noticed the change. But when I questioned things, he denied it, and he made me feel silly."

"What things?"

"Things that appeared on the bank statement," Sarah said. "Restaurants. Clothes from shops I didn't go to. Membership at an expensive gym. He lost a bit of weight, changed his hair."

"I don't understand," Cass said.

"Neither did I," Sarah replied. "At least, I told myself that I didn't. I guess I didn't want to face the truth. He was having an affair. That's what I walked in on. He was talking to her on his slate. He was standing in my kitchen, in the house that I'd paid for, asking his girlfriend if she liked the shoes he'd bought for her using my credit card."

"I think I saw them together once," Cass said. She pressed her fingers against her eyes. "In town. He said . . . he said she went to his gym. He gave me some money and told me to treat myself. There was some makeup that I wanted, and I was more bothered about that. I didn't . . . I didn't think, Mum."

"Why would you have?" Sarah asked. If she'd been unable to see it, she certainly couldn't expect a teenager to. Greg had fooled both of them.

Cass pressed her hands together between her knees. "Because it was obvious," she said miserably. "Do all of them lie? Is this just what they do? Aren't any of them decent?"

"I don't know," Sarah said. Everything that had happened that day, with Helen Taylor, with the arrest of Tom Roberts, with what Cass had just told her, had only served to reinforce Sarah's belief that there was something fundamentally wrong with men. "I've yet to meet one that is. That's why I wanted to live in the Motherhouse."

"I can't believe I was so naive," Cass said. "About all of it. And it's not just Billy's tag. I gave Dad my old slate."

Sarah took a moment to process that. Suddenly certain things began to fall into place. "The one that the policewoman asked about? The one she said was outside overnight?"

"Yes. He didn't have one, you see, and he said he couldn't afford one, and I was worried that there might be an emergency and he wouldn't be able to get hold of anyone."

"But . . ." Sarah began, and then she saw the look on her daughter's face, and her body felt like she had plunged into a pool of icy cold water. "What else did you do, Cass?"

"I didn't take his tag off," Cass said, the words crashing into each other in her rush to get them out. "I swear I didn't. I just loosened it a bit."

"What?"

"He said it was too tight and that it was giving him a rash, so I loosened it. And then he said he needed antiseptic cream for the rash but couldn't afford that either, so we went to the shop and I bought him all this stuff, lotion and oil, and I don't know, but I think maybe . . . I think maybe if he used the oil he might have been able to get it off without breaking it."

Sarah got up, walked calmly into the bathroom, locked the

door, and silently screamed. She gripped the edge of the sink and looked at herself in the mirror. It took several long minutes before she was able to get her feelings under control. She splashed cold water on her face. It helped. Greg. Untagged. Free to go wherever he wanted, whenever he wanted. The thought was almost unbearable.

She unlocked the bathroom door and went back into the living room. Cass was still sitting on the sofa. "Tell me everything," Sarah told her. "Don't leave anything out."

After that, they got Cass's slate and tracked the movements of the old one. Just as Pamela had said, it had been out at night, and it had made trips to the Motherhouse and to the tagging center. Sarah thought about the note left on her car, and the slashed tires. She'd assumed that the Townsends were responsible. Now she wasn't so sure. The more that she thought about it, the more certain she was that Greg had done those things, not the grieving Kate Townsend.

Should she tell Cass? She didn't want to. It was too horrible. There were some things that, once known, couldn't be unknown, and she didn't want her daughter to carry that burden.

But that didn't stop Sarah from thinking about it. Cass went to bed early, exhausted by the events of the day, but Sarah stayed up. She looked at the tracking information on Cass's slate. There was a pattern to the movements he made, to where he went. Greg, as always, was nothing if not predictable.

She knew what she was going to do. The only problem was figuring out how she was going to do it.

CHAPTER FORTY-SEVEN

Sarah

S he still wasn't sure when she knocked on the door of Liz O'Brien's flat and asked to borrow her car. She drove to the side of town near the river. She parked up close to Greg's block at Riverside. It was almost time for Curfew to start, and she saw several men walking toward the housing, each with a half-empty carrier bag in one hand. One of them scowled when he saw her. He scared Sarah enough that she started the engine and pulled away from the curb, but she soon circled back to the street and parked up again, this time under a tree on the other side of the road.

She waited.

It got dark.

Still, she waited.

The minutes ticked past on the clock on the dashboard. She must have fallen asleep, because it was two a.m. and then it was five thirty. She tried to stretch in the seat, but there wasn't enough room. Her mouth tasted like old food. She needed to pee. She should go home. She couldn't go home, because her ex-husband was in that building with a loose Curfew tag that he could quite possibly remove.

Why had he been released here? Why couldn't he have stayed in prison forever? Why couldn't they all just be removed from society rather than being allowed to live among women, where they could bully and manipulate and hurt them? Tags hadn't fixed it. They hadn't spared Helen Taylor. Cass had thought that tags were pointless. She was right. Just not in the way she'd assumed.

Sarah rubbed her knees and tried to ignore the pain in her bladder. It was impossible. She opened the car door just a crack. No one would notice if she quickly went at the side of the road, not at half five in the morning on this side of town.

But just as she was about to get out of the car, she sensed movement on the other side of the road. She sank down lower into her seat, holding her breath, heart pounding, all senses on high alert, and she saw what she now realized she'd come here expecting to see.

Greg had always gone out for a run at seven each morning, as soon as Curfew ended. He could have gone later, when Cass was at school, but no. Seven had been his time. He had often said that he'd like to go out even earlier, then he could run for longer. In hindsight, his obsession with running had started around the time that he'd begun having an affair, and it was obvious that the two things were connected.

And now here he was.

He looked up and down the road, rolling his shoulders and stretching his leg muscles, then started a slow jog toward the end of the road. She let him get a little farther on before she started the car.

She slipped on her seat belt and pulled quietly away from the curb. She found herself wondering where he was going and decided to follow him. He ran in the direction of the town center. After about fifteen minutes, a car coming in the other direction stopped. Greg veered over toward it, opened the passenger door, and got in. He embraced the woman in the driver's seat.

Sarah pulled over to the side of the road and parked up again. She took her slate out of her pocket and tracked Cass's old one. It followed the same route as it had on the other nights, onto a quiet side street next to a church, and remained there for the next forty-five minutes. Sarah didn't want to follow them down there. She didn't want to know.

It had never occurred to her that Greg might continue his affair with Scarlett Caldwell when he got out of prison, but here he was. It had to be tricky for them. He obviously didn't want to meet her at Riverside, and he couldn't go to her house because her husband would be there. Their options were limited. But the backseat of a car? Yuck.

Right on schedule, the slate started to move again, and it wasn't long before Greg was crossing the road a couple of hundred yards ahead. Sarah started the car. It wasn't far into the town center. She kept a safe distance. He ran past the bus station and cut across the road.

Across the tagging center car park.

He stopped in Sarah's spot.

His hands went to the front of his shorts and he seemed to fiddle with them, and it took her a moment to figure out what he was doing, but when she did, she had to pull over and sit there in disgust. He was pissing in her parking space. Dirty bastard.

He finished quickly enough and headed out of the car park, jogging round in an arc, his speed a little higher now, as if he was keen to get home.

Sarah knew what she was going to do. It hadn't been clear before, but now it was. She jammed her foot down on the accelerator and gripped the top of the steering wheel firmly in one hand, and she drove straight at him.

He saw her. He yelled something. He tried to dodge out of the way. It was too late. She hit him. He spun like a top, arms flung out with nothing to grab on to, then dropped to the tarmac, gripping his right ankle. He'd been holding something in his hand. It fell to the ground and smashed. It was Cass's slate.

Sarah didn't stop.

She slowed to an acceptable speed, perfectly calm, then activated her own slate and phoned 999. She told the woman who answered that she'd seen a man on Dunham Road in the center of town and hung up. Then she went home.

She got a call from the police thirty minutes later. Greg had been arrested and was on his way back to prison.

CHAPTER FORTY-EIGHT

Cass

Cass sat on the wall outside the tagging center. She should have been at school, but Sarah had said that it would be okay if she took a few days off. She'd had a lot to deal with, between Miss Taylor and her father. She still hadn't come to terms with it all. She was plagued by nightmares, where she would wake up screaming after imagining Tom in her bedroom, and she kept having horrible flashes of memories from childhood that would leave her feeling shaken and strange. But the women at the Mother-house had been amazing. Every door was open to her. She could always find someone who was willing to listen. And whatever happened, when she woke up shaking and afraid, she knew that she was safe inside that building, where no men could go, and there was a very solid front door and an army of women to keep them out.

She was thankful now for the pink carpets and the deep bath and her room, which overlooked the garden. She was thankful for the communal dining room and the shared meals. And more than any of it, she was thankful for her mother, and the swift way in which Sarah had taken charge of the mess she had made.

Cass knew how foolish she had been, the risk that she had taken, and she knew that she would never do it again. The night before, she and Mrs. O'Brien had burned her magazines in the brazier in the garden. Cass had watched the tiny particles of red rise into the air, and she had thought of Miss Taylor.

She couldn't think of Helen too often. She wasn't ready yet to fully face the pain of it. She and Sarah had already agreed that a move to another school might be a good idea. Somewhere no one knew her history, where she could start again.

But first, there was something else to be done.

She sensed movement in the doorway of the tagging center and looked up to see Billy walking out. He was alone. Cass was glad. She slipped down from the wall and brushed the dirt off her jeans. He walked slowly down the steps, lost in thought.

She went over to him. "Hello, Billy," she said.

"Hello, Cass."

They stood, not quite looking at each other. Billy fidgeted with the hem of his jacket.

"Do you want to go for a walk?" Cass asked him.

"I've got to get to school."

"It won't take long," she said, and so he agreed. There was a woman selling flowers on the corner, and Cass stopped and bought a bunch of pink carnations. They crossed the road and headed toward the park, Billy lagging a little behind.

She waited for him to catch up.

"Your mum fixed my tag," he said when he did.

"She said she would," Cass replied. "She won't tell anyone, you know. About what happened to it."

"I know. She told me. I'm sorry about your dad."

"I'm not," Cass said. "He knew what would happen if he broke Curfew again." She didn't mention the fact that Billy had also broken Curfew. He'd got away with it, but she hoped that he was smart enough to understand that he wouldn't be able to do it again.

They were close to the lake now, and she stood and looked out across the water, which was a flat, murky gray. She felt something catch in her throat and swallowed it down. The side of the lake where Helen Taylor had been found was covered in flowers, pink and red mingling together. She looked down at her own tiny bunch. It didn't seem like enough.

Tears stung her eyes as she walked forward. Billy didn't come with her. Each step was difficult. She laid her flowers down gently, touched the soft petals. "Good-bye, Miss Taylor," she whispered. "I'm sorry. For everything."

She wiped her face with the back of her hand and then turned and walked back to where Billy stood waiting for her. "I can't believe she's dead," he said. "It's so weird at school. We've had a substitute teacher for Curfew class and all she does is sit at the front of the room and let us play on our slates. She doesn't even try to teach us anything."

"What do you want her to teach you?" Cass asked quietly. "What part of Curfew don't you understand?"

"I don't know," Billy said. "It's just . . . doesn't she have to teach us something? Isn't that her job?"

Cass didn't understand why he was making such a fuss. Curfew class was the least of their problems now. She was beginning to see that Helen Taylor's death hadn't really affected Billy in the way that it had affected her. His concerns were still very small.

"My parents are getting divorced," he said. He tucked his hands into his pockets. "My mum moved out yesterday. It's just me and Sam and my dad now."

"Oh," Cass said. "Well, you always said you hoped it might happen."

There was an awkward pause. "I guess I'll see you later, then," he said, and he walked off.

Cass didn't watch him go. She made her way to the tagging center, where she waited in the break room until her mother was ready for lunch, which this time the two of them got through with no interruptions.

"That tag key has been dealt with, by the way," Sarah said over a shared ice cream sundae. "It went into the crusher with the old tags, and it's now on its way to be recycled. No one will ever know you took it."

Cass got out of her seat and hugged her mother.

She didn't let go for a long, long time.

CHAPTER FORTY-NINE

Cass

It was six months since Helen Taylor had been killed by the man who was supposed to love her. Half a year. It felt like far less to Cass. The events of those traumatic few days were burned into her mind. She still replayed those memories several times a week, working through them, questioning what she'd done. But it was happening less and less now.

Her father was back in prison. A ten-year sentence for breaking Curfew a second time, and for removing his tag. By the time he was due to be released she would be almost thirty. It seemed like a lifetime away. Helen Taylor had been thirty.

And who knew what the world would look like in ten years' time? It definitely wouldn't look the same as it did now. Change was coming. Everyone could feel it. The women in the Motherhouse could talk about nothing else. Cass knew enough now to take what they said seriously.

Helen Taylor's murder had been the spark that had relit the fire of female anger. Women knew now that tags could be removed. That men would always break Curfew, given the opportunity. That Cohab counseling couldn't always spot a violent man. Men knew it, too, and thirteen more women had been killed by their partners in the months after Helen's death, more than in the previous decade.

Pamela had said that those men had learned from one another. They had watched the news reports on television and some part of their twisted minds had decided it was worth it. Prison didn't deter them anymore. One of them had said that he'd had to make a stand against the control that women had. He'd wanted other men to see that they, too, could break free. The problem had been discussed in Parliament. The general consensus was that Curfew wasn't working and something else was needed.

"Are you ready?" Sarah asked.

Cass patted the bench with her hand. "Yes," she said.

The ground was frosty beneath her feet, and she was glad for her coat and scarf. She'd chosen one in a bright pink, to match her hat. She got to her feet and took her mother's hand. They started to walk, heading down the hill together. Mabel was waiting for them at the bottom.

The bench, on a spot known now as Helen's Path, was a new addition. A little plaque on the back marked Helen's date of birth and death. It had been Cass's idea. She and the other girls at her new school had fundraised to pay for it.

It was the least that Cass could do.

They walked together to the train station, more and more women joining them as they went, and boarded the packed train. It sped them into London. King's Cross station was heaving. Everywhere Cass looked, she saw women. So many women.

They formed a swelling crowd that carried through the streets, packing out the buses and the tube trains, until they formed a circle around the Houses of Parliament. It felt like every woman in the country had come. Hands were joined in a circle that would not be broken. They didn't want something else. They wanted something *more*.

Cass glanced across at her mother as Sarah squeezed her hand. She squeezed back.

I'm doing this for you, Miss.

She took a deep breath. "No more dead women," she shouted. "Make women safe."

One by one, the other women added their voices to hers. Curfew was supposed to protect them. It had failed. They were of one thought and one mind. Men had been restricted by domestic violence laws, and by Curfew, and by tags, and it wasn't enough.

It was time to find something that was. Male violence had to be stopped.

Whatever it took.

Writing a novel is always an odd experience. Your life splits into two worlds, the real and the imaginary, and often you spend far more time in the imaginary one than in the real one. But sometimes, the imaginary and real words collide, and that is something that happened to me with this book. *Curfew* was written in 2019, before "COVID" and "self-isolation" and "social distancing" became everyday terms. At the time, the idea of locking down great swathes of the population as a precautionary measure seemed like something that could only happen in fiction. Those who were legally restricted had done something to deserve it, usually something serious enough to put them in prison. The rest of us could breathe easy knowing that such a thing could never happen to us.

And then it did.

Curfew went out on submission three weeks into the first lockdown in the UK, when the country was quickly learning just how easily our freedoms could be curtailed, and how willing we were to accept restrictions that would previously have been unthinkable.

The difference, of course, is that in *Curfew*, only men are restricted, and the country is plagued not by a virus but by an epidemic of male violence. Here in the UK, men kill two to three

women a week, every week, and that number has remained consistent for years. It's interesting to me that we present the information
in that way. We talk about how many victims there are, but never
how many perpetrators.

In 2019, the Office for National Statistics estimated that there
were 1.6 million women living with domestic violence. We know,
because the ONS also records the sex of offenders, that the major-
ity of these assaults were carried out by men. It's not a stretch to say
that in 2019 there were approximately 1.6 million men abusing the
women they lived with. You've probably walked past one of them on
the street. You may have worked with them, socialized with them,
had them fix your car or check your teeth or teach your children,
and you most likely had no idea.

Domestic violence is a secret, a dark and dirty thing that happens to other women—unless, of course, it is happening to you, as it
did to me, because I am the daughter of a violent man. My father
taught me more than I ever wanted to know about male violence,
coercive control, and the games that men play with the women they
are supposed to love and care for. I always knew that one day I
would write about these things, but it never felt like the right time,
until one day it was. It began with #MeToo. That should have been
a moment for change, but the response to it, seemingly across the
board, was another hashtag: #NAMALT. (Not All Men Are Like
That, in case you didn't know.) A few high-profile men lost their
jobs, it's true—and deservedly so—but there was otherwise no real
change. #NAMALT is a deflection. It tells women to look not at the
behavior of men, but at themselves. It tells us to #BeKind. After all,
these are serious accusations we are making. We don't want to ruin
a man's life, do we? Be quiet. Go away. Stop talking. He didn't mean
it. He was only joking. He's not like that. You're hormonal. Paranoid. Hysterical. You were drunk. You led him on. What did you
expect, wearing that? *Look what you made him do.*

But what if we changed the conversation? What if we responded to #NAMALT with #EMALT (Enough Men Are Like That)?

I wondered, not for the first time, what we would do if we really valued female lives. We've seen in the past that if you want social change, you must first change the law, and so that's where I started. Perhaps some of it seems unrealistic, but then again, perhaps not, if you consider that it was once legal (here in the UK, at least) to refuse to let women inherit, to sack a woman when she got married, to deny women the right to vote, to pay women less than men for the same work, to refuse to provide female toilets, and for a man to rape his wife. I looked at technologies that are already available so that the world was familiar and plausible. And then I threw in a handful of female characters who were all at different stages of their journey through womanhood, and asked one key question:

Will men always be a threat?

I'll let you be the judge of that.

ACKNOWLEDGMENTS

First and foremost, I'd like to thank my agent, Ella Diamond Kahn of DKW Literary, for your help and support with *Curfew*, from the very first time I pitched the idea to publication and beyond.

Allison Hellegers at Stimola Literary, for taking *Curfew* to America.

Jennie Rothwell at Arrow, for liking the book enough to buy it at auction for the UK.

Emily Griffin and Katie Loughnane, also at Arrow, for taking *Curfew* through the later stages of editing and publication.

Jen Monroe at Berkley, for buying *Curfew* for the US, and for your sharp editing skills, clear thinking, and patience.

Everyone else who has worked on the book: the copy editors, cover designers, translators, and publicists (and anyone I have forgotten!).

Finally, I would like to thank my family, in particular my husband and children, for their continued support and their bad jokes.

CURFEW

JAYNE COWIE

DISCUSSION QUESTIONS

1. Do you think a curfew for men would work in real life? How do you think society would react to the introduction of a curfew like this? Would it be workable, and what problems would be created by keeping men at home?

2. In the book, Curfew is introduced after the murder of a high-profile, politically connected woman. What would it take to bring in a curfew in real life?

3. Although Tom turns out to be the killer, both Greg and Billy had opportunity and motive. Do you think that either of them could have done it? Were they both dangerous?

4. Curfew relies on technology—the tags—to make it work. Do you think modern technology such as smartphones and CCTV has made women safer, or has it in fact opened up new ways to make women's lives dangerous?

5. Throughout the book, Pamela is convinced that the murderer will turn out to be male, despite living in a society that has done everything it can to make that impossible. Did Pamela's fear seem reasonable?

6. Helen initially believes that her relationship with Tom is a positive one and ignores certain negative aspects of his behavior. Do you think that the warning signs were there, and that Helen should have realized that Tom was not the man she wanted him to be? Should she have listened to Mabel, who didn't like Tom from the start?

7. Would you like to live in a Motherhouse?

8. Cass shows a great deal of loyalty to Greg and animosity toward her mother. Was Cass right to feel this way? Was Sarah a good mother? What could she have done differently? Does Curfew help mothers or make it harder for them?

9. Although it appears initially that Curfew makes life more difficult for men, it also seems to have some advantages that Greg fully exploits. How else do you think men would benefit from Curfew?

10. At the end of the book, the women demand even more restrictions for men. Was this the right thing to do? Would it work? What other alternatives could have been considered?

ON MY BOOKSHELF

Pride and Prejudice by Jane Austen

Invisible Women: Data Bias in a World Designed for Men by Caroline Criado Perez

Barrayar by Lois McMaster Bujold

Are You There God? It's Me, Margaret. by Judy Blume

Lady Boss by Jackie Collins

Herland by Charlotte Perkins Gilman

Howl's Moving Castle by Diana Wynne Jones

The Cuckoo's Calling by Robert Galbraith

One for the Money by Janet Evanovich

Where the Crawdads Sing by Delia Owens

Guards! Guards! by Terry Pratchett

An avid reader and lifelong writer, **Jayne Cowie** also enjoys digging in her garden and making an excellent devil's food cake. She lives near London with her family.

CONNECT ONLINE

 CowieJayne

Ready to find
your next great read?

Let us help.

Visit prh.com/nextread